☐ S0-BXT-791

"Too bad we're not invisible like last time." "This is different. Last year we were dead."

Mia gave Quentin a superior-looking smile. "Anything is possible, if you believe hard enough." Looking straight ahead, ignoring him and the rush-hour traffic beginning to build around them, she said softly, "I wish I were invisible. I wish I were invisible. I wish I were invisible."

"Don't forget to click your heels together three times," Quentin said, secretly touched by the way Mia, for all her practicality, had always been a believer.

"Quentin?"

Her voice sounded strange. He glanced over to the passenger seat. *Empty.*

"I think," Mia's voice said, "this falls into the category of 'better be careful what you wish for.'"

Praise for HEAVEN COMES HOME:
"This is a great book, which I dearly loved . . . an award-winner. It hit me with all the emotions."
Rendezvous

"A treasured find. Every page is a delight. You literally won't be able to put down this heavenly farce."
Affaire de Coeur

Other Avon Contemporary Romances by
Nikki Holiday

HEAVEN COMES HOME

Avon Books are available at special quantity discounts for bulk purchases for sales promotions, premiums, fund raising or educational use. Special books, or book excerpts, can also be created to fit specific needs.

For details write or telephone the office of the Director of Special Markets, Avon Books, Dept. FP, 1350 Avenue of the Americas, New York, New York 10019, 1-800-238-0658.

HEAVEN KNOWS BEST

NIKKI HOLIDAY

AVON BOOKS ◆ NEW YORK

This is a work of fiction. Names, characters, places, and incidents either are the product of the author's imagination or are used fictitiously. Any resemblance to actual events, locales, organizations, or persons, living or dead, is entirely coincidental and beyond the intent of either the author or the publisher.

AVON BOOKS
A division of
The Hearst Corporation
1350 Avenue of the Americas
New York, New York 10019

Copyright © 1997 by Nancy Wagner
Inside cover author photo by Debbi DeMont Photography
Published by arrangement with the author
Visit our website at **http://AvonBooks.com**
Library of Congress Catalog Card Number: 96-96866
ISBN: 0-380-78797-0

All rights reserved, which includes the right to reproduce this book or portions thereof in any form whatsoever except as provided by the U.S. Copyright Law. For information address William Morris Agency, 1325 Avenue of the Americas, New York, New York 10019.

First Avon Books Printing: March 1997

AVON TRADEMARK REG. U.S. PAT. OFF. AND IN OTHER COUNTRIES, MARCA REGISTRADA, HECHO EN U.S.A.

Printed in the U.S.A.

RA   10 9 8 7 6 5 4 3 2 1

If you purchased this book without a cover, you should be aware that this book is stolen property. It was reported as "unsold and destroyed" to the publisher, and neither the author nor the publisher has received any payment for this "stripped book."

This book is for
Cyndia & Steve,
Barry & Myrna,
and most especially, Dave.

1 ～

The clock struck noon, and Quentin Grandy, recipient of not one but two Academy Awards for Best Director, knew he was a dead man.

With a hand that shook, he loosened his bow tie from the starched collar of his tux shirt and averted his gaze from the mirrors that condemned him from every wall of the guest room of his pal's Brentwood estate. Fitting enough judgement for his cowardice. Only half an hour ago, Quentin had urged his groom's party on, assuring them through the locked door that he'd follow shortly.

But he hadn't budged.

His fears had him paralyzed.

What if he couldn't be faithful to Mia, the love of his life? What if his playboy ways lured him out into the bimbo hunt after he proclaimed his vows in front of the five hundred guests Mia had assembled? He knew in the year he and Mia had been engaged he had honestly struggled to quell the fear and to answer this question once and for all, but now it emerged to destroy him like a specter from a swamp-thing movie.

He loved her too much to hurt her.

The nearer the time came to their wedding day, the more he worried over his secret fear. Every time a woman glanced his way, no matter beautiful or scraggly, hostile or charming, he asked himself again: Could he be faithful? And even though he knew he should have shared this fear with Mia, the way they shared everything else, he'd been reluctant to bring up the subject. Mia had struggled early on with her own jealousies and the last thing he wanted to do was ignite that flame.

With a sigh, he flopped back on the goose down coverlet and covered his eyes. Now with all his dithering, he was more than an hour late! It wouldn't be Quentin who called off the wedding; Mia, with her penchant for promptness, had probably done so already.

"You're a schmuck," he muttered, and let his chin droop onto his starched and pleated shirt.

The door sprang open, ricocheting off the wall, causing a Warhol original to tilt crazily. Andy would have approved, Quentin thought in a wild moment of disbelief as he stared open-mouthed at the apparition glaring at him from the doorway.

A white-haired man, beetling bushy brows above a glare that could bring a stampeding herd of buffalo to a dead halt, loomed in the doorway, crimson dressing gown billowing around skinny ankles.

"One thing you got right," cried the old guy between a wheeze and a rattle, "you're a schmuck, all right!"

"Mr. G!" Quentin stared at the other-world being he'd thought he'd seen the last of a year ago, a sinking feeling overtaking him. "What are you doing here?"

The wiry brows grew even closer together. "A better question is, what are *you* doing here?"

Quentin leapt from the bed, his first instinct to defend himself. But before Mr. G's unceasing scrutiny, he arrested that impulse. Out of habit, he pushed at the bridge of his nose. But thanks to Mia's encouragement, he'd replaced his heavy glasses with contact lenses. Not quite meeting Mr. G's gaze, he said, "I'm mulling things over."

"Things!" Mr. G stabbed a finger toward Quentin's face. "Your wedding invitation—not that you sent me one, of course—said 11 a.m. and unless I've forgotten how to tell time on this planet, you're more than an hour late. For your own wedding. Things! Hah!" He dashed at his face with his ever-present silk hanky, fished from a pocket of his voluminous robe. "You're leaving Mia at the altar! Blowing your second chance at life louder than Gabriel ever blew that annoying trumpet!"

Quentin backed away a step and dropped back to the bed. "No, no, that's not the way I meant it. I've simply been worrying over whether I'm right for her. Whether I'll hurt her."

"Hurt her?" With one spritely lunge, Mr. G pounced and grabbed Quentin by the ear. He dragged him to the cheval mirror and snapped the fingers of his free hand before letting go of Quentin.

Their reflections disappeared and Quentin stared in amazement as the Riviera-Palisades Country Club, site of the wedding, swam into view. The scene switched to a close-up of a flower-banked room, zooming in on a dark-haired woman almost lost in a swath of white lace and satin.

"Mia," he said under his breath, aching to be with her, beside her, holding her, wondering why he'd fallen prisoner to his ridiculous fears.

"Take a good look," Mr. G said, nudging Quentin in the ribs, a little harder than necessary.

He peered, and the knife of guilt turned in his gut as he saw Mia's face was paler than he'd thought possible. Dark eyes large with worry, she stared out the window of the room, her brow creased. Only her fingers moved, working the crystalline rosary beads in her satin-covered lap.

"She thinks I'm hurt!" Quentin knew that look. Mia wasn't sitting there thinking Quentin had stood her up; the idea that his delay was due to cold feet had never occurred to her. No, that expression came from one thought: her heartsick concern he'd been delayed by an accident. He knew her so well; she'd probably convinced herself he lay near death on Sunset Boulevard, surrounded by ambulance, police, and fire teams.

The mirror went dark, then his own image returned, wavered briefly, then solidified. Quentin raced for the open door. "How could I have done this to her! I've got to get there. Explain. Apologize. Thanks for coming—"

"To show you the error of your ways?" Mr. G crossed his arms over his chest and coughed dryly.

The door slammed shut, seemingly on its own.

Quentin swung around and tried, unsuccessfully, to stare down Mr. G. Then, pretty sure of what he'd find, Quentin reached a hand behind him and tried the doorknob. Locked. "Is there something going on here I need to know about?"

Mr. G smiled. The old guy was enjoying himself; which shouldn't have surprised Quentin, given the conditions under which he and Mia had met Mr. G. A little over a year ago, they'd been injured on a set, and both landed in intensive care at Cedars-Sinai. Or so the world thought, but while their bodies had lain hooked to modern medicine's tubes and monitors, he and Mia had found themselves in an after-life adventure Quentin still wasn't sure had really happened.

Mr. G smiled again. "Oh, it happened all right."

Quentin started. He'd forgotten about Mr. G's mind-reading habit. "Look, I've got to get to Mia. Now. I can't let her worry one more second."

"An admirable sentiment. Especially for such a tardy bridegroom." He scratched his bulbous nose and said, "You really think you're gonna show up an hour or so late, kiss Mia on that furrowed brow, and the ceremony's gonna go forward as planned?"

"Well, I'll have to throw myself on her mercies, but I'm praying she'll understand."

Mr. G perched on the dressing table next to the cheval mirror. "You really don't know much about women, do you?"

"You don't think it'll work?"

"Let me put it to you this way." Mr. G smiled, showing his teeth in a way that didn't bode well for Quentin, then said, "No."

Quentin leaned against the locked door. He might as well hear what the old guy had to say.

"I thought you'd never ask." Mr. G jumped up and rubbed his hands. "I have a proposal for you."

"Oh, no." Quentin should have seen this coming. An idea, one he didn't want to entertain, nudged its way into his brain. Mia insisted everything happened for a reason. Had Mr. G caused him to be late? Set up this situation for his own devious reasons?

Mr. G shook his head. "You still don't trust me, do you? Never mind that. I've always found myself bored by those arguments over predestination. Concentrate on this thought instead: a man in your shoes shouldn't be too quick to look a gift horse in the face."

"Mouth." Quentin corrected him automatically, thinking of the worried-sick look on Mia's face as he'd viewed it in the mirror. She'd be equally pissed when he showed up hale and hearty and begging her forgiveness. No, not equally, tremendously more so. Stifling a groan and smothering his own disbelief that he was conducting this conversation with a being he'd last met in Purgatory, he said, "Shoot. Let's hear the concept."

"You're not considering a story pitch here, you know," Mr. G said. "This is your life we're talking about. But don't fret cause I'm gonna help you out. You do this one little job for me—successfully, of course—and I'll take a tuck in time and none of your five hundred wedding guests will ever know you were an hour late."

"So Mia won't know?" He moved forward, ready to do anything for the old guy.

Mr. G laughed in a way that made Quentin's socks go damp.

"Oh, Mia will know, but that's your problem to work out."

He should have guessed as much. Mr. G didn't make things easy. "What's the job?"

"If I made things easy, what would be the point?"

Despite himself, Quentin grinned. Mr. G cared enough to offer him a way out and that made him feel all things were possible.

"Your mission," Mr. G said, rubbing his hands together in a way that started to worry Quentin, "is to lead Alexander Graham Winston to realize he isn't happy—and get him to do whatever it takes to fix that."

"A. G. Winston? The computer whiz? The richest bachelor in America?" Quentin knew Winston had been featured as *WorldView*'s most recent Person of the Year.

"The same."

"But he's got everything. He even makes a point of how perfect his existence is. What's to be unhappy about?" He and Mia had won their way out of Purgatory and back to life intervening in Chelsea Jordan's life. But Chelsea, child porn star turned actress turned genuine celluloid celeb, had already hit bottom. She knew she was miserable.

Mr. G showed those pointed front teeth of his. "That's for you, and Mia—because this deal requires that you persuade her to work with you—to figure out."

"And how am I supposed to do that?" Quentin knew he shouted the question, but really, something about this old guy always drove him to the edge.

Mr. G smiled and said not a word. He patted his pockets, produced another silk hanky, this one neatly folded, and before Quentin's eyes, disappeared.

The square of crimson silk fluttered to the ground, the monogrammed "G" winking up at Quentin.

Mia Tortelli had prepared for her wedding with the same precision, diligence, and care she took to produce one of Quentin's big-budget films.

But there were two major differences. First, she usually stayed safely behind the scenes, but today, she'd hold center stage. And surprisingly, she welcomed that. She wanted the entire world to see how happy she and Quentin made one another.

The second difference was the one that had her worried sick.

Quentin never ever showed up late for a day of filming. But when Mia had last checked her mother's watch, thirty minutes had passed since the groom's party should have arrived. With a brave smile, Mia sent her mother off to instruct the waiters to circulate with champagne, then she locked the door, clutched her rosary, and sat down to worry.

Almost an hour passed, during which time

she fantasized every conceivable tragedy that could occur between Brentwood and the country club. Given the brief stretch of Sunset Boulevard that ran between the two locales, Mia's thoughts were forced to turn to the worst possible disaster.

Sick at heart, she rose and walked to one of the broad windows overlooking the golf course. To her amazement, and quickly mounting fury, she spotted her bridegroom skirting the edge of the green, then skulking across the parking lot, plainly trying not to be spotted by any wandering guests.

Sure enough, a few minutes later, she heard a tap at her door, followed by Quentin's rather sheepish-sounding voice calling softly, "Mia?"

She said not a word.

"Please, Mia, I need to talk to you. I know I'm late and I'm terribly sorry. Can you ever forgive me?"

"Forgive you?" Mia knew she screeched the words, but how could he do this to her!

The knob twisted. She heard the plea in Quentin's voice as he said through the door, "Please, Mia. Open up and let me explain."

"If you weren't hit by a truck or a meteorite, go away." She turned her back. Satiny whispers accompanied the move, reminding her she should be standing in a reception line, not behind a locked door, her groom on the other side.

Knocking, hard and loud, erupted, then

ceased abruptly. "Even if you won't listen to me, Mia, I have a message from Mr. G."

"That is a sign of desperation, Quentin." Mia was surprised he'd bring up Mr. G. To this day, Quentin remained skeptical about their after-life adventure.

"Maybe so, but it's true."

Something in Quentin's voice gave her pause. Mia eyed her beautifully crafted French manicure, regretting for just one moment having abandoned her bad habit of nail chewing. In times of distress, one needed a thinking aid. She thought now of the vows she'd been prepared to exchange.

The knob twisted again.

For better or for worse.

"You'll have to wait till I change."

"We need to hurry. Please, Mia."

"I don't care what the crisis is. You can't see me in my wedding dress."

Mia heard Quentin chuckle. He thought her concern for rules and procedures silly, did he? Well, she would never keep her groom waiting at the altar.

With hands that trembled, she removed the headpiece of roses and tulle from her hair, settled it with care on a dressing table, then turned to the task of unfastening the mother-of-pearl buttons that lined the satin from elbow to wrist.

Rules were rules, and it was bad luck for a groom to see his bride before the wedding.

Mia was glad she'd insisted her mother and bridesmaids mingle with the guests and the caterers assuage their thirst with champagne. By now the guests were no doubt well enough into the bubbly to be speculating wildly on the cause of the delay in the ceremony. The tabloids would have a field day.

She'd hear what Quentin had to say, explain to her parents and their publicist, then slip away to lick her wounds alone.

Better yet, she'd let Quentin handle the publicist.

Mia finished undressing, hanging the wedding gown with care. She'd open the door to Quentin, but she couldn't imagine anything he could say or do to salvage the wedding.

A groom did not stand up his bride.

It simply wasn't done.

Not to a heart as tender as hers.

The knocking started again. Mia let him pound as she pulled on the melonberry skirt and top she'd worn earlier. The expensive cotton caressed her skin. This wasn't just any skirt and top; each piece had cost more than a hundred dollars. Still unaccustomed to the money she made as producer of Quentin's big budget movies, Mia had trouble paying the prices Hollywood's successful took for granted.

But for her wedding day and her wardrobe for their honeymoon, she'd splurged. The cotton, gentle as a lover's whisper, comforted her skin as she hugged her arms to her chest and prepared to open the door to her belated bridegroom.

When Mia opened the door at long last, Quentin just caught himself from falling face forward. "Mia," he said, drinking in her big eyes, mournfully large now, her silken, olive complexion, the spiky top of her mink-brown hair he found so quixotic.

Relieved to have snapped out of his last-minute attack of self-doubt, he caught her in his arms.

Slowly, firmly, with a grim determination that registered like a pan of ice water flung against his heart, Mia freed herself from his embrace.

Arms folded across her chest, she said, "And what is this supposed message from Mr. G?"

Quentin met her gaze, but it was a tough thing to do. "Mr. G called me a schmuck, and he was right." He ran a nervous hand through his hair, wishing Mia didn't look quite so stern. "I'm late because I started worrying and fretting and asking myself whether I would end up hurting you, and I admit it"—he figured the truth was the only way to go here—"I got cold feet."

She was tapping her foot, gazing steadily at him. One or two freckles stood out on her cheeks, a bad sign, he realized too late.

"So you admit you weren't coming?"

Quentin scuffed a toe against the doorjamb.

He managed to wedge his shoulder against the door she tried to slam shut. "There's no excuse for what I did, but please listen to what I have to say from Mr. G."

"That you're a schmuck?"

Quentin knew he deserved the scorn in her voice. He could also see curiosity battle with the hurt.

"Let's hear it," she finally said.

"Thank you," he said, wishing he could squeeze through the door and take her in his arms while he begged her forgiveness. What had he been thinking? He'd never want any other woman.

She tapped her toe again.

"It's like the Chelsea Jordan deal, only the catch is the man we've been assigned doesn't know he's unhappy. But if we lead him to see he isn't and help him figure out how to be happy, then the best part is, Mr. G will take a tuck in time and none of the guests will know I was late for the wedding." He said that last part in a rush, cause it did sound kind of selfish, even though he was pretty sure Mr. G offered that payoff to protect Mia more than to keep Quentin from looking like the schmuck he was.

He heard Mia's foot tapping again, an ominous sound. Sweat trickled down the collar of his tux shirt as he waited for her response.

The two of them had been in the same boat in Purgatory when Mr. G offered them the challenge that led to their second chance at life. But right now Quentin was the man up a creek without a paddle. Would Mia believe Mr. G had appeared to him or conclude Quentin was desperate enough to invent the story?

"So who's the happy guy?"

He swallowed, then said, "A. G. Winston."

"You are making this up!"

He held up two fingers. He'd been an Eagle Scout.

"Come on. A. G. Winston has everything. He's rich, brilliant, and incredibly sexy."

"You think he's sexy?"

She batted her lashes. "Oh, very."

He couldn't afford to rise to her bait. Not with the task he had cut out for him, regaining her trust. It wouldn't do him much good for the wedding guests to be frozen in time if the groom couldn't win back the bride. "Mr. G said the challenge is to lead him to realize he's not happy."

Mia wrinkled her nose. "That does sound like something Mr. G would say."

Quentin sagged in relief. "Then you believe me?"

She started to nod, and, catching him off-guard, slammed the door.

Luckily for Quentin, he remembered the monogrammed hanky he'd retrieved from the floor after Mr. G's Cheshire-cat act. He unfolded the silk square, then fed it inch by inch under the door.

He only had to wait a few minutes before the door opened and Mia appeared, purse in hand.

"I'll do this crazy thing," she said, "but not one word to me about us."

2 〜

The headquarters of Winston Enterprises dwarfed the other buildings snaking along the six-lane Boulevard of Technology near Orange County's John Wayne Airport.

Quentin pulled his Ferrari out of the stream of traffic and slid to a halt in front of a No Parking sign. Mia scrunched her eyes and he did the same, protecting himself from the onslaught of sunlight reflecting off the massive building's mirrored exterior.

Mia pointed to the stretch of office structures on the opposite side of the busy avenue. Rambling stone buildings married nicely with the rolling terrain, merging with the surroundings rather than trying to overpower. "Do you think Mr. Winston was trying to make a statement?"

"Possibly." It wasn't the building Quentin was studying. Sliding his hungry gaze over Mia's precious spiky hair and intense brown eyes, he kicked himself for being this near to her and yet so far. If he had to hogtie A. G.

Winston and pour sugar down his throat to make him happy, he'd do it. If he could have one more chance to win Mia, he'd be thankful to Mr. G till his dying day. After the stunt he'd pulled, another chance was more than he deserved.

She snapped her fingers and Quentin snapped to attention. He pointed to the guardhouse and read. "All visitors must have a pass."

"Oh, bother." Mia let her head fall back on the butter-soft leather of the seat. The sooner this misadventure came to an end, the sooner she could go home and figure out how she was going to live the rest of her life without Quentin. Watching him study the guard booth, with that look of faraway intensity he got when creating a story line, she wished she could forget what he'd done and take him back.

But she refused to live her life as an emotional yo-yo. And until Quentin resolved his own fears, she'd be nothing but the ball spinning on the end of the string.

Quentin threw her a wink and slid from behind the wheel. Sporting his usual confident smile, he said, "I'll stroll over to the guardhouse and have them ring up and say we're here to do a film about the story of his life. Who could resist a line like that? We'll pop up, conduct an interview to find out what we need to know about his life, and work from there."

Mia gave him a slow nod. It did seem everyone wanted to be in the movies. Since the smash success of *DinoDaddy*, their production offices had been overwhelmed with scripts and letters, many of which began with, "Mr. Grandy, have I got a story for you, the story of my life!"

Yes, A. G. Winston would be most unusual if he resisted that ploy.

Quentin wasn't in the booth more than a few minutes. He strolled back, looking bemused and whistling softly. Mia's heart started to melt when he turned to her. She loved the way his zest for life glowed in his eyes, in the quirky upturning of his lips, in his eagerness to joust with a challenge.

He slipped behind the wheel and leaned toward her.

She inched back, seeking the arm of the door for an anchor. A little more sternly than necessary, she said, "Well?"

"Always stick to business, don't you, Mia," he said softly. With a gentle fingertip, he smoothed a spiky strand of hair from her cheek.

"As should you. Are we going in?"

Quentin returned his hand to his side of the two-seater. "Mr. G may be smarter than I gave him credit for."

"Of course he's smart. Did you get through to A. G. Winston?"

"Yep." Quentin drummed on the wheel. "He

came right to the phone. Complimented me on our films, especially *Quetzalcoatl's Overcoat*." He flashed her a smile.

Our films. Mia loved the way Quentin didn't hog the glory. He'd been that way from the beginning, even during the days they'd scraped together pennies for college film projects.

"But A. G. Winston said he hadn't lived long enough or done anything worth making a movie about. Said he was disappointed that I asked, since real life can't be dramatized nearly as effectively as fiction."

"He lectured you, eh?" Mia smiled at the idea. What did a computer nerd know about drama compared to a man who'd already won two Oscars?

"He's right, you know. People want larger than life in movies and books. The mundane they can view every morning in the mirror."

Mia agreed but her heart wasn't in the philosophical debate. The longer she spent with Quentin, the harder it would be to face the future. Every moment since they'd left the country club had amounted to torment. Quentin had insisted on changing clothes, saying he wasn't going to run around town in a monkey suit. Mia had waited in the car at his friend's Brentwood house while Quentin changed his clothes. When he'd reappeared, wearing jeans, a soft denim shirt, and deck shoes, and looking even more attractive in the clothing that suited him so well, she'd suffered yet another pang of loss. Forcing her mind back to the business at hand, she said, "Did you get us a mundane appointment?"

"Nope. He said it was a bad day. Or rather, a good day for him, but already booked. It sounded to me as if a party were in progress."

Mia pursed her lips, wondering again why she'd chosen this year to give up nail-biting. "Do you see anything funny about this situation?"

"You mean ha-ha or weird?"

"Weird."

"What are you getting at?"

Mia pointed toward the gleaming building. The sun had begun its daily dip into the Pacific and taken with it the glare that bounced off the chrome and mirror surface. What with having to change clothes and then the time they'd spent arguing over the best approach to take on tackling Winston, the day was beginning to wane. "Here's a guy with an empire, and he's also humble and a student of drama *and* he enjoys a party. I don't get it. What's wrong with his life?"

Quentin twisted in his seat. He wondered whether an outsider would ask the same question of his life. "I told you, Mia, that's the point to this challenge. A. G. Winston doesn't know he's not happy."

Quentin wanted to get in that building and get on with the job. But when Mia wanted to chew over a thought, there was no stopping her. So instead of barging from the car and trying to make the guards believe he'd forgotten his invitation to the party, he said, "What do you think is missing in Winston's life?" Thinking back on their adventure in Arkansas with Chelsea Jordan and the country preacher who'd successfully wooed her from the Hollywood maelstrom, Quentin was pretty sure what Mia would say. Love, she'd say, and sigh, and then add, most importantly, the comfort of trust.

He glanced over, surprised she'd not answered right away.

"Mia?"

With her pert face scrunched into a thoughtful pose, she said, "It can't be anything too simple or obvious. It's probably not as simple as love. The man is wealthy, sexy, and accomplished. I think . . ." She turned her head toward the passenger window.

"Yes?"

She faced him again. Speaking slowly, as if picking her way through her thoughts, she said, "Have you ever thought you're happy, yet later you realized you weren't? I mean"—she produced a fierce frown—"before you and I became engaged, you were happy, successful, popular. You certainly didn't want for female companionship." At this she beetled her brows and glared at him. "You were happy, right?"

Quentin wasn't sure if he should agree. If he said yes, would he be condemning himself? But sensing the importance of the point she was trying to make, he said, "Yeah, I would have said I was happy."

"And then when we almost died, and later came back to life, and fell in love, were you, you know, happier?"

"No question." He hated to see the way she struggled to be so logical and cover her hurt feelings in order to hold this discussion. If only he could turn back the clock! If only he'd gone to the wedding. Damn it, he could have handled temptation and fears of fidelity as the case arose. What a schmuck.

"Well, then, I think that's what we're facing with A. G." She lifted her thumb to her lips, but didn't nibble, as she would have in the past.

She brushed it lightly over her lips, in a slow erotic motion that made Quentin itch to kiss her, then said, "So we have to figure out what or who makes A. G. Winston think he's happy, then what do you say we go for the opposite?"

"You mean if he has a brunette girlfriend we find him a blonde?" He knew he sounded sarcastic, but the idea struck him as simplistic.

"Got a better plan?"

"Step One is to get in to see him." Quentin frowned. Normally he would have had his secretary book an appointment, but with Mr. G, time was always of the essence. How long could he keep those wedding guests locked in a time warp?

"Too bad we're not invisible like last time."

"This is different. Last year we were dead."

Mia gave him a superior-looking smile. "Anything is possible, if you believe hard enough." Then her smile faded.

"Sweetheart, please forgive me," Quentin said, knowing her so well he could read her thoughts. "I know you're thinking you believed in me, and I still screwed up. I'm so sorry I hurt you. Let me make it up to you."

Mia laughed, a sound that didn't sound quite like her usual self. She touched the silk hanky Mr. G had left behind to the corner of one eye, an action that twisted the knife of guilt yet again. Mia never cried.

Looking straight ahead, ignoring him and the rush hour traffic beginning to build around them, she said softly, "I wish I were invisible. I wish I were invisible. I wish I were invisible."

"Don't forget to click your heels together three times," Quentin said, secretly touched by the way Mia, for all her practicality, had always been a believer. To an agnostic like Quentin, he found her faith foreign, yet he knew he envied it.

On this adventure, though, it looked as if he'd have to be the practical one. He pulled his flip phone from the dash and dialed information. If he couldn't get through to Winston, he'd dangle a movie role in front of whatever assistant answered the phone. One way or another, they were going to that party.

"Quentin?"

Her voiced sounded strange. He glanced over to the passenger seat.

Empty.

Funny, he hadn't heard her leave the car. And the passenger door on his Ferrari had developed an annoying groan. He put down the phone. "Where'd you go, Mia?"

"I'm right here," she said.

He eyeballed the passenger seat, spotted the crimson hanky fluttering chest high. Or rather, where chest high would be were there a person in the seat.

"Mia?" No. It wasn't how it looked. Or rather, how it didn't look.

The silk fluttered. "I think," Mia's voice said, "this falls into the category of 'better be careful what you wish for.'"

Quentin hit the steering wheel with both fists. "Mr. G," he bellowed. "Give her back!"

Mia said, "Don't worry. I'm really right here." The hanky fluttered again, then she said, "But this does take a little getting used to. This invisibility is different than last time."

"What do you mean?" Quentin heard the edge of concern in his voice.

"Last year when we were invisible we were still solid, but now I'm sort of shimmery. Almost fading out."

Quentin reached out and trapped the red cloth in his hands. It tugged free of his grip.

Goosebumps danced on his forearms. "This is
too weird. You've got to wish yourself back.
Right now!"

"Oh, no, this is much too useful." Mia's
voice was almost drowned out by the groan of
his passenger door as it opened and closed.
"I'll just pop into the party, have a look at Mr.
Winston, and report back."

"You're not going without me."

He could swear he heard her laugh. "Don't
get a parking ticket while I'm gone," she said.

He watched the bobbing crimson until it
disappeared within the confines of the foyer of
Winston Enterprises. He shook his head, then
got back on the phone. Mia would work this
her way, and he'd try it his. Invisibility really
wasn't his cup of tea.

At least fifty people milled about the spacious boardroom, most of them, judging from
the cameras, microphones, and reporter's note-
books, members of the fourth estate. Mia recognized the chief features writer for the *L. A.
Times*, as well as several less savory journalists.

What was America's wealthiest bachelor
up to?

Near the back of the room, a glacial blonde
leaned over a seated black-haired man.

Mia moved closer.

The black-haired man hunched over a notebook computer, his handsome but pale face set
in a mask of concentration, his fingers flying

over the keyboard. The woman, dressed smartly in a St. John knit, stroked his shoulder, the way old ladies wrapped in mink pet their Pekingese pooches.

Mia hovered closer to the man behind the computer. She double-checked his face against her memory of the *WorldView* magazine cover. Yep, that had to be A. G. Winston. No one else had that beauty, intelligence, and—she peered more closely—a nose broken once upon a time.

"Darling, everyone is ready for our announcement," the blonde stage-whispered, as if she wanted to be heard by the throng of people in the boardroom.

Mia winced. The woman's voice might be sugarcoated, but it definitely carried the tone of a sergeant directing her troops. Mia's hackles rose and her protective instincts surged. She not only saw a bad actress, but sensed a bad seed.

She heard two men standing nearby say in a low voice, "They make a lovely couple, don't they? Brains and beauty. I don't know which one of them is luckier."

The blonde woman turned and extended a hand to the two men. "Darren. Larry. So good to see you. I hope you purchased that stock I recommended. It's up by a third."

"Sharyn, darling, congratulations." The guys fell over themselves trying to air kiss the woman's cheeks.

Yech. Obviously the film kingdom didn't have an exclusive on piranhas. Had she and Quentin arrived in the nick of time?

Mia looked again at the blonde's hand that had lain so possessively on A. G. Winston's shoulder and noted the diamond that put her own two-carat engagement ring to shame.

She glanced down and realized she'd never once thought of removing the ring Quentin had given her soon after they'd returned from their last other-worldly adventure. And now, staring at the clear fire of her ring, she knew she didn't have the heart to tug it from her finger. Even though in her invisible state, only she could see the ring, she wanted to leave it on her hand, where it would stay forever, if only Quentin could deal with his fear and come to his senses.

The obvious fiancee had started to turn back toward A. G. Mia knew she'd have to wait until later to nurse her broken heart. Then she realized she still held the crimson silk square in her hand. Quentin had been able to see that, and so might others. She balled it up and tucked it under the neckline of her top, wondering if that would make it invisible.

The moment the silk touched her chest, noises rang in Mia's head. She clutched her ears, wondering why so many people were talking so loudly all of a sudden.

The two men with Sharyn were both talking at once, only neither one's lips moved. Mia shook her head. Clearly the one called Darren was saying, *You bitch, wouldn't I love one more three-way before you tie the knot*. Mia's mouth formed an "O" of shock as she checked for Sharyn's reaction.

But the cool blonde was merely smiling and saying, "Of course A. G. and I will be doing quite a bit of entertaining." But Mia also heard, even though Sharyn's lips never moved: *Just as soon as I return from settling that problem of the Dew Drop Inn in Eureka Springs. Not that you two will be on the guest list. What bores I put up with in this business.* "Darlings, so good of you to come today," Sharyn moved off, bypassing A. G. to greet a newcomer.

Mia rubbed her ears. People's thoughts zinged at her from every direction. When she turned toward A. G., though, the sounds were calm and steady, a parade of mathematical calculations marching in conjunction with his fingers on the keyboard of his computer.

But Sharyn! Mia reeled again as Sharyn's inner voice gave vent to a bondage and discipline fantasy involving the white-haired man shaking her hand. Mia backed away a step, beginning to wonder whether the fantasy wasn't in fact fiction as the details grew. All the while, butter wouldn't melt on the sweet look on the woman's face.

What had caused this onslaught?

Mia pulled the hanky from her blouse to wipe her damp palms. The noises stopped.

She stared at the hanky and began to smile.

Then she laughed. Good old Mr. G.

He didn't put his people up a creek without a paddle.

Then her laughter faded as she thought of the power of the hanky, thought of using it to listen in on Quentin's inner secrets. She could ask him why he didn't show up for their wedding, then capture his secret thoughts as he answered her question.

A chill blew around her and she rejected the idea. She shouldn't do it. It was wrong. Yet . . . Mia was tempted. Very tempted.

Oh, no. Sharyn had headed toward the podium, which was banked in microphones. If A. G. thought that woman made him happy, he needed a good bop on the head.

A murmur went around the room and Sharyn paused. Her lips parted in a sexy pout that made Mia want to be ill. The image reminded her of the Barbie-doll types Quentin used to attract, and still did, despite his best efforts not to. And of course that reminded her of her own sorrowful plight.

Just then Sharyn pulled an about-face from the podium, and advanced, one hip thrust at a time, toward the latest arrival to the party. Mia flitted over to see who it was and her jaw dropped.

Quentin, wearing a shit-eating grin, was making a beeline for Sharyn.

Mia stood, unable to turn away, unwilling to watch, as the woman cooed over Quentin. If she batted her lashes one more time, they'd fly right off her eyelids. Quentin, in that charming way he had, cut Sharyn out of the crowd and walked her to the side of the room, acting for all the world as if she were holding this soiree for his benefit.

Mia could hear him saying, "I have always wanted to meet you. Any woman who could get A. G. Winston to tie the knot must be something special."

"And I've always wanted to meet you," Sharyn said in a breathy voice, pulling Quentin to a seat beside her. "Imagine, a movie director here at my engagement party." She patted his thigh and didn't move her hand. "I've been told I resemble Marilyn Monroe," she said, doing a fairly accurate imitation of the star's voice.

Quentin tilted her chin with one hand, studying her profile. Mia wafted over and pinched the back of his neck.

"Ouch."

Sharyn pouted. "Don't you like what you see?"

"Oh, most definitely. I said 'ouch' as in all the pain and pleasure you could bring to movie audiences."

"Ooh, flattery." Sharyn delivered an arch look that caused Mia to roll her eyes.

Catching sight of a passing waiter, Mia tipped a glass of champagne onto Quentin's lap to cool him off.

He jumped up and Sharyn chastised the waiter with a voice colder than the bubbly.

A. G. appeared at her side, surprise and recognition in his eyes when he saw Quentin. He offered him dry clothing, but Quentin brushed the offer aside. Instead, he kept darting his gaze about, and Mia realized he was searching for her.

She fluttered the hanky and he excused himself. Sharyn began to herd A. G. toward the podium.

"We have to work fast," Mia said, deciding to stick to business and not comment till later on Quentin's fawning over Sharyn the Shark.

"Did you have to get my pants wet?" Quentin whispered, looking for all the world like a man conversing with a six-foot palm.

Mia forgot about sticking to business. "Did you have to flirt with that witch?"

"I wasn't flirting; I was gathering information."

"Ladies and gentlemen," Sharyn was speaking into the microphones, while A. G. stood at her side.

"We've got to get him out of her clutches," Mia said.

"How do you know she's bad for him?"

"Call it intuition."

A. G. whispered something to Sharyn, then stepped away, heading to his computer. Sharyn paused, the look on her face clearly saying, "We have to humor our little genius."

Mia whipped over to A. G.'s computer and before he reached it, she typed on the screen: "Most important breakthrough in chip technology. Will sell to you if you go immediately to the black Ferrari parked in front of building."

A. G. took his seat, poised his hands over the keyboard, then scanned the screen. A smile lit his face. Sharyn was entertaining the crowd with the story of how she and A. G. met while the computer whiz slipped quietly from the room.

Mia hustled Quentin out the door, explaining he'd have to think up something about chip technology once A. G. got to the car. Maybe he could offer to drive to Denny's for a cup of coffee and a demonstration.

Quentin, for his part, was at a loss. Functionaries roamed the halls and filled the elevators, making it quite impossible for him to hold up his end of the conversation with an invisible person without drawing attention to himself as a loony.

And, following the bobbing hanky out the entrance of Winston Enterprises, Quentin thought it possible he had gone loony tunes.

3 ⌒

"**S**ugar, stop that."

Gemini Dailey, known to everyone in the surrounding countryside as Jemi, pulled a pillow over her head, doing her best to ignore the damp doggie nose nudging her bare feet.

Instead of behaving as a properly trained German shepherd should, Sugar slopped a wet tongue over her ticklish toes.

"That does it." Jemi tossed the pillow onto the floor and sat up in bed, focusing crossly on the clock. Bats and whiskers! Already five-thirty!

She leapt from bed, pausing to give Sugar an appreciative pat on the head. "Good girl," she said, and searched about on the bedside table for an old bone. She was positive she'd seen one there yesterday. Or maybe the day before.

Ah, yes. She retrieved the sticky chew treat and Sugar accepted it with enthusiasm.

It was a good thing, Jemi thought, eyeing the gnarled bone before shrugging into her overalls and T-shirt, that her guests at the Dew Drop Inn never saw her private quarters.

A natural-born housekeeper she surely wasn't.

Jemi tamed her long red hair in a tight braid then turned to her east-facing window. The early morning pink of the sky had already stiffened to rose. She balanced on the balls of her feet and breathed deeply. In her blend of yoga and ballet, Jemi raised her arms above her head and greeted the sun and the new day. Her brother and sisters may have rejected their parents' hippie ways, but Jemi clung to some of the traditions she'd learned from them.

She performed several cat stretches, then skipped the rest of her morning yoga routine. Once again, she'd overslept and would have to rush.

Leaving Sugar crunching happily on a bone that should have been forbidden in a resort hailed as a vegetarian paradise, Jemi skipped down the stairs to the first floor of the cottage that housed the office, dining room, and kitchen of the Dew Drop Inn.

She set the coffeepot to dripping beans she'd ground the night before. Her mother never would have approved of caffeine, but on some points Jemi had to forge her own path. Chamomile or peppermint were perfectly in synch for lazy moments or wintry evenings, but were of absolutely no help in adjusting to early morning hours.

Humming a country-western tune she'd heard on the radio the day before, she walked to the back door of her roomy kitchen. She opened it and reached down to where she knew her delivery of raw milk from Hester's Farms would be waiting, encased in a Coleman cooler packed with ice.

She found it.

She also found the note from Casey, her kitchen helper.

"Oh, no," she murmured, crumpling the yellow tablet paper in frustration. She carried the heavy gallon jars, cream bobbing on the top to her walk-in refrigerator and wondered how in the world she would cope without Casey. But the note said all that needed to be said. Casey's mother had gone into premature labor during the night and would need help with the latest in her brood of nine.

Casey was seventeen, already out of high school, and the most wonderfully talented cook. She was also a hard worker, able to clean cottages and help with the yard work while inventing some yummy new vegetarian recipe.

Jemi's shoulders sagged and for a moment, she felt like driving into town to give her brother Ari a piece of her mind. This whole thing was his fault. If it hadn't been for Ari, she never would have advertised in that highfalu-tin' magazine, nor raised her rates to such scandalous heights.

If not for Ari, the Dew Drop Inn wouldn't be

99 percent booked, with patrons willing to pay scalper prices of three hundred dollars a night! Plus tax!

But without Casey, she had far too much work to do to waste time taking Ari to task.

She set about whipping up a batch of honey wheat bread and when she'd finished, she covered the crockery bowl with a cloth and left it near the stove to rise. That job completed, she rubbed a thoughtful finger across her nose and considered her employee situation.

Even with Susannah, the twelve-year-old who came over every day during the summer, she'd still need help.

But it was already June. The tourist season in Eureka Springs, Arkansas, was running full tilt and most places had already staffed to meet the demands. Jemi, however, wasn't accustomed to needing extra workers.

When her parents had run the Dew Drop Inn, the cottages had been filled mostly with friends of that charming, garrulous and happy-go-lucky couple, friends who never seemed to be able to pay.

Her parents said money wasn't important; too much wealth clouded one's karma. Ari, of course, was fond of remarking money wasn't important to their parents because they'd both been born with trust accounts solid enough to salve any situation. Nevertheless, to teach this principle to their children and maybe because they really believed it, they let their artist and musician friends live in the cottages and never got around to collecting payment.

As a result, Jemi grew up surrounded by laughing, loving, free-wheeling adults who never worried where their next meal would come from. Someone would toss together a salad of field greens or boil some rice and those who were hungry would eat.

All three of Jemi's sisters and her brother rebelled early on against this easy-come easy-go lifestyle. Her eldest sister Pio, short for Scorpio, was a surgeon in Chicago; her sister Libby, which she preferred to her given name of Libra, had just won the Most Successful New Commodities Trader Award on Wall Street; her sister Virgo would probably make partner at Peat, Marwick, and Mitchell within a year. And her brother Ari, of course, was fabulously successful in his career as an antiques dealer. He divided his time between Manhattan's Upper West Side and his shop in Eureka Springs. A shop, he assured Jemi, he'd visit much less often if she'd ever wake up and smell the coffee and shake the country dust off her feet.

But Jemi, the youngest, clung to the only life she knew. Even after her parents grew bored, their friends having drifted off to various points of suburbia across the country, and cast off for new adventures on the Pacific island of Yap, Jemi remained.

Partly because the Dew Drop Inn was home; partly because she feared she'd never be able to

move in the circles her sisters and brother took
for granted.

She'd worked so hard to put the inn to rights,
scraping along on tourist income of fifty dollars
a night, that she'd neglected her education. Her
parents had offered to send her away to any
university she chose, but instead she'd stayed
home and attended a nearby community college for two years, then dropped out when her
parents decamped to Yap.

Now, five years later, she longed to fill that
void in her life, longed to be free of an obligation she'd imposed on herself, yet seemed
unable to slip free of the bonds of the past.

A foul stench rose to her nostrils and Jemi
jerked to attention. Now she'd done it!
Scorched the tofu!

With a sigh, she uttered a prayer to the
universe for deliverance.

Then, as practical as the circumstances required, Jemi cleaned the skillet and began
again.

"Now what are we going to do with him?"

Mia hated it when Quentin glared at her.
Come to think of it, he so rarely did it, it quite
made her feel as if the world were totally out of
sorts.

Which it was, of course, Quentin having
abandoned her on their wedding day.

Considering she was invisible, being glared
at was especially odd.

She glanced down at America's richest bachelor. He lay in a heap, half in and half out of Quentin's Ferrari.

"If you'd thought of something halfway intelligent to say to stall him," Mia said, "I wouldn't have had to bop him over the head."

Quentin wrested the flashlight she still wielded from mid-air, and said, "It's not every day I conduct a conversation about which I know nothing."

"Where's your imagination?" Mia stamped her foot, to no effect. "You got us into this mess, the least you can do is think on your feet. Oh-oh!" She saw a guard in the booth hang up the phone, speak to another officer, then head in their direction. "We've got to scram!"

Quentin glanced over his shoulder, and without hesitating, shoved Winston's rangy legs into his car. "Hang on," he said, he supposed to Mia, and, leaping behind the wheel, peeled out just as the guards raced toward them.

There was nothing like his Ferrari engine, unless it was the new Maserati he'd yet to have time to drive. He slipped into traffic like a thread slicing into the eye of a needle. With luck, those guards wouldn't have had time to record his license. Kidnapping sat so poorly on one's vitae.

A. G. was stirring and groaning. Before he could come completely to, Quentin said, "So,

Mia my invisible friend, what do we do now?
Turn ourselves in to the FBI?"

"Don't be such a poor sport." Mia's low-
pitched voice, always music to his ears, drifted
from behind his right side.

"Do you have a better idea?"

She said nothing, and as if she were there in
person, crouched in the rumble space of the
two-seater, Quentin pictured her as clear as
day. She'd be frowning the tiniest bit, to indicate how serious her thoughts were; yet a hint
of a smile would tuck up the corner of one side
of her mouth. Mia loved a challenge, Mia loved
performing the impossible. Nothing else would
have persuaded her to throw in her lot with
him way back when, when Quentin Grandy
had no awards or little gold statuettes to his
name. Now everyone wanted to produce with
him; only Mia had believed in him then.

And she'd be smoothing that pinky of hers
across her luscious lips. He knew she wished
she hadn't given up that disgusting habit of
nail-chewing; knew she'd done it for him as
much as for herself.

His heartstrings clutched and he cursed in-
wardly. Why was he only imagining his Mia?
By rights, he should be holding his bride in his
arms.

"Turn right," Mia commanded.

He did so, then said, "Why?"

"Airport."

"What?" He started to stomp on the brakes, but the heavy traffic disallowed such a luxury.

"Doesn't MegaFilms keep a jet at the John Wayne Airport?"

Quentin nodded.

"We're going to Arkansas."

"Over my dead body!"

He knew the laugh he heard was Mia's.

"What's going on here?" This time the voice belonged to his visible passenger. A. G. Winston struggled to sit upright in the seat, holding a hand to the side of his head.

As he wasn't quite sure himself what had possessed Mia to crack the genius over the head, Quentin didn't answer.

Winston seemed to be trying to focus his eyes. He rubbed his temples, then after a searching glance at Quentin, said, "You don't take no for an answer, do you?"

"What do you mean?" Quentin hoped Mia hadn't hit Winston too hard.

"You're Quentin Grandy. I'd know you anywhere. You wanted to make a story of my life, and I said no, so now you're kidnapping me?" He shook his head, then winced. "I get investigated for antitrust violations, when the vultures of Hollywood never take no for an answer!"

"I assure you—"

"Let him think that," Mia's voice interrupted in an urgent stage-whisper. "What do you care? Let go of your ego. It serves our purposes. Tell him if he spends the weekend with us, we'll let him go."

"Are you crazy!"

"I really don't think so," Winston replied. "I've always been in remarkable possession of my faculties." He sighed, and added, "Too much so, I'm afraid."

"No, not you!" Quentin applied the brakes in a hurry to avoid a car stalled ahead of them in the lane of traffic. Winston almost hit the dash. "Best put your seat belt on," he said. "We may as well keep you safe, since we're stuck with you for the moment."

Winston fastened his belt, glancing over his shoulder as he did so. "Would that be the royal we?"

Out of the corner of his eye, Quentin caught a flurry of crimson silk. "Of course," he said, thinking he didn't know what he'd do first when Mia returned to her corporeal self, kiss her or throttle her.

"I might point out," Winston said, "that you're not stuck with me. Simply pull over and let me out and your problem will be solved."

Quentin swung into the entrance to the airport. "Have you ever noticed, Mr. Winston, that things aren't always the way they seem?"

"Illogical, but accurate. And you may as well call me A. G." A. G. pulled a tiny flip phone from a coat pocket. "I've no wish to be hit over the head again, so I'll go along with you peaceably. I'll allocate two days to this unusual project. I'll just phone my fiancée and explain we'll have to delay the announcement of our nuptials."

Winston made a face, and said, "Other than being hit over the head, I must say, Grandy, that I feel grateful for your giving me a way out of that circus. I really don't see why who I marry should be of interest to anyone. A new invention, now, that's another matter entirely." A dreamy look came over his face, and Quentin wondered whether the genius had forgotten his surroundings that quickly.

Evidently, he remembered soon enough, because he poised his index finger over the phone. Quentin had to stifle a laugh when he saw the phone almost yanked from A. G.'s hand.

A. G. tugged. Obviously Mia tugged harder.

The phone tumbled into the narrow space behind Quentin's seat.

Winston studied him with a thoughtful expression in his intelligent eyes. "You may be right about things not always being what they seem."

Quentin claimed a parking space near the private plane terminal. Over his shoulder, he said, "What now?"

In answer, the flip phone was passed discreetly to his left side. "Call the hangar. Tell them we're taking off for the landing strip nearest to Eureka Springs, Arkansas."

Wondering why they had to fly to Arkansas,

and pretty sure Mia wasn't about to let him in on the reason why, Quentin lowered his brow and punched in the central number for Mega-Films Transportation. They were more than happy to ready a Gulfstream for Mr. Grandy. For Mr. Grandy, it seemed, they would work miracles.

Feeling strangely discomfited by all that solicitude, Quentin switched off the phone and shook his head when A. G. held his hand out, plainly requesting the return of his property.

"No, my friend," he said, "If we're kidnapping you and transporting you over state lines, what's a little larceny?"

Quentin opened his door and indicated Winston should do the same. The tall computer designer unfolded his body and gave a mighty stretch once he was free of the car. The well-cut suit and trousers looked out of place on the man who appeared to be only a few years older than Quentin's twenty-seven. "Bet you don't wear that get-up often, do you?"

Winston shook his head. "Sharyn insisted I dress up today."

"So when's the wedding?"

The two men walked toward the terminal. Quentin could see the silk hanky fluttering just behind him and to his left.

"It's supposed to be New Year's Eve."

"Romantic way to end one year and begin another."

"I guess it is, but I believe my fiancée chose

the date for tax purposes. She holds an advanced degree in tax."

That went to show you couldn't tell anything by looks anymore. Quentin would have been willing to guess the only advanced degree that blonde held was in the study of the *Kama Sutra*.

Mia was thinking exactly the same thing. As every minute passed, she grew more convinced Mr. G wanted them to free A. G. from Sharyn the Shark's clutches. A. G. talked rather stiffly, as if he were processing each word in his mind before letting go of it, but she found herself liking him. How many people would have come along with them as sensibly as he had?

They had reached the small private plane terminal. The MegaFilms pilot, a knockout brunette, strode forward, hand extended, an expression between a pout and a smile on her full lips. Mia felt her own lip start to curl at this reminder of Quentin's appeal to women everywhere, when to her surprise, the pilot cooed her greeting to A. G. Winston.

Poor Quentin looked downright flabbergasted.

"Now that's a first," Mia said.

"Does that make you happy?"

"I cannot tell a lie. Yes."

Quentin smiled. "Then I'm happy," he said softly.

Mia held back a sigh of longing.

The pilot couldn't seem to keep her hands to herself. Smoothing the front of Winston's suit jacket, she was saying, "You'll be perfectly comfortable with me at the controls." She smiled archly at the word "controls."

"Yech," Mia said.

Quentin grinned.

A. G. gave the woman a polite smile, but other than that, his attentions seemed to have drifted elsewhere. Mia imagined he was performing complicated mathematical calculations on his next invention, while the rest of the world carried on in its own mundane way.

"Where to, Mr. Grandy?" The pilot turned her full-wattage smile on Quentin, after casting one last despairing glance on their sexy genius.

And he was sexy, Mia realized, studying him as Quentin and the pilot moved off to file the flight plan. In looks, A. G. Winston fit her mental image of the moody romantic. Only, Mia couldn't reconcile what she'd heard about his temperament with that image. He was reputed to be cold, distant, concerned only with producing superior technological achievements and a corresponding stellar bottom line of profits.

But to look at him, she'd never suspect that was the totality of his personality. Those hooded eyes, lying beneath brows even craggier and darker than Quentin's, were sapphire dark, fired with an intensity that didn't equate with a cool-headed businessman.

A woman could lose her heart to the steady warmth of those eyes.

Unlike Quentin, who was motion personified, A. G. Winston stood still, body slightly forward, arms at his sides, head cocked just a bit to the left.

His hair, thick and silky, he wore captured in a ponytail that reached below his shoulders. Mia was willing to bet he had long hair simply because he couldn't be bothered with remembering to get his hair cut. He probably had no idea how appealing that glossy mane was to the opposite sex.

Unless, of course, Mia thought darkly, Sharyn whispered that into his ear at regular intervals.

What a waste, letting a woman as brittle and grasping as Sharyn Stonebridge snag this guy. Unless he were equally as shallow, but nothing Mia had detected from her hanky-hearing trick led her to believe that.

She was tempted to sneak another listen when she saw Quentin and the pilot approaching. A. G. shifted, visibly returning his attention to his surroundings.

"Time to go," Quentin said.

"May I ask our destination?" A. G. said.

The pilot looked puzzled.

"I'm not sure we should tell him," Mia whispered in Quentin's ear, unsure why she felt that way.

"Why not tell him?"

"Precisely." A. G. steepled his fingers and looked Quentin straight in the eye. "I didn't run away when I just now had the opportunity to do so."

"True." Quentin looked irritated, and Mia knew why. He hated not knowing what the plan was. A true director, he preferred being in charge.

"Is there something going on here I don't understand?" the pilot asked, squaring her shoulders and making what Mia thought was a very belated attempt to behave professionally.

Quentin gave her one of his easy slow grins. "Just taking a pleasure trip."

She smiled back, no doubt thinking that with two men as famous as Quentin Grandy and A. G. Winston, she might get to share in the pleasure. Before Mia could stop herself, she whipped around and snagged the woman's nylons, creating a satisfying ladder run down the back of one leg.

The pilot glanced around and moaned in disgust. Quentin said, "That's bad karma," in a low voice. Mia shrugged, even though she knew he was right.

To the pilot, Quentin said, "We're conducting an intensive interview with Mr. Winston. We've, uh, reservations in Eureka Springs, Arkansas, for that purpose."

Mia smiled. Of course they didn't have reservations, but Quentin's word choice reminded her of their last adventure wrought by Mr. G. They had found themselves at the local airport and discovered they possessed a mysterious reservation for a rental car, something that came in very handy with both of them invisible.

A. G. nodded. "Very well."

Mia followed them to the plane. She had no idea what they'd find at the Dew Drop Inn, a rustic retreat she'd read about when exploring destinations for her now-abortive honeymoon. But if Sharyn was up to no good there, she thought it could only help to have A. G. discover that fact.

She crossed her fingers, hoping she'd heard Sharyn's thoughts accurately, and they weren't going off to Arkansas on a wild goose chase.

4 ⚬

Why they were headed to Eureka Springs was more than Quentin could figure out. He knew the Ozark resort town was several hours east of where they'd found themselves in their Chelsea Jordan assignment from Mr. G. He knew this because Mia had pored over every type of travel brochure imaginable, trying to pick where they should venture on their honeymoon.

Quentin had thought a week of lying on a beach would be lovely. Simple, quiet, deserted, peaceful. Seven days of sand and sex, his idea of heaven.

But Mia had felt otherwise. She wanted to have an experience. Quentin would usually have been the one itching to be moving about, visiting some place requiring constant energies, but for his honeymoon, he'd wanted the opposite. He wanted to concentrate on Mia and Mia alone.

Good job he'd done of that, he thought,

disgusted with himself. He'd thought himself completely out of a wedding.

The plane shuddered to a halt on the bikini-sized landing strip and Quentin threw down the cards he held. He and A. G. had played poker throughout the flight, and during the games, he'd discovered the man to be bright, congenial, and the kind of guy he wouldn't mind having as a brother.

Mia, as Mia always did whenever they traveled anywhere, had fallen asleep. He couldn't see her, of course, but the silk had ceased bobbing about soon after takeoff.

The plane halted on the tarmac and the hanky fluttered on one of the long couches in the comfortable private plane. "The Dew Drop Inn," Mia's sleepy voice whispered.

"That's where we're going?" Quentin thought that sounded like a name from "Hee-Haw."

"You'll like it. It's cozy and charming, and just a little ways outside of Eureka Springs. And just what the doctor ordered for A. G."

"Where is it we're going?" A. G. collected the cards, shuffled the deck, then returned it to the box before rising and stretching.

"Dew Drop Inn. A five-star resort, I believe." Quentin was sure the sarcasm dripped from his tongue.

Mia tugged on his sleeve. "Don't," she said. "Just trust me, because I know what I'm doing."

He shook his head, but didn't argue. After all their discussions concerning a honeymoon destination, they'd agreed on Maui. And that's where they'd be headed right now, if he'd followed the straight and narrow, so he guessed he had no right to complain about a night or two at the Dew Drop Inn.

"I think I've heard of it, actually," A. G. said, his expression showing he hadn't liked what he'd heard. "Several of my business acquaintances recommended it for its"—he paused and appeared to be replaying a memory tape—"yes, that's right, for its rustic simplicity."

"Like I said, a five-star resort."

"For your information," Mia said, "it's not some dump with an outhouse. The rooms go for three hundred dollars a night and they advertise in *Town and Country*."

"Since when do you read *Town and Country*?"

"I don't," A. G. said over his shoulder as he disembarked. "As a matter of fact, I'm not sure I'm acquainted with that publication."

"I wasn't talking to you," Quentin said, then threw up his hands. "This is going to drive me crazy!"

"I suppose you think it's a picnic for me?"

It took Quentin a moment to register that both A. G. and Mia had said the same thing. He laughed, shook his head, and answered neither one of them. Right now all he wanted was a good run, a hot shower, and then a good bed from which to watch an old movie on cable.

Mia whispered to him to slow down, and he fell back a few steps behind Winston.

"When we get there," she said, "you check in by yourself."

Quentin pointed to Winston.

"I have an idea."

At least now she would let him in on the scheme.

"What Winston needs is a good dose of real life, a chance to learn how the rest of the world lives."

"I disagree." Quentin stopped, checked over his shoulder to make sure Winston wasn't watching him argue with thin air. "The man's filthy rich, sure, but he deals very well in the real world. He's got both feet smack on the ground."

"Quentin, you can say that because you've never been poor."

"What's that got to do with his happiness?"

"Look how quickly you were able to have a jet at your disposal. Think of that pilot fawning over A. G. Why? Because you're an Oscar-winning director and he's the richest bachelor in America."

"So that's the key to your plan, to turn A. G. into a pauper?"

The hanky fluttered. "I already lifted his wallet and signet ring."

These items floated in front of him and

Quentin hastily stuffed them in his pants pocket.

Mia, seemingly with no compunction about her new life of crime, continued, "As long as no one staying at the inn recognizes him, my plan should work."

Quentin had a feeling he wasn't going to like what he was about to hear. "You're not going to bop him over the head again, are you?"

"Only if I have to."

"Are you coming?" A. G. called from the terminal doorway.

"Right!" To Mia, he whispered, "I'll go along with this, simply because I haven't a better idea. And, to be fair, I did get us into this situation."

The hanky dipped, but Mia said nothing.

"I'd like a room," said the tall, suntanned man dressed casually in jeans and a denim shirt.

Jemi smiled. "How many people?"

"T—, er, just me."

She hesitated, wondering whether to question his answer. "A cottage for one costs the same as a cottage for two," she said, deciding that was the most tactful response.

"Money doesn't matter. It's just me. I'm here to do some, uh, research." He drummed his fingers on the counter, then leaned forward. "I'd like it to be for two, but you see, I've suffered some complications in my love life."

"Oh, I'm so sorry." Jemi patted one of his hands, her instinctive sympathy rushing to the forefront. "I hope you'll find the Dew Drop Inn the perfect place for healing. If there's anything you need, my name's Jemi. Let me know and I'll help you in any way I can." She patted his hand again, and said, "I need to see your driver's license and a credit card, please."

"Right." The man patted his pockets, then produced a wallet. Glancing in it, he shut it hastily, returned it to his pocket, glanced over his shoulder with a frown, then pulled out another wallet.

Jemi narrowed her eyes. As nice as the man appeared, with his curly brown hair and wide-set brown eyes, something strange seemed to be going on. Why did he have two wallets?

"How did you hear about the Dew Drop Inn?" she asked as she wrote up his registration.

"Business."

She picked up his driver's license, and almost gasped when she saw the Southern California address. "And are you here on business?"

"Right, like I said research. I'm thinking of uh—research," he repeated, seeming to think better of whatever he'd been about to say.

Jemi thought of the letter she had received only that morning, informing her that the Southern California interest that wished to purchase her inn would be sending a representative right away. Was this the man, traveling incognito? Her cottages were generally booked ahead by the week, and rarely did anyone pop in for a night, especially not businessmen from California.

"Let me give you the Sunrise Cottage, the third one down the lane on the right," she said, thinking to impress him with the best. Then, too late, she thought of the heart-shaped bed, not the thing to do to a man recovering from a broken heart.

"That's fine," he said and glanced again over his shoulder.

"Oh, but you might be more comfortable in the Wildflower," Jemi muttered to herself. But that cabin had been having a problem with a mockingbird that refused to move its nest from the window next to the bed. Jemi realized those were the only two cottages she had available.

"The first one is fine." He paced to the door and back to the registration desk. "The key?"

"Um, we don't have keys here."

"No keys." He gave her an odd stare.

Jemi almost groaned out loud. These city people would never want to buy a place like the Dew Drop Inn. "No one will bother you here." She handed him one of the wooden bluebird cut-outs she gave to all the guests. "The house-keeping staff will enter only if you hang this little bluebird on your doorknob." Not that she had much of a housekeeping staff left.

He accepted the bluebird, but she could tell by the look on his face he was wishing he'd spent the night at the Best Western.

The man was out the door before she realized she hadn't asked him how long he intended to stay.

At first, Mia had her hands full convincing A. G. Winston to remain in their rented Town Car. Obviously assuming Quentin was the only guard on his actions, he'd started to hop out of the car as soon as Quentin disappeared into the office of the Dew Drop Inn.

Even the sight of several free-roaming fowl pecking at Quentin's ankles hadn't discouraged the genius from attempting to gain his freedom.

The first time A. G. opened the door, Mia snatched it shut again. He looked around him, then slid his hand toward the handle. Mia hit the automatic lock button.

"So things aren't always the way they seem," A. G. said, a thoughtful expression on his face.

Mia wished the man could hear her words. She for one could sure tell him the truth of that statement. From weddings that didn't happen to kidnappings that most certainly did, she could enlighten him as to some of the stranger marvels of the universe.

Thinking of the idea she'd had while waking from her nap on the flight, she looked around her for a piece of cardboard or heavy paper.

Without thinking what the action would signify to A. G., she opened the dash and pulled out the papers inside. Luck was with her; the rental company had stashed a heavy cardboard paper inside. One side carried instructions for what to do in an emergency; the other side sported an advertisement for a pizza delivery company. She pulled a pen from A. G.'s pocket and wrote on the heavy paper: Will Work For Food.

"I say," A. G. said, "I do not believe in ghosts. They are not logical nor are they consistent with principles of physics. Therefore, you must know, whoever you are, that you're not scaring me in the least by these sleight-of-hand tricks."

Mia realized what the free-moving actions must look like to A. G. She dropped the pen and wished for a safety pin or some other means to fasten her crudely drawn sign to the back of A. G.'s shirt.

She spared a glance toward the office, and saw Quentin leaning over what looked like the registration desk. No doubt charming the check-in girl. She stifled a sigh, reminding herself that long ago she'd sworn she'd never be jealous of other women. Funny how she'd stuck to that, yet Quentin had still stumbled over his fear of playboyhood.

I might as well be jealous, Mia grumbled to herself.

A. G. tried the door again, and she almost bopped him over the head out of frustration.

She wanted to get him set for his adventure before Quentin returned. The two men had gotten rather buddy-buddy while she'd slept on the flight, and she had no doubt that Quentin would object to her means of assisting A. G. Winston down the path of true happiness.

Quentin paused on the porch of the office and looked around. Night had settled completely on the cluster of cottages. All was quiet and at peace. Perhaps the isolation had been what had interested Mia in considering this place for their honeymoon.

Or, he thought belatedly, perhaps her well-hidden romantic aspect had wanted to return to Arkansas in memory of their time spent in the northwestern part of the state last year, when Quentin the chucklehead had finally realized the gem of his life was right under his nose.

He gazed up at the evening sky where the stars were beginning to emerge. The only other lights were the few shining in the scattered cottages.

Cottage. Bed. Cable TV. Quentin skipped down the steps, heading to the car, when he realized he should have asked for double beds. Even though Mia had insisted he check in alone, Winston would have to sleep somewhere. He dashed back up the stairs but the gamine redhead who'd registered him had disappeared.

Fitting enough for the anxious little thing. Quentin had almost thought she was afraid of him, or perhaps all men made her nervous, but surely that was a strange temperament for someone whose job it was to receive guests. She wasn't his type, but she was cute. Good figure, even disguised beneath the overalls and T-shirt. Not of course, that *he* was interested, but Mia might think of some way to use her to divert A. G.'s thoughts from Sharyn the Shark.

He smiled at that name, then remembered he'd left Mia alone far too long to guard Winston. The brainy guy might have found a way to escape and then there'd be hell to pay. He gave up on the redhead and strode outside, heading for the car once more.

Winston wasn't there.

And in the almost total darkness, he couldn't see anything that even faintly resembled a red silk hanky. Then, in the distance, he saw a bobbing light, like that of a flashlight. Sure enough, the flashlight Mia had insisted he request from the rental agency was gone.

Moving quietly, wondering what Winston was up to, he walked toward the light, which bobbed near the back of the office cottage.

He found Winston advancing steadily on a light that appeared to be moving of its own accord.

Mia!

What was she trying to do, drive the man crazy?

Bad enough that they'd wrested him from his engagement party, now Mia the minx would have him believing in ghosts. For a man of science, that would never do.

"Winston!" Quentin strode up to their kidnappee, ready to offer him the comfort of the Sunrise Cottage.

"No, no, go away, you'll spoil everything," Mia's voice said from behind the flashlight beam.

"And what exactly is it that I'll spoil?" Quentin took a step closer to Winston, wondering at the man's fascinated expression.

"He thinks I'm a ghost and he's investigating and that's just what I want him to do."

"So you can knock his skull in again for some devious purpose?" Quentin spoke in jest, but Mia's silence that followed his statement made him suspicious.

"Er . . ." she finally managed.

"I say," Winston said, "have you learned how to communicate with this extraterrestial being? If so, I'd like to know how you learned, and how you do it. The information could be most useful."

"Thinking of marketing it, Winston?" Quentin couldn't help but admire the man's entreprenurial instincts. No wonder he was America's wealthiest bachelor. Another man in his place would be running away; yet another, belligerent. "I might be able to help you, if we go fifty-fifty on profits, that is."

"Quentin!" Mia hissed his name and Quentin had to smile. The situation was simply too absurd. Wherever he was at that moment, Mr. G had to be laughing.

"Sixty-forty."

"Me sixty?"

Winston shook his head. "Normally I'd offer the one with the insight to the product the greater percentage, but for my bother and travel time, I think you owe me the greater amount."

Quentin thought that sounded reasonable. "Okay," he said. "Now, let me tell you a story."

As he opened his mouth to speak, he felt a crack to his head and he slumped to the ground.

"Grandy?" Winston rushed forward, and Mia took a deep breath. Hitting her beloved over the head was more than she could deal with, and now . . . she gripped her eyes closed and bopped Winston over the head with the flashlight.

"Oh, dear. Oh, dear. I've become excessively violent," she said, looking down at the two bodies. First things first, though, she thought, and huffed and puffed until she'd dragged Winston's body onto the back porch of the office cottage. From her quick survey of the Dew Drop Inn, she'd determined that was where the manager lived and prepared meals.

She tugged until she had A. G. Winston

slumped into a seated position, his "Will Work for Food" sign stuck to the back of his shirt with a leftover bobby pin meant to fasten her veil.

Then she ran down the steps and splashed some water from a garden hose on Quentin's face to rouse him and get him out of the way before A. G. recovered.

She almost hated to bring him around; he sure wasn't going to be happy.

5 ~

Alexander Graham Winston was not in the habit of thinking of himself as anybody's fool.

But in less than twelve hours, he'd been shanghaied, led to believe ghosts might exist, cracked on the head twice, and now, to add to the list of indignities, just discovered that he'd been robbed of his wallet and signet ring.

Even worse, he could not identify his whereabouts.

Alex looked around, peering through the inky night, seeking clues. Beneath his feet, wooden steps; to his back, a closed door. From the bushes around the steps, mysterious rustlings issued; otherwise, only the calls of a few birds broke the silence of the evening.

He rubbed the bump on the back of his head, wondering whether the earlier hit had caused him to hallucinate the light that moved of its own accord. But, no, Quentin Grandy had heard the other-world creature's voice and had carried on a conversation with it.

Where had Grandy gone? The director had slumped to the ground just before Alex himself had succumbed. Odd, most odd. Had he imagined his presence, also? Alex shook his head, then winced.

The door behind his head creaked, then hit him square in the back.

He leapt up, then staggered as a spell of dizziness caught him unawares.

"Oh, I'm so sorry!" a sweet female voice cried out.

The next thing Alex knew, warm hands guided him back to where he'd been seated on the top step.

"Put your head between your knees if you're dizzy," the voice said from behind him. "Oh, I do hope I haven't hurt you too badly."

He started to twist his head around to see who his assailant-rescuer was, but the movement did make him queasy.

"There, there," she said, stroking his head the way no one had since his mother had stopped doing it when he reached the manly age of six. "Don't rush. Take a nice slow deep breath."

As she spoke the soothing words, she breathed long and deep herself, continuing to smooth his hair. He thought he also heard something rustle behind his back, and for a fraction of a moment, he pictured himself possessed of angel's wings. Then he recovered his usual good sense. Neither ghosts nor angels existed. After a long moment, he lifted his head and turned half around.

The sight that met his eyes amazed him.

He knew she was a woman, by her voice, her hands, her sympathetic style. But her hair was pulled into a stern braid. Her clothes were the overalls that farmers adopted, though hers did stop short of her knees and were softened by the addition of a white undershirt. Her feet were bare.

He looked at the woman's face, and realized he might not believe in ghosts, but from this moment on he would believe in angels.

As he focused on her face, her sensuous mouth curved into a warm smile. Her eyes, under beautifully arched brows, were large with concern. However, the light cast from the door left her in enough shadow that he couldn't say whether those eyes were blue or brown or green. Her hair was a rich color somewhere between red and brown. But, even without discerning all the specifics, he could say he would describe her as beautiful.

Alex slowly shook his head. She removed her hand.

He almost asked her to put it back. Then he remembered himself.

Alexander Graham Winston: entrepreneur, genius, billionaire, and man about to be officially engaged. Why he should find comfort with a stranger on a porch in the middle of nowhere was quite beyond him.

He half-rose and said, "My name is Alex. I'm sorry to bother you, but I'm in need of a telephone."

"I'm Jemi," the woman said, "and of course you need a lot more than just a telephone."

She joined him on the step, her legs and body moving with a flexibility and grace Alex couldn't help but admire. He himself was so tall that he'd felt like a bumbling calf since his junior high growth spurt of ten inches.

"I do?" he said.

"Do you know how to cook?"

He lifted one hand to the bump on his head. Perhaps he had been injured more than he'd realized. "May I ask why you ask that question?"

"No need to worry about pride with me," the woman said. "One form of work is as good as another. I cook, I clean, I make the beds, so why would I look down on anyone else willing to work at exactly the same thing?" She smiled gently and pointed to his back. "And if you work for me, it won't be just for food. I need help, and I'm willing to pay. The only question is, can you cook?"

Alex reached a hand tentatively over his shoulder. Sure enough, something was stuck to the back of his jacket. He tugged, and to his amazement, he found himself staring at a crudely lettered sign. He held it up to the light from the back door and read, "Will Work for Food."

"I have no idea how this found its way onto my back," Alex said, "but as a matter of fact, I'm a fair cook. I enjoy the process of combining ingredients to reach a sum greater than the whole."

She stared at him for a long moment, as if processing his sentence, then said, "Bread?"

"Yes."

"Quiche?"

"Quite handy at that."

"Rice?"

"Absolutely."

"You'll do." The woman rose, lifting herself effortlessly from legs crossed under her body. "Come in and I'll show you the kitchen. Then I'll find you a place to sleep. Oh, I mean, I'm assuming you don't have a home."

Alex started to reply of course he had a home, and quite a nice one, too, thank you very much. But he caught himself before the words crossed his lips. As long as he was here, in the middle of nowhere, he might as well exchange work for shelter. That was a basic transaction of society, one he'd never experienced at such a primal level. He cocked his head to the left, assessing the value to be gained from such a lesson. He also observed that under the mannish overalls, Ms. Jemi possessed curves that were as soft and womanly as her sweet voice. "I would be most appreciative of a place to stay," Alex said and rose to follow her inside.

Jemi held the door open, thinking how sad it

was such a fine-looking young man should
have fallen on hard times. He held himself
well, posture erect despite his height, which
was about a foot taller than her own five feet
four. He stepped closer, and she noted his
clothes certainly seemed in good condition for
a homeless man. A small voice in the back of
her head warned her that this man wasn't what
he appeared, and another voice, most likely
echoes of her brother Ari, joined in. *Jemi, you
can't rescue everyone. Jemi, you should think before
you act. Jemi, what if you take in someone who isn't
as harmless as you assume?*

"Where are you from?" Jemi asked as they
entered the spacious, homey kitchen where she
prepared the meals for her guests.

The man blinked and said, "California. I'm
an—uh, engineer."

Well, that explained it. Jemi knew California
had suffered a recession, and that high-
technology companies weren't the golden ap-
ples they'd been for so many years.

"Do you want to see my identification?" he
asked, not reaching for any.

Jemi waved a hand. "What for? I operate on
instinct and you seem okay to me, Alex." She
looked at the mess of dishes she'd left in the
sink earlier. Casey would have had those
whipped out in no time, but without Casey,
Jemi had fallen sorely behind schedule. "Why
don't you start on those dishes, then get the
bread ready for tomorrow? I have to conduct

the evening yoga session in the summer house." She waved at the cupboards lining the wall. "You'll find everything you need in there, and I won't be more than an hour."

The man nodded. "I can take care of that," he said, removing his jacket and rolling up the sleeves of a white shirt that looked remarkably clean for a man in his straits.

Jemi almost reconsidered. Yet only that morning she'd asked the universe to provide the help she needed, and as usual, the universe had responded. It was not for her to question in what package the help arrived.

She studied the man's face for a long moment, noting the deep blue eyes, the brows that almost joined over a nose that undoubtedly had been broken at some point. His mouth was steady and the corners curved upwards, which indicated a good heart. Other than the wavy thick hair he had fastened into a ponytail, he could have been any young professional. The hair certainly didn't fit her idea of that image, but then, she did live in the woods, way off the beaten track.

"Do I pass inspection?" he asked in a quiet voice and she jumped.

"Since you ask, yes." She smiled. "Okay, Alex, take over." She turned and walked quickly from the room, whistling happily as she headed for the summer house and her guests awaiting their evening yoga lesson.

* * *

"What has gotten into you?" Quentin struggled to sit up, one hand held to his throbbing head, another to his queasy stomach.

"You were about to spoil the plan I'd put into effect," Mia answered from behind him.

"Plan-schman." Quentin twisted around, knowing he did so in vain. All he would find of Mia was her voice. He rubbed the lump on his skull. "Whatever happened to us working together?"

She didn't answer, and Quentin knew he'd said the wrong thing. He cringed both at his own stupidity and at the pain in his head.

A cricket chirrupped near his feet, but Mia still didn't respond.

"Plan aside," Quentin continued, addressing the darkness and the lone cricket that jumped onto his shoe, "I've never known you to be violent. But you've taken to head cracking like a natural born felon."

Chirripp.

Quentin looked at the tiny creature. "At least you're talking to me." His eyes had adjusted to the darkness. He lowered his head to look more closely at the critter sitting on his deck shoe. "What do you think? Do you think she'll answer me? Work with me? Forgive me?"

He had no idea whether Mia was still there, whether she could hear him, but he might as well take the opportunity to plead his case indirectly. He said to the cricket, "If you see Mia, please tell her how sorry I am."

Quentin extended a finger and the cricket sailed onto his hand, working its triangulated hind legs musically. Whispering, Quentin said, "Ask her if she'll marry me?"

The cricket stopped singing in mid-note, so abruptly that for a crazy moment, Quentin wondered whether Mia had conjured herself into the tiny creature's body.

"You're losing it, Quentin," he said aloud, and just as the cricket began singing again, Mia's voice said excitedly, "He's going inside with her!"

Quentin lowered the cricket to the grass. "Who's going where with whom?"

"I wish you'd pay attention. A. G. and Jemi."

He rubbed his head and waited for an explanation. Mia might be invisible, but he was clearly the one left in the dark.

"Jemi is the woman who runs the Dew Drop Inn."

"A redhead with a long braid and odd taste in clothing?"

"The same."

"She checked me in. Seemed kind of anxious."

"Really? Most nervous types wouldn't take a homeless man off their back steps and give him a job."

Quentin stood up and stretched. The pain in his head had lessened. "How do you know she's the kind to do that?"

Silence.

Another chreeep from the cricket.

"Mia, does this have something to do with your plan?"

"Yes, and listen, it's brilliant, if I do say so myself. I don't think of myself as the creative half of our team, but what could be better than casting America's richest bachelor as a homeless man who'll work for food?"

Quentin wasn't sure whether the question was hypothetical or had practical application to their situation, but his heart did feel relieved by her reference to them as a team. Perhaps she no longer viewed him as a complete pariah. He turned, desperately wishing he could see Mia. Nothing.

He sighed and said, "Did you make him a cardboard sign and ask him to knock on her back door and ask for work?"

"Don't be silly. I don't think he would've understood the request. So I did have to tap him ever so lightly on the head, then I fastened the sign to his back."

Quentin groaned. "Violence, Mia, is rarely a creative solution. What if someone with less than a heart of gold had chanced upon him? Lifted his wallet or done him harm?"

Something waved in front of his face. "Remember I'd already taken his wallet and his signet ring, so there's no need to worry about someone mugging him."

"Because you've already done it."

"For his own good, you understand."

Quentin couldn't believe his ears. His little rule-conscious Mia arguing for situation ethics? Despite his amazement at her behavior and the sluggish feeling in his head, he admired her quick thinking. "Maybe you should direct our next movie and I'll stay home."

"I have no desire to direct. I'm simply trying to move this project along, the way any good producer would do." Her voice grew decidedly colder. "After all, I've no desire to prolong our time together here. I need to get home and get on with my life."

"Oh, Mia—"

"Forget it, Quentin."

Tonight was too soon to beg forgiveness. Tomorrow, when the sun came up and time began to heal the hurt, he'd try again. He covered a yawn, and said, "We've got the Sunrise Cottage."

"You mean *you* have the Sunrise Cottage."

"Where are you going to stay?"

"I don't think it matters where an invisible person sleeps." She sounded tough, but sorrowful.

The cricket added a slow cry of its own.

"It matters to me. Please, Mia, come to the cabin. I won't sleep for worrying about you." Nice sentiment coming from him, Quentin thought in disgust, after the worry he'd caused her by not showing up at the wedding. Her image, as he'd seen it in the looking glass courtesy of Mr. G, filled his mind and he tightened his jaw. He'd make it up to her, he swore to himself.

"But I'm invisible," Mia said with her own brand of stubborn logic.

"Sweetheart, that's not the same thing as invincible." He held out a hand, and to his relief, he felt the whisper of silk touch his fingertips.

Together, alone, they walked toward the cottage.

It was the oddest thing, but hunt as he might, Alex couldn't locate the dishwasher. He thought perhaps she'd contrived to place an industrial type Hobart behind a cabinet face, but his very thorough check of the large kitchen revealed no appliance designed to wash, rinse, and sterilize dishes. That puzzled him; he knew about such machines due to an investment he'd made and felt certain health regulations must require such a device.

Almost hidden under the mounds of dirty dishes, the sink did consist of three compartments, which he finally concluded must fulfill those three steps in the cleaning process. But this technique surprised him in a place reported to be as desirable as the Dew Drop Inn.

Only last month one of his friends, the president of a successful software company, had been telling him and Sharyn of their relaxing week at the inn. Best vacation he could remember, he'd said. Rest, relaxation, fresh air, a total escape from the stresses of everyday life.

Alex turned his back on the dumping ground of dirty dishes and decided he'd prepare the bread. When Jemi returned, he'd ask her where she housed the dishwasher.

Jemi was rather an unusual name, he thought, beginning another search of the cabinets for the bread machine. Sure she'd have a commercial-size device, he looked first in the large floor-to-ceiling pantries.

Again, he came up with nothing. But she'd clearly asked him to make bread. Not muffins, not biscuits, but bread.

He rather enjoyed baking bread. He'd tried most of the recipes in the bread machine cookbooks. When the units first appeared on the market, he'd had one delivered express. No doubt he'd been trying to recreate a childhood he'd never known, to manufacture the experience of home cooking.

Thinking of his childhood was never a comfort to Alex, so he banished the thoughts from his mind. But had it not been for those years, he'd certainly have no idea how to cook. So he supposed he should be thankful, or he might be spending this night under the stars.

His mother had been far too distracted by her research to consider a young child's needs. The housekeeper had maintained a certain lax order, cleaning when the dust bunnies grew into basketballs, but dinner for many years at the Winston household had consisted of peanut butter and jelly sandwiches for Alex. He assumed his father ate at the university where he taught and researched, the same for his mother.

Two different universities. Alex had decided, at some point during his teen years, no one school could have housed both brains or egos.

Though they rarely thought of feeding his tummy, they treated his mind to all the food groups, and added gourmet delicacies as soon as he'd grasped the basics. From his toddler years, Alex had been trained, schooled, and prepped to be brilliant.

But he remembered most how hungry he'd been before he'd learned to fend for himself in the kitchen.

Alex sighed and glanced around this kitchen. A pine table with four chairs claimed the middle of the room. A cup of coffee, cream congealed on its surface, had been left next to a placemat featuring a smiling cow. A magazine lay next to the cup. Curious, he looked at the cover.

Cosmopolitan.

He wrinkled his brow. The title provided an odd contrast for a country woman dressed in overalls.

Then he reminded himself he'd made a most unscientific leap from observation of facts to conclusion. Perhaps other females occupied this room.

Surely someone had put the bread machine away in a most inconspicuous place.

Drawn toward the table, he seated himself and turned to the front of the magazine. *Cosmopolitan* was not a journal familiar to him. He didn't think Sharyn read it, and as it wasn't one in which Winston Enterprises advertised, he knew nothing of its composition.

The first twenty pages or so consisted of glossy color ads.

Beautiful women.

Young women.

His pulse raced a bit.

He thought of Sharyn, wondered whether she was worried sick over his disappearance.

As soon as Jemi returned, he'd ask again to use the telephone.

He turned a page and studied the table of contents. The magazine consisted of stories of fashion, sex, beauty, sex, diet, and sex.

He hadn't realized magazines targeted so much material on sex to women.

He wondered, staring at these articles, whether he shouldn't order Sharyn a subscription to *Cosmopolitan*. To Alex's great frustration, even after she'd finally agreed to marry him, she scarcely allowed more than a kiss.

Sharyn.

Alex quit turning the pages and stared unseeing across the room.

Many a night after Sharyn came to work for Winston Enterprises he'd returned to his luxurious home, alone, hurting, aching, frustrated, and determined to win the woman who seemed his natural mate.

Sharyn had been heralded by *MoneyMag* as "one of the rising stars of financial management." Alex observed her brilliance on a day-to-day basis, and his companies benefited from her expertise.

Sharyn defined gorgeous.

Sharyn knew how to control a boardroom and how to host a dinner party.

When he'd almost given up hope that Sharyn would ever look at him as a male object of desire rather than a brainy but absent-minded colleague and boss, Sharyn herself had playfully suggested they made the perfect couple.

It was after that Alex dared to hope.

He knew himself for the geek he was.

Knew women might want him for his money, but scarcely for his own eccentric self.

What woman wanted to live with a man who worked twenty hours a day, who had been known to wander off from a corporate function and return four hours later, having just invented a new hardware device?

Sharyn never seemed to mind. She was the essence of control, of charm, of the partner who could accept and understand.

She also had a figure that set his heart to thumping.

But she never played around. A ring on the finger, she'd said, and then we'll live in paradise. The way her lips had curved, her tongue peeking out just enough to hint at ecstasy beyond his imagination, had set Alex over the edge.

The next day, he'd proposed and given her the ten-carat ring he'd selected because he remembered her saying she wanted the biggest and best ring ever. And there they had been, about to announce their engagement to the world when Grandy had whisked him away. True, he'd played along with the director, somehow relieved at being rescued from announcing his engagement, a tender and romantic event, the way he would herald a corporate buyout. But Sharyn was to be his wife, and he'd run out on her.

What was he thinking of?

He had to get out of here.

Back to California.

Back to Sharyn.

He leapt up from the table. The chair crashed to the floor.

6 ～

Jemi was still whistling as she skipped up the path from the summer house. She raised her arms toward the night sky, and thanked the universe for such a wonderful life. For all the things she complained about, most often her fear of being stuck in the hills forever, away from the city lights that held such attraction for her, she did love the Dew Drop Inn.

She enjoyed meeting her guests, watching them arrive at the beginning of their stay, many of them pale and drained of energy, then observing them as they relaxed and prospered under her care.

The current group really enjoyed the yoga. Even the lovebirds on their honeymoon participated, letting go of one another long enough to practice the asanas as Jemi led them.

Continuing toward the office cottage, Jemi smiled as she pictured the professor of antiquities and his wife. Their first night, almost a week ago, the old man had blustered on about the origins and history of yoga, but declared he himself had no use for such things. His wife, reminding him their son **was** paying for their week's stay out of his concern for their health, had bullied her husband into trying it. And at tonight's session, the professor had stopped to thank Jemi. "Haven't felt better in years," he'd said, beaming and pulling his wife to his side for a quick hug.

Yes, she did love the inn.

She also loved yoga, appreciating the way it provided a special way to settle her soul and renew her peace of mind. Thank goodness her parents had instilled the habit into her at an early age.

The thought of her parents dimmed her joy a watt or two. She missed them, but couldn't help but feel Ari was right when he said their mother and father were the two youngest children in the Dailey family. Only last week, after reading a letter he'd received from Yap, the South Pacific island where they'd gone to experience life with the natives, Ari had declared that their parents would never grow up. And he'd used that occasion to lecture, gently enough, on the topic of Jemi letting go of the Dew Drop Inn.

The inn had been her parents' thing, until they'd grown bored. They'd left it to her when her siblings had heartily disclaimed any interest. She had no obligation to keep it going, not when she wanted to return to college and move on with her life. Ari and her sisters certainly hadn't clung to the past.

Jemi slowed, thinking of the man from California who'd checked in that evening. What if he, or the interest he represented, did want to buy the inn? What if she could earn enough money from the sale to move, to start over in a city where she could experience all the adventures she yearned to live?

A shiver of anticipation coursed through her.

Yes, I'll do it, she said to herself.

Sugar bounded up to her just then, leaping to wet her face with a well-placed lick or two. An owl hooted overhead; in the stream by the path, a fish leapt into the air, landing with a cheerful splash.

Jemi paused and hugged her arms around herself. She must be crazy to think of abandoning such a peaceful home. She'd visited Ari and her sister Libby in Manhattan, ogled the buildings that grew to the sky and sandwiched in so many lives. She'd also walked the crowded sidewalks, but instead of feeling overwhelmed, as she'd expected, she'd been invigorated. Her blood had hummed with the tempo of the city and she had known she could be happy there.

What to do, what to do? Sugar nudged her knee, and Jemi decided that for the moment, she wouldn't worry. She had her hands full, and her task for the moment was to check on her new assistant. She gave Sugar a rough and tumble hug and continued toward her cottage, her dog dancing along at her side.

The thought of returning to a clean kitchen, bread rising in the oversized blue and cream stoneware bowls, nothing for her to do but select the oranges for the morning's fresh-squeezed juice set her to whistling again.

The man, Alex, had appeared competent enough, taking off his jacket and rolling up his sleeves. Jemi liked that in a helper; it matched her own style. When something had to be done, she did it.

Susannah, the twelve-year-old who claimed the inn as her home away from a place so miserable it couldn't be called home, was of the same nature. Jemi frowned, thinking of the child. Something needed to be done about her situation. For two years now, Jemi had nurtured the child under her wing. It saddened her that the sweet and very bright youngster had no one other than her grandmother Queenie Gillmore, the town drunk, to look after her.

Ari often ribbed her for attempting to rescue every stray of the universe, and in keeping with that pattern, Jemi had tried to reach out to Queenie, too. But the older woman had rebuffed her. Actually, Jemi remembered with a sigh, Queenie had chased her off the crooked metal steps of her dilapidated house trailer with a kitchen knife, hollering that she didn't need nothing from nobody.

The lights were on in the Sunrise Cottage. As she passed by, Jemi realized the Californian had said nothing about luggage. He probably wouldn't stay more than one night, then, and tomorrow very well could be her only day to make the Dew Drop Inn sparkle.

With that thought in mind, she bounded up the steps to the office cottage. Perhaps she'd turn some of the bread dough into cinnamon rolls and decorate them with nasturtiums.

Sugar at her heels, Jemi walked through the office and dining room. She pushed open the swinging door to the kitchen, wondering whether the violet and saffron Johnny Jump-Ups might not work better with the cinnamon rolls.

Visions of flowers flew from her mind when she stepped into the mess that had been her kitchen.

Dishes and utensils had been pulled from the cupboards, her canning racks and five-gallon steaming pots yanked from their nesting places in the pantry. Everywhere she turned, things were out of place, mostly left in oddly neat stacks on the floor. And to add insult to injury, not one dirty dish had been washed.

She sniffed the air, but could detect no indication of the yeasty promise of bread dough set to rise.

And no sight of the man she'd taken in.

"Gemini Dailey, you are a fool." She righted a chair that had been kicked backwards, then dropped into it and covered her eyes. Had the man been ransacking in search of money? Drugs? Perhaps he'd taken her for the hippie type to have marijuana squirreled away. But drugs interfered with nature and Jemi had never touched them, despite the casual acceptance, especially of marijuana, by her parents and their friends.

The office! She leapt up and ran into the room where she kept her books, receipts and payments. Almost all her guests paid by credit card, but she kept cash on hand for Susannah's and Casey's wages. She ran a familiar eye over the area behind the reception desk. Not one page of the calendar had been displaced, nor one dollar disturbed.

Slowly, she returned to the kitchen. Sugar had remained there, body poised alertly as if awaiting orders to seek and destroy.

"Oh, I'm sure he's long gone," Jemi said, stroking the dog. "We won't see his face again."

Despite the mess in her kitchen and all the work she faced, she experienced a sense of regret. The man had been different, would have had stories to tell. The way he'd asked, "Do I pass inspection?" hinted at both humor and sensitivity.

Jemi met men who came as paying guests, but they always came as couples, some with women, some with other men. They asked questions about Ozark folklore or the origins of the inn or sought advice on advanced yoga postures, but they never regarded her in the way she knew a man looked at a woman.

Most of her male friends from Eureka Springs were Ari's pals, which meant no matter how charming and attentive they were, they were more interested in one another.

And here she'd had a man, an intelligent and attractive man, all to herself and he'd fled, fast.

Grimly, Jemi tied an apron over her yoga tights and set to work mixing the bread. While she measured the flour and poured out the oil, she pictured the man's crooked nose and wondered how he'd broken it, regretting that now she'd never have a chance to discover the mystery her imagination assured her lay behind it.

The first thing Quentin commented on about the Sunrise Cottage was its complete dearth of modern necessities: no telephone, no television—not even VHF, let alone cable, and no lock on the door.

Mia gazed at the heart-shaped bed, covered in a quilt of red and white hearts stitched within circles of blue. A bed designed for honeymooners who'd not even notice the lack of a television.

Quentin dropped into one of the two easy chairs by the fireplace. "No gas starter, either," he grumbled. He kicked off his shoes and unbuttoned his shirt.

Mia halted, caught between the sight of Quentin undressing and the images the bed brought to her mind.

"It's a good thing I'm worn out," Quentin said, "or I'd insist on finding another hotel."

Mia fluttered the crimson reminder of her presence at Quentin. He had himself to thank for these countrified conditions; were it not for his behavior, they'd be on their way to Maui. "We're not here for a holiday, we're here to do a job."

"Yes, yes, yes." Quentin stripped off his shirt and let it fall to the floor of the cabin. "If I could convince you how sorry I am about this morning, and you could find it in your heart to forgive me, we could go back, get married, and fly away to a real hotel for a real honeymoon."

"It's that simple, is it?" Mia didn't bother keeping any of the starch out of her voice. "If it was simple you wanted, why didn't you show up for the wedding? Now that would have saved a lot of trouble."

Quentin held out his hands, looked around him, fastened his gaze on the red square floating nearby. "How many ways do I have to say I'm sorry?"

"Words won't cut it, Quentin. What's going to happen next time you worry over whether you can be faithful? I used to be the one consumed with jealousy. Every time an actress cozied up to you, I went ballistic. And I thought you spent far too many energies guarding over

Chelsea Jordan. But I worked that out, I really did." Mia wasn't sure whether she was reassuring herself or Quentin. "And just when I thought I had nothing to worry about, you fall apart."

"I love you too much to hurt you."

Mia stomped her foot. Of course Quentin couldn't see, but it made her feel better. "Loving someone means working things out, sharing those fears. If you'd talked to me ahead of time, you probably wouldn't have frozen up. But I had no clue these fears were haunting you. Did someone set you off? Did you run into an old girlfriend?"

Mia gripped the silk square and wondered whether she dared listen in on Quentin's thoughts. Earlier that evening she'd used its magic to confirm what her sighting of Gemini Dailey had indicated: Where Sharyn's heart was made of steel and muscle, Jemi's consisted of love and hope.

Quentin was shaking his head. Mia lifted the hanky toward her heart, but hesitated. How much better it would have been for both of them if Quentin had shared his inner turmoil. Listening in wouldn't help him learn to open up.

"There's no one else, you must believe that." He rose and paced the small setting room of the cottage. "How could it be a question of someone else? We were getting married today, for pete's sake."

"Then what was it?"

He ran a hand through his hair, then said, "If only I could see you, maybe I could explain. It sounds so crazy, and talking to thin air is driving *me* crazy."

"So you're saying you don't want to talk about it." She felt him closing her off. She heard her mother's words from that morning, "If the guy is no good, you're better off knowing now, before the wedding."

Quentin shook his head. "Not right now."

Mia cast one more glance at the heart-shaped bed and another at Quentin's bare chest and sorrowful face. "Then go to sleep," she said.

He pointed to the bed. "There's plenty of room."

Mia thought of the first bed they ever shared, a nest she'd built of hay and leaves the last time they'd been in Arkansas on one of Mr. G's inspired assignments. She thought of the brand new king-size waterbed, their marriage bed, they'd purchased for their Hollywood Hills home, awaiting their return from Maui for a proper christening.

"There's a hammock on the porch," she said quietly. "I'll bunk there."

And before he could protest, she slipped out the door.

Alex had run up the winding road that led to the highway they'd driven in on from the airport, possessed by the feeling he had to call

Sharyn as soon as possible or something terrible might happen.

The thought made no logical sense. Of course he needed to let her know where he was and apologize for disappearing under such awkward circumstances. He couldn't imagine what she had said to the assembled crowd of reporters and well-wishers to explain his abrupt disappearance.

But assuming that something terrible would happen was most nonlogical. Sharyn might be upset with him, but she had the coolest head of any woman he knew. A rational explanation would be all she needed to set things right.

Perhaps, Alex thought as he trudged toward the distant lights now coming into view, the difficulty of the situation grew from there being no rational explanation.

Alex looked up at the stars lighting his way and as he did, a distant memory, long repressed, wafted into his mind.

His eighth birthday and his parents had declared he should have a party.

Alex stopped his long strides and gazed up at the night sky, remembering now, in great detail, that afternoon.

The formal dining table, the one his family rarely used, had been draped with a bright blue cloth. Plates and cups with screaming clown faces on them set at ten places. A man dressed as a clown had been hired to entertain him and the other children, though at eight years of age, Alex felt himself beyond such silliness.

Alex knew his parents must have made the other parents agree to send their children. The kids in his class didn't like him. He knew they laughed at his thick glasses and at the way it took him so long to think of an answer to any question put to him.

He sat stiffly on the sofa, uncomfortable in the new shoes and gray slacks, white shirt and bow tie the housekeeper had forced him to wear.

When he heard the doorbell ring, warning of the first guest, Alex ripped off his tie and raced out the back door of the house. He ran as fast as he could, kicking off his new shoes and dropping them in a neighbor's trash can.

He'd been wading in someone's koi pond a few blocks away when the security patrol found him.

His parents had hauled him into the house and in front of the assembled guests, lectured him on responsibility. Then they made him return all the gifts his classmates had given him.

Until today, he'd never again bolted from his life. Technically, he'd been abducted, but he knew in his heart he'd gone along with Grandy, tempted by the rare opportunity to steal a moment away from his life.

Alex looked down at his dress shirt and

expensive wool trousers. He glanced around at
the dark woods stretching out from both sides
of the road. He could almost feel the cool water
of that koi pond as he began to move forward
again.

He reached a fork in the road. A sign indicated Dalton lay one mile to the left, Eureka
Springs one mile to the right. He turned to the
right and soon saw the lights of a town. A car
approaching from behind him slowed and
through an open window, a man offered him a
ride into town. Alex thanked the man, but
declined the offer. The vigorous walk in the
mountain air was helping him to clear his head.

It was also making him hungry, he realized
as he reached the first establishment on the
outskirts of Eureka Springs. He gazed around
at the Victorian-styled buildings. Most of the
shops were closed, but here and there he
spotted what appeared to be restaurants or
cafes.

He unrolled his sleeves. Darn, he'd left his
jacket behind in his rush to leave the Dew Drop
Inn. He should have left a note of appreciation
for Jemi, too. She had been more generous with
him than anyone he knew would have been.
He couldn't say that he would have taken in a
homeless man appearing on the back steps of
his Newport Beach estate; not that anyone
could get through the elaborate security system
he'd designed to knock on his back door.

What a funny woman, opening her door and

showing no surprise at his appearance. Funny, but kind and trusting. Also, Alex remembered, she possessed those wonderfully laughing eyes and womanly curves that could distract a man from his work.

His stomach rumbled, but he ignored it and stepped into a wooden phone booth. He punched in the numbers of his phone card and dialed Sharyn's home. To his surprise, her housekeeper informed him that Sharyn had taken a week off to visit some spa. No, she hadn't left the name or the location.

Slowly, Alex replaced the phone. Standing in the booth, he reflected on that information. Had she been upset that he'd disappeared? She knew he was not a man to act impulsively. He might drift away in the midst of a party and go to work on his current invention, but that was not done on impulse. People who knew him understood his working style. One of the reasons he thought he and Sharyn would deal together so well as husband and wife was her acceptance of his behavior.

But going away for a week without leaving a destination indicated definite pique.

He'd expected to find her worried, sitting by the phone waiting to hear from him. Feeling strangely dejected, he dialed Winston Enterprises and informed the evening receptionist to let his staff know he'd be on a research trip for the next few days.

Then he entered the first eating establishment he came to, proclaimed by a woodcut sign as the Dogwood Cafe.

He seated himself at the counter of the tiny establishment. His body was so long that he had nothing to do with all the height hulking over the countertop. Immediately he wished he had selected a table. But a diner alone seemed an imposition. He forced his back into the straight-as-an-arrow posture drummed into him by his mother in the odd moments she'd caught him slumping as a youth, and folded his hands on the counter.

"New in town?"

Alex looked at the middle-aged man seated two seats over. The man wore a polo shirt, shorts, and thongs, and had been poring over a copy of *Fortune* before addressing Alex.

"No and yes," Alex answered. He hadn't realized until just that moment just how sheltered his existence was. He lived behind gates and alarms; he commuted in a chauffeured car; he worked in a glass and chrome fortress. When he and Sharyn went out for dinner, they selected an exclusive restaurant where no one would bother them. For movies, they had the screening room at his Newport home. Counting Quentin Grandy and Jemi, he'd met more strangers today than at any other time in his recent life.

Alex steepled his fingers.

The man leaned closer and said, "The food isn't bad here, but I recommend sticking to the burger. When they get fancy they don't quite come through with the goods as promised." He pointed to his plate. "See this, it's supposed to be fettucine carbonara. I've had better Spaghettios out of a can."

Alex found himself smiling. "Thank you for the warning."

The man threw some bills on the counter and rose. He passed a business card over and said, "If you stick around, give me a call. Name's Paul. I run the Deerly Beloved." He held out a hand and Alex responded with a handshake.

Fingering the man's card and wondering at such casual friendliness, Alex was pleased to see the waitress appear. She pulled a pencil from a nest of platinum blonde hair and said, "What'll it be?"

"Burger. Medium rare. And a Coke."

She blew a bubble, then glanced over her shoulder. Alex surmised such behavior was against the rules. He certainly wasn't used to restaurants where the waitstaff chewed gum.

"We got Pepsi. That OK?"

He nodded.

She disappeared through a swinging door.

He was ravenous. While he waited for his food, Alex studied the placemat on the counter. It appeared to be a map of Eureka Springs. To his surprise, he saw that the Dew Drop Inn was included. Judging by the scale of the map, the inn was four miles from the center of town. No wonder he'd worked up an appetite.

The waitress slapped his plate down. "Getcha anything else?"

He shook his head and picked up his knife and fork. The woman paused and stared at his hands.

"Is anything the matter?" Alex asked.

"Nah," she said, watching him over his shoulder as she moved away.

He cut the burger neatly in two and attacked it with zeal, slicing a bite and tucking it onto the back of his fork before delivering it to his mouth. He thought he caught the waitress staring at him again, but he was too hungry to wonder about the odd habits of the local people.

Soon he'd cleaned his plate and drained his Pepsi.

"Dessert?"

"No, thank you," Alex said.

The waitress scribbled on a pad and dropped a ticket on the counter. "You can pay me when you're ready," she said.

7 ~

Through the haze of a most confusing dream, Jemi heard the pounding on her door. She was light, she was matter, she floated beyond the boundaries of her earthly existence.

But the pounding dragged her down, chasing away the dream.

Wondering what ill-mannered guest might be trying to check in during the middle of the night, Jemi hauled herself from her warm bed and scuffed into her bunny slippers. By the chair where she'd draped the stranger's jacket, she hesitated, then shrugged it on over her nightshirt. She knew she must make an odd sight, with the jacket brushing her knees, the sleeves swallowing her hands. But the fabric, weighing heavily on her shoulders yet caressing her arms, pleased her. Besides, she told herself, guests at the Dew Drop Inn expected the quixotic, not the exotic.

Sugar left her post at the foot of Jemi's bed and followed her downstairs. There, Jemi peered out the door, expecting to see yet another city dweller seeking the mysterious healing powers of the Dew Drop Inn.

What she saw was Officer Billy Rutledge, his chipmunk cheeks redder than usual, hammering on her door. Beside him, looking quite uncomfortable, was the man who had trashed her kitchen.

Jemi flung open the door.

"Billy, what's going on?" she said, sparing a quick glance for the man with the curiously broken nose, who, she somehow knew, had been a player in her interrupted dream.

The officer tipped his cap. "Sorry to wake you, Jemi, but this man said he's staying here at the Dew Drop Inn." The officer, a man she'd gone to grade school with, looked askance at the well-dressed bum.

"He did?" Jemi rubbed her eyes and wondered how late it was. The last time she'd checked the clock of reality, she had offered Alex a job, not an invitation to lounge about as a guest. "And why is he with you?" Had the man left the money in the office untouched then gone off to steal somewhere else?

Billy gave Alex another sideways look. "He tried to skip out on a ticket at the Dogwood and Miss Wallie called us. She said it would have been one thing if he'd justa been a hungry homeless man, but it was obvious by his clothing that he could have paid his bill a hundred times over. I reckon that's the only reason I gave his story of staying at your place half a nod, cause he refused to identify himself."

Jemi blinked and studied the black-haired man's clothing. How had it been obvious to Wallie Sims that this man was well off? Possibly wealthy? Jemi shook her head.

"So he's not staying here?" Rutledge sounded stern.

"Oh, no, I didn't say that." Jemi thought quickly, or tried to, through her sleep-dulled mind. If she called the man a liar, he'd spend the night in jail. And possibly that was exactly what he deserved. But all he'd done wrong was try to feed himself. It wouldn't have hurt stingy old Wallie to have let the man eat for free. Because she hadn't, though, this man had appeared at her doorstep twice in the same evening.

She beckoned Rutledge over and whispered in his ear. "Most of my guests never carry cash," she said. "I'm sure he didn't know what to do when his gold American Express wouldn't work at the Dogwood. Tell me the total and I'll pay it, plus a tip for Wallie's troubles."

Rutledge scratched his head. "Well, I don't know. You're sure you can vouch for him?"

Alex cleared his throat and looked as if he were about to speak.

Wondering where her senses had flown, Jemi answered quickly, "No problem," knowing she'd exact her revenge from the man who

called himself Alex. She'd have him wash every
dish, whether it was dirty or not. And scrub the
floors. What Ari would say about her taking a
second chance with a guy who was no doubt a
known felon, she pushed from her mind. Maybe Ari wouldn't have to hear the whole story,
though he always came for dinner on Sunday
when he was in town and pumped her about
her week.

"Five seventy-five is what he owes," Rutledge said, slipping the cuffs from Alex's wrists.

Jemi scurried to the office desk and produced
that amount and then some. She shoved it into
the officer's hands, and said, "Give my best to
Marla."

The officer beamed. "We're having another
little one this summer."

"Wonderful," Jemi said, and wondered
whether she would ever be lucky enough to
have one baby.

The officer wagged a finger at Alex, and said,
"Don't think you can come to our community
and get away with the kind of things you might
in your big city, fella. Next time, take a peek in
your wallet before you chow down." Then he
backed off and Jemi heard his car roar to life
and then retreat.

Off he went, disappearing into the distance,
taking away her simple problem. And leaving
her very much alone, staring into the keen eyes
and at the crooked nose of her now very real
problem.

"Why did you destroy my kitchen?" she demanded, straightening her shoulders and glaring at the man she'd just bought off from the police.

"What?" He appeared the picture of innocence.

"You pulled everything from A to Z from my shelves then . . . vamoose."

"I do apologize for that. I was searching for your dishwasher and bread machine, then I had the most urgent need to locate a telephone."

"Dishwasher. Bread machine. Telephone." Jemi glared at the man.

"Yes," he said. "Dishwasher—"

"Forget it," she said. "You can sleep on the couch down here as long as you don't make a mess or cause a scene."

"Excuse me?" The dark-eyed man blinked.

"I said you can stay here. I've got to get some sleep."

"Do you mean you'll still offer me shelter after I ran away and then caused you this embarrassment?"

Jemi shrugged. "I can't put you out into the night, can I?"

"Many people would."

"Most people wouldn't be spending their lives running the Dew Drop Inn." Jemi shifted from foot to foot, then looked down at her nightshirt and the jacket. *His* jacket!

She blushed, and started to back from the

room. "I'll toss down a blanket," she said, "but if you want to stay here, you've got to get up early and help with breakfast."

He took a step toward her, reached out, and fingered the lapel of his jacket. The man was regarding her with an odd expression on his face, almost as if he were studying some extinct species.

Jemi held her breath.

He smiled. "Thank you for rescuing me. Again. I'll be more than grateful to sleep on the couch." He dropped his hand and Jemi looked up, but could read nothing from his face.

"I'll get that blanket," she said, backing up the stairs.

Sugar positioned herself at the foot of the narrow staircase, eyes steady on the unexpected guest.

Mia couldn't believe what she'd just witnessed. A. G. had run off and been returned by a policeman! She kissed the crimson hanky wound between her fingers and wondered about destiny.

All she had to do was herd him close to the Dew Drop Inn. That should be simple enough, judging by the way he'd watched Jemi. Something about the look in his eye made Mia sigh. Alex was definitely intrigued.

Mia retreated from her watchpost on the porch of the office cottage and headed for her hammock. She found it odd A. G. didn't identify himself. If he'd wanted to return to California, all he had to do was get the officer to call Winston Enterprises. Even though Quentin held Winston's wallet and signet ring, he could have proven who he was. And by now, his people must be looking for him.

As long as Winston didn't try to claim his identity, though, Mia felt her plan held promise. Who in the middle of this mountain paradise would believe Alexander Graham Winston masqueraded as a homeless man? Once he'd accepted Jemi's offer of shelter, he'd sealed his fate; a few days with the down-to-earth Jemi Dailey, and A. G. Winston would be a heck of a lot closer to understanding the meaning of happiness.

Mia settled into the cold comfort of her lonely hammock, her satisfaction dwindling as she thought of her own situation. Here she was matchmaking, yet she couldn't even make it all the way up the aisle to the altar.

She sighed, and tried not to think of Quentin inside the cottage, alone in that heart-shaped bed.

An owl hooted and Mia looked into the star-sprinkled sky.

"Mr. G," she whispered, "don't forget about me, okay?"

Alex pulled the blanket over his eyes. What an odd dream he'd been having!

He tried to recapture the feeling of reckless

abandon, of the release of every stricture under which he'd lived. He pictured himself as he'd appeared in last night's dream: a vagrant forced to rely on the kindness of strangers and work with his hands to feed himself. He snuggled against the hard pillow and decided that if every stranger was as kind and as cute as the woman in his dream, he'd consider trading at least one of his holding companies for the chance to spend a week or two at her mercies.

Or longer.

A door opened and slammed shut with a bang. The dream fragments shattered and Alex frowned. He wondered why his housekeeper was making such a racket. She knew he often worked all night and hated to be disturbed early.

He tugged the blanket from his face and sat up.

Only to find himself right in the middle of his dream.

Sure enough, he wore the dress pants he'd donned yesterday for his engagement press conference. He looked around the rough-hewn walls of the cottage, hung with blankets and weavings he supposed were Native American. That's when he spotted the young girl standing beside the door.

"Sorry," she said, turning to flee, "I didn't know Jemi had company. I can come back later."

Alex studied the blonde-haired child. She

looked to be between ten and twelve. Her green eyes were bright and inquisitive, and she watched him as if she knew a secret. "No, that's not necessary. I'll be leaving soon."

She advanced a step. Her shorts and T-shirt were worn but clean. Her feet were bare; her teeth white but crooked. Alex couldn't say why, but the child looked vaguely familiar. "I'm Susannah," she said. "I work for Jemi."

"Ah," Alex said, wondering about the existence of child labor laws in Arkansas. "What do you do?"

She shrugged. "Everything but cook. Clean the cabins, help in the yard." She straightened her back. "I'm learning yoga, too. Jemi's teaching me."

"Ah," Alex said again. He glanced down at his bare chest and reached for the dress shirt that had seen better days. He'd slept in his pants, having never taken to the custom of wearing boxers or briefs and not wanting to cause Jemi any concern should she come down the stairs before he awoke. As she had him pegged as a thief, he hadn't wanted to add to his list of crimes by sleeping naked. "Are you a little young to have a job?"

Her look was pure scorn. "I'm twelve. Besides," she plucked at the hem of her shorts and set her jaw, "I like to work." She glanced at him from under her long lashes. "I like to work with computers, too, but Jemi won't buy one."

"Computers? So do I! My name's Alex and

I—" Alex cut short his sentence when he saw Sugar rise and point her nose up the stairs. Evidently the shepherd had sat guard all night long. He'd been about to say he made computers and electronics, but there seemed no point to reveal himself to Jemi. No doubt she'd send him packing and after learning what he had last night about Sharyn taking off for a vacation alone, he felt absolutely no need to rush back to his world.

"I'm working for Jemi, too," he said instead.

"You?" She giggled and stared wide-eyed. "No way. Why would Jemi hire you?"

"To work as chief cook and bottle washer?" He smiled.

"But you're . . ." Susannah began, then trailed off, glancing between Alex and Jemi, who'd appeared on the stairs.

"Time to get to work." Jemi jumped lightly from the third step to the floor and gave them a bright smile. Today she wore purple overalls with an orange cropped T-shirt underneath. The effect with her bright red hair made Alex blink. Like Susannah, her feet were bare.

Jemi stretched and moved into the room. "Good morning, Susannah. Take a look at that mockingbird nest and see if the babies have flown the coop yet. That's our only free cabin. Then I want you to spruce up the office, polish all the furniture, and shine the brass lamps."

Susannah's eyes had widened. "Is someone special coming to visit?"

Jemi glanced out the broad windows of the cottage. "Someone important is already here. So let's get moving." She patted the girl on the head as Susannah skipped by.

"As for you," she said, "up and at 'em. Let's get into the kitchen and see what you do know how to do."

Still holding his shirt, Alex rose from the couch. He noticed he towered over her by almost a foot. With Sharyn, who was almost five feet ten and favored high heels, he never felt awkwardly tall. Looking down at the barefooted Jemi, he had to summon all his hard-learned posture control to keep himself from stooping.

Despite the difference in their heights, she met his gaze eye to eye, only she seemed to be shifting her attention to his chest. Seeing that, Alex shrugged into his shirt and finger-combed his hair. He scraped a hand across the stubble on his chin and wished for a razor.

Jemi continued to watch him openly, and he wondered, for a fleeting moment, whether she approved of what she saw. He thought he had a nicely built body, muscular without being beefy, but as he'd spent most of his life with machines rather than women, he hadn't gotten much feedback on the subject.

Even his fiancée hadn't commented one way or another, and he'd been too embarrassed to ask. Sharyn knew him as a captain of industry and emperor of electronics and probably would have laughed at such a silly question as "Do you like my chest?" He frowned, thinking again of her lounging about at some spa when she should be worried sick over his disappearance.

Jemi snapped her fingers. "Yoohoo, we've got a lot of work to do today, and if you mess me up the way you did last night, I'll overcome every one of my rescuer instincts and kick you out in the woods." She planted her hands on her hips.

Alex sketched a salute. For the moment, he was hers to command. Not too many people chanced upon the opportunity to drop out of their own lives and experience an alternate reality. Last night when he'd phoned in to Winston Enterprises to let them know he'd be gone for awhile, he had given them no clue as to his whereabouts.

Several days of sheer escape. Rolling up his sleeves, he followed his new boss into the kitchen, leaving his shoes and socks by the couch.

Though he'd never gone barefoot in his life, it seemed the proper thing to do.

Jemi marched into the kitchen, thankful her newest employee couldn't see her face. She'd been staring at his chest like some country bumpkin seeing a subway train for the first time.

But his chest begged to be studied, what with

the way his muscles rippled as he moved and the dark hair that matted over his pectorals and charted a path toward his navel. Jemi stopped in mid-stride and Alex bumped into her.

"Excuse me," he said, stepping back.

She turned around. He'd buttoned his shirt and tucked it neatly into his trousers. That reminded her of his jacket and she said, "I'm sorry about wearing your jacket."

"You made a reasonable assumption that I would not be back to claim it."

"Not after what you did to my kitchen! If there's anything you can't find, just ask."

He nodded. "You look much better in my jacket than I do, anyway."

"Really?" Then Jemi caught herself; the man had to be kidding her. "Never mind. We need to get breakfast set up." She pointed to a large crockery bowl filled with oranges. "I serve fresh-squeezed orange juice and breakfast rolls. Some of the guests prefer the juice with protein plus powder. You make that in the blender." She made a little face and mumbled to herself, "Yes, I do have a blender."

"And a juicer?"

"Hand-operated." She pointed to the counter next to the bowl of oranges.

"Do you take a philosophical exception to modern conveniences?"

"Do you always talk so funny?" Jemi asked the question before she thought just how rude it sounded. The man might be odd and homeless but it really wasn't nice to make fun of anyone.

Alex lifted his hands, palms up. "We are the creatures of our environment, wouldn't you agree?"

"Oh, yes, that's for sure." She smiled. "Which is why you need to start squeezing those oranges one at a time." She handed him an apron. "I'll have to see if Ari can get you some clothes."

"Ari?" He tied the apron around his waist. Rather than looking ridiculous as Jemi thought many men would, he looked even more interesting. Oh, it was a pleasure to have someone to talk to. Not, Jemi thought guiltily, that Casey and Susannah weren't nice, but a twelve-year-old and a teenager who thought only of "Melrose Place" weren't exactly stimulating company.

"My brother." Jemi pulled the tray of fresh cinnamon rolls she'd stayed up late preparing from the pantry shelf and set them into the oven to warm.

"That's an unusual name." The man was examining the juicer, taking the top off and studying the way the parts fit together.

"It's short for Aries, the way my name is short for Gemini."

He stared blankly.

"Astrology. Signs of the zodiac."

"Oh," he said.

"My parents," Jemi said, "are hippies of the old guard. They named all of us after the sign under which we were born."

"And when were you born?"

"You mean you don't know when Gemini is?" Jemi found this hard to believe. Where had this man been all the years of his life?

"I'm afraid I don't even know what my sign might be." Alex squeezed an orange half against the hand juicer and a satisfied look crossed his face as juice pooled into the pitcher. The pungent bite of citrus filled the air. The warming rolls added their own aroma to the morning chorus of the kitchen. Jemi breathed in deeply, feeling suddenly at peace.

She tipped her head and studied Alex. She could usually guess someone's sign of the zodiac, but he might prove a tough nut to crack. "Off the top of my head, I would have pegged you as a Leo," she said, "but instinct tells me that's not right."

He continued to operate the juicer.

She thought of the gleam that came and went in his deep blue eyes, of the ripply muscles of his chest. She looked down at his bare feet and noticed curly black hairs marching up to his toes. His feet were large, but well in proportion to his height.

Ah, yes, all indications pointed to the Scorpion. And then she factored in the measured way he spoke, of the way his diction indicated a man of reason and logic. Yet, last night when he'd traced a finger over the lapel of his jacket, Jemi's heart had almost leapt from her chest.

"Scorpio," she pronounced.

The juicer stopped. "And that means what?"

"When's your birthday?"

"October thirtieth."

"Bingo." Jemi smiled, pleased at her powers of deduction. She, more than her brother and sisters, would always be the heart child of her parents. There was a reason she remained here at the Dew Drop Inn, continuing in their abandoned footsteps.

That thought led her mind straight back to the visitor from California. "Oh, what am I doing? Standing here talking as if I have all day! Yes, you're a Scorpio and I'll tell you anything you want to know about that later, but there's so much to do to make today go just right." She bit at her lip and raised one foot to the opposite calf, her favorite thinking position.

"Why is today important?" Alex asked the question without pausing in his juicer duties.

"Oh, it's all so complicated. You see, there's someone from California who's interested in buying the inn, and he's here, or rather I think he's here, staying in the Sunrise Cottage. And if he does buy it, I'll have lots of money and be able to move and travel and go back to school . . ." Jemi trailed off, thinking she was rattling on when she should be working.

"Do you want to sell?"

"Yes and no." She dropped into a chair at the table and ruffled the pages of the *Cosmo* that lay there. "I've always lived here and I love it, but then I wonder if I'm not missing out on life. I didn't finish college, which bothers me, and I think I should."

"Why?"

"Well, because."

"I didn't finish college."

Jemi started to say that proved her point, but did check her tongue that time. "It's something I need to do for myself."

He nodded and pointed to the almost empty bowl of fruit. "More?"

"That's good." She got up from the table. "Why didn't you graduate from college?"

He wrinkled his nose for just a moment, reminding Jemi of how she wanted to ask him how he'd broken it. Perhaps some goddess had done it to him to keep him from being too perfectly formed. She smiled at the fanciful idea.

"I was bored," he said.

"With so much to learn?" She stared at him as if he'd sprouted an extra head.

"Learning can take place anywhere. You don't need college for that. Look at all the people who've dropped out and gone on to start successful companies."

"Oh, them." Jemi waved her hand. "Who

cares about business? That's something one just does. I'm talking about learning about art and music and poetry, the important things in life."

"Oh."

"You weren't bored with those subjects, were you?"

"I don't believe I ever took any courses in the arts."

She stared. "No wonder you dropped out. Look at the time!" She jumped up and found her list of breakfast requests. "Let me show you where the trays are and the bread baskets. Then I'll set one up to show you how we do it. You can do the rest and start delivery to the cottages."

"Deliver them?"

"People come here to experience nature, but I'll tell you, the wealthy still like to be waited on."

"That's for sure," Alex murmured, a funny smile on his face.

Jemi opened a cupboard and found herself whistling. Sharing her problems hadn't solved anything, but she did feel better. Somehow, things would work themselves out.

She turned toward Alex, lips puckered in a cheerful whistle, arms full of breakfast things, feeling very much more on terms with the universe.

"Jemi! Help!"

She froze at the sound of Susannah's frightened voice shrieking her name. She dropped
the dishes on the table and ran outside.

Quentin awoke to the most amazing sight. Hearing screams and bloodcurdling yells, he leapt from his bed and ran to the front window of his cabin. An old woman with orange hair staggered about, stabbing at the air with a pitchfork and screaming, "You'll pay for what you've taken from me!"

He yanked on his pants and flung open the door. From the corner of his eye, he saw the woman who'd checked him in yesterday approach the old lady ever so slowly. Mia had said the woman's name was Jemi. Behind her, wearing an apron over his clothing, followed A. G. Winston.

He didn't know which sight amazed him more. Peering, Quentin saw quite plainly pink and purple hearts embroidered on the apron. He chuckled, then stopped his silliness; this woman looked like trouble, and he should try to help.

Isn't that what Mia would say?

He glanced around, somehow hoping her

wish had worn off and she had become visible during the long restless night, but saw no proof to back his wish. Squaring his shoulders, he advanced on the pitchfork, circling with caution.

"Please, don't do anything," Jemi said, waving him off. "Go back inside; I can handle this."

Looking at the tiny redhead in violet overalls, almost more child than woman, Quentin doubted that. He stayed where he'd stopped, ready to help if needed.

A few other heads had appeared at doors, then quickly retreated. Perhaps this character was a regular? Or part of their Ozarks humor?

A young girl, blond pigtails bouncing, dashed past the pitchfork and threw herself into Jemi's arms, sobbing. Quentin knew, then and there, this was no performance.

The sight of the girl seemed to set the old woman off again. She plunged forward, screaming, "Steal my girl and see what happens to you!"

The redhead, both arms around the child, sidestepped the old woman, reaching out a bare foot as she raced by. The woman stumbled, tripped, and fell face-first in a heap. In a flash, Jemi plucked the pitchfork from her hands. Then, to Quentin's surprise, Jemi disentangled herself from the child and bodily lifted the old lady. She carried her the few steps to the creek that meandered through the property and dumped her face first in the stream. The woman spluttered, then lifted her head from the water.

Jemi dusted her hands, as if finishing off a job well done, then turned to the child with her arms open.

Winston stood watching the spectacle as if he were assessing it for use in some computer program. Quentin could almost hear the man's brain ticking away as he studied the scene. No emotion flickered on his face, but the way he stood quietly, leaning slightly forward, showed Quentin, the director and student of human behavior, that Winston was engrossed.

And the man didn't even look silly wearing that apron.

He'd have to remember to keep Mia away from the guy. Someone that logical and practical could be a real threat to Quentin's intention to win Mia back as his bride. Of course, Quentin thought, kicking his toe on the ground, he was his own worst competition.

"Are you going to retrieve her?" Winston asked.

"In another minute or two." Jemi stroked the child's hair. "It's difficult, honey, but try to remember she's sick and can't really help what she does."

The child broke away from Jemi and stamped her foot. Eyes blazing, she cried, "She can too help it. She doesn't have to get all likkered up!

You don't. And she doesn't care about me at all. It's my lousy monthly check she cares about!" With a whoop of pain, the child ran off toward the woods.

Jemi shook her head and placed a hand over her heart. Then, with slow steps, she measured the distance to the creek, leaned over, and hauled the old woman out. "Miz Gillmore, you can come in now and dry off and have a nice cup of chamomile tea."

The carrot-headed crone blinked and ran a hand over her face. "It's time to get up?"

"Yes, it's time." Not seeming to mind the water streaming from the woman's clothes, Jemi put an arm around her and led her toward the back of the office cottage.

Winston, that inscrutable look on his face, followed.

Quentin wished for his camera and film crew. What a scene he'd missed capturing. His mind churning on the dramatic possibilities, which camera angles he would have used, he turned to walk back to his cabin. Completely absorbed, he didn't even notice the crimson silk blocking the doorway.

"Please take the breakfast trays," Jemi said as soon as the three of them entered the kitchen via the back door.

Alex nodded. He would do what he could to assist in this unusual situation. He spared a glance for the miserable-looking old woman huddled against Jemi's side. "Is there anything else I can do?"

Jemi shook her head, then settled the woman into a chair. She put a teakettle on to boil, then set to work by his side arranging cinnamon rolls in natural fiber baskets.

The old woman had slumped forward, her cheek flat against the *Cosmopolitan*. Alex thought the sight quite a contrast to the magazine's beauty ads he'd studied only the night before.

"Make sure you take the tray to the Sunrise Cottage first," Jemi said, puckering her lips in what Alex had quickly come to realize was a gesture indicating anxiety.

"That would be the person you assume to be interested in the inn?"

"Assume?" She said it sharply.

"You did say he didn't identify himself as such; I'm only suggesting that logic dictates one not rush to a conclusion."

"Oh, puh-leeze! How many people arrive on my doorstep from California the day after I receive a letter from an interested buyer who says he'll be here soon?"

"That I wouldn't know," Alex said, wishing he might help himself to one of the rolls. The aroma had enchanted him and he found the memory of his pilfered burger very distant. Of course, the hunger was only another echo of his childhood, so he squelched both the pangs and the memory as best he could.

Lifting the first tray, he said, "How will I know which one is the Sunrise Cottage?"

Jemi rolled her eyes and Alex thought that this day was the first time in his life he'd ever been made to feel as if he were lacking in mental capacity.

"Look at the picture over the door," she said, pushing him none-too-gently from the room as the teakettle began to whistle.

Alex concentrated on not stepping on anything sharp as he picked his way off the porch steps and onto the grassy pathway toward the first cottage. He peered at the door through a cluster of wicker chairs and spotted a wood cutting of a bright blue flower. Sure enough, stenciled in white alongside the door he found the name, "Bluebell."

The second cottage carried the image of a white lacy flower swaying above a tall stalk. "Queen Anne's Lace."

The third cottage boasted a painting of a sun rising from a pristine mountain lake. He walked up the steps to the porch and paused before knocking on the door.

Shouting voices—voices he recognized from last night's abduction—sailed through the door.

"Are you crazy?" Quentin Grandy's voice he plainly recognized.

Alex couldn't hear the reply.

"I think your imagination is running away with you," Quentin shouted.

Alex found himself straining to decipher the identity of the other party. He leaned toward the door, tray held forth.

"Of course I'm willing to do whatever it takes to meet Mr. G's assignment, but this cloak and dagger stuff isn't my style." Grandy again.

Try as he would, Alex couldn't hear the other party to this argument. Glancing behind him first, he stooped and put his ear to the door.

"Now that's a low blow," the director was saying.

Alex regarded Quentin Grandy as one of the few sincere geniuses of modern cinema and was overcome with curiosity to know why he'd been acting the way he had. Since the man was responsible for Alex's current predicament, Alex figured he had an arguable right to eavesdrop.

Balancing the tray, he dropped lower, searching for a keyhole. He didn't want to peek in the window for fear of being discovered. He'd just realized there was no keyhole when the door flew open and Alex fell into the room face first, sending juice and rolls flying.

The only coherent thought that came to Alex's mind as he surveyed the mess and Grandy's amazed expression was that Jemi might not believe this man wasn't here to buy her inn.

"You could have knocked, Winston," Quentin Grandy said, leaning over to shovel bread back into the basket.

"Uh—yes, yes, I could have knocked."

"What, up to a spot of eavesdropping?" Quentin laughed, somewhat nervously, Alex thought.

"As a matter of fact, I was," Alex said, glancing around the room. The other party to the conversation must be hiding in the bathroom of the large one-room cottage. His quick survey took in the heart-shaped bed and his secret romantic's heart gave a wistful tug before he remembered his mission. "I'll just wash my hands in the bathroom, if you don't mind," he said.

"Be my guest," Grandy said, biting into a roll he'd recovered from the floor.

The bathroom was empty. Alex backed out and said, "I think a roll went under the bed." But a poke of his nose showed no one hiding there.

"You look a bit puzzled," Quentin said.

"Things have been strange since the moment you showed up at Winston Enterprises yesterday."

Quentin waved a hand. "Some people claim I have that effect."

"No, it's more than that." Alex leaned

against a wall of the cabin. "Are you thinking of going into the resort business?"

"Me?" Quentin laughed and leaned forward. "If I had my way, I'd never leave the city."

"Hmmm, that's what I thought."

"Why do you ask?" Quentin selected another roll. "These are tasty. Want one?"

"Don't mind if I do." Alex checked for any debris, found nothing major, and bit into the roll. "Delicious," he said. "Jemi does know a thing or two about baking."

"Jemi, she's the girl who works here? The redhead?"

"I believe she is the owner of this establishment."

Quentin shook his head. "I guess that makes as much sense as anything."

"She's mistaken you for a prospective investor from California, here to consider placing an offer to buy the Dew Drop Inn."

"How'd she get that crazy idea?" As soon as the words were out of his mouth, he yelped, as if someone had stuck him with a pin.

Alex raised his brows, decided the noise was no more odd than anything else he'd experienced in the past twenty-four hours, and took the last cinnamon bun from the basket. It was a pity he'd spilled the orange juice all over the floor. It would have gone well with the rolls.

"She received a letter yesterday letting her know to expect a visitor from California," he said. "But if you're not this person, I think it's reasonable to surmise that visitor may be the next person from the Sunshine State to check in."

"And?" Grandy asked, eyeing the empty basket.

"Don't worry, I'll bring you some more, and some juice. I'm, uh, working here for the moment. What I want to ask of you, Grandy," he said, feeling somewhat awkward, wondering whether the man of the world would laugh at him, "is if you'll keep my identity a secret. You see, Jemi thinks I'm a homeless man working for food and I rather like the idea of playing out that scenario."

Grandy raised his brows, then reacted as if to another blow. Perhaps the director had a medical problem. That could explain him talking to himself so much.

"Absolutely. Anything you say." Quentin propelled Alex by the arm to the door of the cottage. "As far as I'm concerned, I don't know you from Adam. We'll do that in-depth interview some other time. If I see you, I don't know you. Will that cover it for you?"

"Yes, I believe it will." Alex extended a hand to Grandy and shook on the bargain. In the normal course of events, Alex would have had his lawyers send a formal letter of intent, but then, things weren't normal here. Not at the Dew Drop Inn.

Alex wasn't even all the way out the door of the cabin when he heard Quentin Grandy, a

man who had won two Oscars, begin talking to
the walls again.

He'd turned back to draw the door closed to
ensure Grandy's privacy when Quentin beckoned him back inside.

"One more thing," the director said, an odd
smile playing on his face, "let's go ahead and
let Jemi think I'm here to buy the inn."

"I don't quite see the logic to that proposi-
tion, but fair is fair. You're doing as I asked, so I
won't do anything to contradict that supposi-
tion."

"Heck," Grandy said, reacting once again as
if he'd been pinched or punched, "if it takes
that to get me back to a world with cable TV,
I'll gladly buy this place."

Before A. G. was even out the door, Mia
danced around the interior of the cabin, enjoying the look of admiration on Quentin's face.

Mia had led them to the Dew Drop Inn based
on listening in to Sharyn's thoughts; quite a
leap, she knew. But as pleased as she was that
her impulsive plan seemed to be paying off, she
was even more pleased with Quentin trusting
her and going on faith with a plan he didn't
comprehend.

Of course, she had had to poke him a time or
two to keep him on cue, but there at the last,
before A. G. left, she'd seen the light of understanding dawn on Quentin's face.

Now he turned and gazed like a blind man,

twisting and turning his head in all directions.
"I know you know what you're doing, Mia," he
said, "but I really hate being left in the dark. It's
bad enough not being able to see you without
having to operate without cue cards, too."

She smiled, which of course was a gesture
wasted. So she drew the crimson cloth into a
smile, and said, "For some reason, Sharyn
Stonebridge has something against this place.
And I'll bet you a hundred dollars she's the
investor who wants to buy the Dew Drop Inn."

Quentin scratched his chest. "Now you're
really making a leap. And how do you know
she even knows the Dew Drop Inn exists?"

Mia thought guiltily of the secret power of
the hanky, and thought too of her intentions to
always share everything with Quentin. But he'd
relieved her of that, she supposed, by deciding
not to marry her. "I-uh-overheard something at
Winston Enterprises."

Quentin stretched and looked around the
room. "I thought you wanted me to go ahead
with Winston's idea that I was the investor to
give me some plausible reason to be staying
here in this treehouse."

"You don't need an excuse to stay at the Dew
Drop Inn. This place is fast becoming an 'in'
haunt for those of us who rush about and need
to drop out of the world. This environment is
perfect for breathing deeply, smelling the flowers, and practicing yoga."

Quentin wrinkled his brow. "Is this Mia the

perpetual motion woman I'm hearing? Mia who dropped out of her relaxation class because she couldn't sit still?"

"Just because I'm not any good at it doesn't mean I don't appreciate its value."

After a short laugh that sounded pretty sad, Quentin said, "You mean like me and fidelity?"

Mia edged toward the door. She didn't want to discuss *them*. "I think instead of pursuing a pointless philosophical discussion, we should drive into town and poke around."

"You mean go shopping?" Quentin's look of distaste couldn't have been much stronger.

"No, I mean try to figure out what possible connection Sharyn Stonebridge might have with this neck of the woods."

Quentin walked toward the bathroom. He paused in the doorway and threw over his shoulder, "Okay, Mia, I'll go along with your program. But as a point of order, an issue that so clearly affects you and me is not simply a pointless philosophical point."

He aimed a look in the direction of her voice, the look that had been known to make an errant camera person shiver in his top-siders.

Mia said nothing, but let the hanky inch toward her heart, longing to know what was going through his mind. She shouldn't have cut off his attempt to discuss their situation. She'd been hurt when he'd done that last night, and now she'd been equally as wrong.

She sighed, then lowered the silk.

As long as the two of them continued to out-stubborn one another, nothing good could happen.

"Mia?"

"Yes?"

"Do me a favor and try to wish yourself back to visibility, okay? I think it would be a heck of a lot easier for us to talk face-to-face." So saying, he went into the bathroom and shut the door.

Mia heard the shower gush on. She slumped onto the edge of the heart-shaped bed, thinking how odd it was to be invisible to others and only partially visible to her own eyes. Today she seemed even more shimmery and translucent than when she'd first wished herself invisible. It was almost as if she were fading, which pretty much mirrored the way she felt about her chances at ending up Mrs. Quentin Grandy. She studied the hanky, wondering whether its secret listening power would persist if she did wish herself back to being three-dimensional.

Mia clutched the silk and promised herself she'd wish again soon. But first, she wanted to take advantage of her condition to investigate Sharyn the Shark and keep an undetectible eye on Jemi and A. G.

And face it, she said aloud, "You want to eavesdrop on Quentin's heart before you lose out on the chance."

She lay back on the bed. Her outstretched

arms touched the pillow Quentin had used the night before. With a sigh, she clutched it to her face, breathing in the scent of the man she couldn't help but love.

9 ～

Quentin stepped out onto the porch of the cottage, Mia somewhere by his side. The morning sun slanted through the trees, promising a beautiful summer day. He stretched and wished he'd risen earlier and worked in a good run. Sleeping alone in a honeymoon bed was hard on a guy, but no more punishment than he deserved.

From the cabin next to his, a robust white-haired gentleman and a plump woman appeared. They smiled in his direction and began performing toe touches.

The hanky fluttered.

"Ready?" Quentin asked.

"I think so."

"At least you don't have to decide what to wear."

"Very funny," Mia's voice answered. "I just have a sense there's something I've forgotten to do."

Quentin did a few toe touches of his own.

When Mia got that feeling, he knew they'd wait until she settled the question.

The older couple moved off the porch and toward a cluster of guests gathering near the office cottage. Curious as to the people who paid three hundred dollars a night for a place *sans* television out of choice, Quentin examined the Dew Drop Inn clientele.

They seemed fairly chummy with one another, with the exception of a gaunt blonde and a young man and woman entwined in one another's embrace. Quentin squinted and studied the blonde, recognizing her as a famous model. He checked for the red silk, wondering if Mia would recall he'd dated Malinda once or twice. Nothing had happened between them; the woman had been obsessed with what not to eat for dinner and talked of nothing other than health food and various holistic remedies that cost Quentin his own appetite.

"I've got it!" The hanky fluttered. "We can't leave for Dalton until we know A. G. and Jemi will spend the day together."

"And how are we going to do that? The woman has a business to run."

"Go mingle," Mia said, "and leave the matchmaking to me."

Wondering what she planned to do and knowing whatever it was she'd do it well, Quentin jogged down the steps. Rather than mix with the other guests, he'd make a lap or two around the property.

Jemi sent Queenie Gillmore into town with Blue, the postal carrier, quelling with an amused glance Alex's objection that the postal service liability insurance most likely didn't cover passengers. She and Blue had swapped spit when they were eleven, and he'd been her devoted slave ever since. A favor for Jemi Dailey was nothing. And like a lot of the locals, he was used to looking after Queenie Gillmore.

Jemi had been thankful to see Rickie the Ranger, the old friend of her parents who led the guests on their nature hikes, arrive on time, a feat quite out of character for him.

She started to give a sigh of relief as the gray-haired hippie herded all the guests toward the hills, but she cut that short when she realized the mystery buyer from California had failed to join the walkers. Jemi puckered her lip and worried whether he'd left without saying anything to her. But with the rooms waiting to be cleaned and no Casey or Susannah, she didn't have time to dwell on that problem.

Alex had remained in the kitchen. She headed there now, to gather the cleaning cart and supplies. To her pleasure, he was just finishing the breakfast dishes.

Alex turned from the sink as she walked in. Jemi caught her breath at the sight of him framed in the sunlight sparkling through the kitchen window. Some men would have looked silly wearing an apron, but Alex towering over the sink with his shirt sleeves rolled up exposing muscular arms made quite a picture.

"I've got to clean the cabins," she said brightly, hoping he didn't see the way she stared at him. Geez, you'd think she'd never seen a man. Jemi backed toward the large storage cabin then turned and tugged on the cart.

Alex remained by the sink. He dried his hands, folded the dish towel, and removed his apron, looking every bit as if he was finished with his day's duties.

Keeping an eye on her targets, Mia shook her head, hoping Jemi wasn't planning to clean the cabins alone. Yet, with Jemi pushing the cart toward the back door, it did appear that way.

Skipping over to where Alex lounged by the sink, Mia gave him a gentle push in Jemi's direction. He glanced at his feet, then over his shoulder, but remained pretty much where he was.

"While I'm gone," Jemi said, "please get things ready for lunch. When the guests return from hiking, they'll be starved."

Now this wouldn't do at all. It was a good thing she and Quentin hadn't sallied off to town and left these two to their own devices.

Jemi had been studying Alex like he was a coconut cream pie she wanted to devour and Alex watched Jemi as if she were truly a rescuing angel, and a sexy one at that.

This time, Mia forgot about gentle. She poked Alex in the lower back and he lunged forward, landing next to Jemi and the cart. Then Mia lifted one of his hands and placed it on the handle.

"Alex?" Jemi looked up at him.

"Excuse me," he said, removing his hand.

Mia slapped it back onto the cart, then shoved his other hand on for good measure. The computer whiz looked down at his hands as if they were objects he'd never seen before.

"Are you trying to say you want to help me?" Jemi asked, a grin lighting her face.

"Uh—I don't know a thing about cleaning. Cooking I can do, but—"

Mia slipped her fingers over his lips, then pushed his head up and down, up and down.

"You are a most unusual man," Jemi said, "but of course you can help. Grab the handle and help me bump this down the back stairs."

With a shake of his head and one last glance over his shoulder, Alex did as Jemi asked.

Mia broke out laughing, then went in search of Quentin.

On their way to the first cottage, Alex pointed to the brooms and brushes sticking from the cleaning cart. "I am happy to assist you, Jemi," he said, "but I really know less than nothing about this type of task."

"Well, if a twelve-year-old can do this job, I reckon you can learn." No wonder the man had lost his job, Jemi thought. "Besides, you're the one who acted like you wanted to help."

At least then he fell into step beside her without carrying on any more. She cast a glance sideways at him. He had that faraway look in his eyes, as if his mind had flown to Neptune or Pluto. His dress shirt had gone from starched to crumpled and she felt a pang of remorse over asking him to clean cottages dressed in his nice clothing. She'd ask Ari to find him some castoffs more suitable for kitchen work. Her gaze remained on his chest and she noticed for the first time how dark curly hairs peeped above the neckline of the shirt. They looked soft, yet sturdy. Contradictory, rather like the man himself. But then, he was a Scorpio.

"I was thinking," Alex said, severely disrupting her train of thought and causing her to stumble a bit on the path. "I was wondering whether it would be wrong of me to share with you that your California guest did seem to be interested in the possible purchase of your property."

"He did!" Jemi stopped the cart and performed a quick pirouette. "What did he say?"

"When I served his breakfast tray, he appeared to indicate a sincere interest in the possibility."

"Is that a funny way of saying he asked you questions about the inn?" Jemi did wish the man would talk straight. Her parents had been educated at Harvard and they never talked half as complicated as Alex.

Alex ran a hand over the dark growth on his chin. "Perhaps," was all he said.

Jemi started to bump the cart up the steps of the Bluebell Cottage. With another one of those strange jerking motions he made, Alex lunged forward, caught hold of the cart again, and pushed it effortlessly to the porch.

"Thank you," Jemi said, used to making do on her own, but pleased with his rush to her aid.

Looking over his shoulder again, Alex said, "You're welcome."

Jemi handed Alex a dust cloth, pushed open the door, and headed for the bathroom. She always cleaned that room first, then worked her way back out of the cottage. That way, when she was done, she was on her way out. Whistling, she plucked the biodegradable cleanser she used and the bath and bowl brushes from the bath bucket and bent over the tub.

Left standing in the bedroom portion of the cabin, Alex examined the chamois-colored cloth he held, but rather than considering its use, his mind shifted to a problem he'd been considering in a new chip design. Some of his competitors had been content to rely on foreign entities for development in that area, but not Alex. He didn't feel that way out of any xenophobic or ethnic promptings; he simply loved to wrestle with complexities of design.

He sank to the bed, envisioning the layout of the sliver of silicon as he'd last pictured it. Thinking pure and simple without the aid of his computer felt surprisingly good, and he wondered whether his tools hadn't evolved into crutches. He breathed in deeply and let the image of the chip fill his mind.

He saw clearly the mental enlargement of the design, pictured the coiling conductive device he'd invented only last year, pictured it linking with the right side of the wafer, with the deliciously curvy backside of Jemi Dailey.

Alex snapped his head back and to the right. Sure enough, through the open door to the bathroom, he saw Jemi tucked over the side of the tub, whistling and scrubbing. The rest of her body flowed in movement along with her arms, causing the most interesting dance of her derriere.

He blinked and commanded the vision of his chip layout to reenter his mind.

He closed his eyes to focus.

The image he saw was that of Jemi, her arms around Susannah, stroking her hair and mur-

muring soft words after her grandmother's drunken attack.

Most undisciplined of him.

Alex knew for a fact that as much as he desired his intended, he had never been troubled with mental interference of such images of Sharyn.

When he needed to work, he worked.

Sharyn understood that; she treasured his ability to divorce himself from the earthly plain and drift in the realm of the inventive intellect.

Jemi rose and stretched her arms over her head. The purple overalls rose and tugged upward, revealing firm and shapely upper thighs.

Alex squirmed.

Perhaps he would reconsider staying any longer in this hideaway. If these aspects of life foreign to him were going to filter into his working mind, he'd best call an end to the visit.

"And just what do you think you're doing?" Wielding a bristly-looking brush, Jemi advanced on him.

An aberrant image of himself pulling her down on the bed zapped Alex's mind, destroying any vestige of his thoughts on chip design.

"Thinking," he managed to say.

"Do you normally get paid to think?"

"Well, as a matter of fact," Alex snapped his lips shut. "I was awaiting instructions," he substituted.

She shook her head, then tucked the brush into a bucket, stripped off her rubber gloves, and washed her hands in the bathroom sink. Over her shoulder, she called, "Instruction number one: Don't sit on the guest's bed."

Alex rose at once. Of course that had been inconsiderate of him, sitting on another person's sleeping quarters. But when he was thinking, he tended to forget about his surroundings. Sharyn handled that trait so very well, running interference for him. He certainly couldn't imagine her shouting at him for absentmindedly resting on an inappropriate piece of furniture.

Jemi carried the bucket to the cart she'd parked on the porch of the cottage, then returned with an armload of linens. Alex noticed that her cheeks were rosier than before, and a bead of sweat had pooled above her lip. She licked at it with her tongue and he was most surprised to feel what he could only describe as a rush of erotic sensation.

"Now we strip and remake the bed," she announced, setting the linens down atop the old-fashioned chest at the foot of the bed.

"Str-strip?" Alex had never stuttered in his life.

She regarded him as he might have anyone who asked him what RAM or ROM or gigabyte meant. "Take off the used sheets, replace them with clean." She tapped her foot. "Don't tell me you've never made a bed before."

Alex had recaptured his momentary loss of composure. Something had gotten into his brain in the past twenty-four hours; he hoped the cracks on his head hadn't permanently affected him. "Actually, I don't believe I have," he said, wondering if she'd write him off as a complete dork, and noting in his own analytical way that if she did, he'd care. A lot.

Jemi leaned toward the head of the bed, grabbed two of the four pillows and pulled the pillow cases from them. "Who made your bed when you were a kid?" Then she pointed to the other pillows.

Alex stepped around to the other side of the bed. While he considered the best way to answer Jemi's question, he tugged at the fabric and managed to free the pillow from its wrapper.

"I've noticed you take a long time to answer a question," Jemi said before he could say anything else. She plucked the top of the sheet from where it curved around the mattress and pulled it off the bed. "That's sort of nice. I mean, most people are so willing to jump in with mouth open and brain not engaged."

She gazed at him across the width of the bed, dark blue eyes wide and friendly. She was looking at him, Alex registered with surprise, as if he were a man she'd like to get to know better. Many women had looked at him as if his bank balances were more than satisfactory and his position in the world of commerce a source of salivation. He couldn't remember any woman gazing at him as if she was studying the delicate grace of a daffodil or contemplating the majesty of a tree arcing toward the sky. "Thank you," he said, thinking those words didn't say nearly enough.

"You're welcome. Pull up the corners on your side."

He eased the elastic-edged sheet from between the mattress and box springs, managing to send the pillows rolling to the center of the queen-size bed.

"Have you thought about your answer?" Jemi asked as she leaned over the bed and reached for the pillows.

She wasn't wearing a bra. When she tilted forward, her breasts pushed against the restraining overalls, but Alex would have bet with a Vegas bookie that judging by the way the flesh swelled, she wore nothing under the overalls and T-shirt.

"Answer to what?" he asked, tugging on the elastic holding his hair back, thinking that action might restrain his wayward thoughts. Just because he was sex-starved was no reason to be reacting this way.

He would soon be marrying a woman who held to the highest standards of morality. If he'd had his way, he and Sharyn would have been sleeping together since their first date. Sex was a subject Alex had made quite a study of, and he couldn't count the days until he put his research into practical application. He knew that as a male virgin almost thirty, he was an anomaly.

And he wished with all his heart that weren't the case.

Jemi was staring at him, a funny look crossing her pert features. She held one of the pillows just above waist level and her breasts rested on the soft mound. Her gaze shifted from his face, then drifted lower, then cut abruptly back to somewhere over his right shoulder.

Alex looked down. He swallowed. There he stood, fully aroused. He had no idea what to say. A man of the world might have passed it off with a joke, or offered to tousle together on the unmade bed. A man of the world might have pretended not to notice.

He sneaked a glance at Jemi and saw her lips were slightly parted and her eyes had darkened. "It's been such a long time," she said, the note of longing clear in her voice.

Alex swallowed, hard this time. "It has?" he managed to say, thinking that perhaps he'd tossed out the comment with the proper amount of savoir faire.

"More than a year," Jemi said, sinking to the edge of the bed. She stroked a hand over the pillow she continued to hold close to the front of her body.

Alex had to force his hand not to join hers on the pillow, so great was his desire to feel that gentle stroke. He remembered her soothing touch the night before when she'd discovered him on the porch.

"I don't meet a lot of people out here," she said, almost defensively.

"I suppose not," he murmured, wondering what she would say if he told her he'd spent his life in a sexual desert.

"In California, I guess it's different. Women, women, women." She reached out a hand toward him, then dropped it to the bed. "I guess you pretty much have your pick of the litter."

If he swallowed any more, he'd feel like a Saharan nomad at a drinking fountain. He let his head bob, attempting a noncommittal look. He could not tell a lie, but the last thing he wanted was this earthy woman to know the truth of his lonely circumstances. A child genius raised by precocious parents, sent off to a boy's prep school, then shepherded to CalTech (much to his parents' dismay, he'd refused to attend MIT, due to his dislike of cold weather), who'd found himself rich and famous by age twenty-one, wasn't a boy who had much chance to experience sex.

If it weren't for Sharyn, he would almost have given up hope. He wanted to be wanted for himself, not for his image, money, or status. Sharyn, financially successful, independent and well educated, had no reason to covet any of those markers. Sure, his personal fortune far outdistanced her income, but in her own right, she was quite well-off.

But here was an attractive woman sitting across from him on a bed, regarding him with what he could honestly describe as sexual interest, and this woman had no idea who he was, had no idea the supermarket tabloids liked to trumpet him as America's wealthiest techno-nerd.

He smiled. He was pretty sure Jemi, with her total lack of technological toys, had never even heard of Alexander Graham Winston.

"What's so funny?" Jemi asked.

He shook his head, unable to explain the joke.

Jemi sat there, hugging the pillow, thinking how young he looked when he smiled like that, almost her age. Jemi was pretty embarrassed that she'd blurted out her comment about not having had sex in so long. She knew no accomplished woman of the world would ever admit to such a thing. Maybe she lived in the boonies for a reason; maybe she'd not survive life in the fast lane. She hadn't meant the comment as a come-on, but seeing how aroused Alex was, and letting herself enjoy the fantasy that she had caused that interest had loosened her imagination and her tongue.

Now, of course, he would think her desperate. She sighed and fell back on the bed, the pillow still clutched to her chest. "I always say the wrong thing," she said. Looking up at the ceiling, she said, "I wasn't trying to solicit you, or anything like that. Sometimes thoughts pop out of my mouth before they pop into my head."

Alex smiled and sat down on the edge of the bed on his side. "That's a nice expression. Unusual, too."

"You think so?" Jemi screwed up her forehead. "My sisters and brother tell me I operate from the spleen, and not the cerebrum. Not, of course, that I don't find you attractive, because honestly I do, but it's such an awkward thing, expressing that." She blew away a wisp of hair that had strayed over her eyes and turned onto her tummy. "But I don't want you to think I'm desperate."

"That thought never crossed my mind."

She sat up. "Now you're making fun of me!"

"No. Absolutely not." Alex shifted and somehow he ended up on her side of the bed, sitting next to her. "How could I make fun of someone as open and kind-hearted as you?" Looking down, he smiled into her eyes and Jemi knew she'd be interested in him as a man whether or not she was a year from her last intimate encounter.

The way his brows marched together across his broad forehead looked intimidating at first glance, but when she studied the sparkle and life so evident in his dark blue eyes, the brows took on more the image of gatekeeper of a truly remarkable soul.

However, open and kind-hearted were not words she wanted to hear used to describe herself. Sexy. Magnetic. Gorgeous. Alluring. Those were the words she longed to hear, a longing she usually kept well contained behind her funky-looking clothing and her tightly braided hair.

"Not many people would have taken me in off the street, or highway, as it were," Alex said. He reached out a hand and smoothed the stray hair back from her face. His touch was gentle, his fingers remarkably soft and smooth. Jemi knew, as much from his touch as from her instinct, that he hadn't been out on the road very long at all.

He sat so close that his leg mated against her thigh. She welcomed the warmth of the contact, and found herself wishing he felt the same way. But he just kept speaking about her goodness. Jemi almost made a face, almost yanked down her overalls and screamed, "Look at me, I'm a sexy, desirable woman, the equal or better of any California golden girl." But she didn't, of course, because Alex only spoke the truth.

She was good, and generous and giving. She'd kept her parents' dream alive, sacrificing her own goals in order to do so. If anyone needed help, she extended an open hand. Jemi Dailey, rescuer, always putting herself last. If she'd been Catholic, she might well have found herself in a charitable order.

She jerked to attention. Alex had taken her left hand. He held it over his lap, lightly following her lifeline. She had a long one, with many forks. His feathery touch set off sensations that rocketed from her hand to her tummy to her toes. She curled her bare toes under and tilted her head back, the better to watch the expression on his face. Given the foot he had on her in height, she'd already found herself doing that several times that morning.

But none of those times had produced the entrancing results of this peek into his bristle-stubbed face. He gazed at her hand like a collector appraising a work of art. He didn't seem to notice the callus beginning to form below the base of her ring finger. He didn't seem to notice the scratch on her thumb. He didn't seem to notice that he'd ceased to trace her lifeline and held her hand quite still.

Jemi caught her breath.

Alex lifted her hand to his lips and kissed the backs of her fingers. "That's for taking me in and showing me things about life I've never known before," he said.

The stubble on his chin scraped against her hand. His lips were firm and hot to the touch. And she knew, without a doubt, that he wanted her.

10 ～

Quentin almost hit the girl.

One moment the lane leading to the highway into town was clear, the next, a young girl stepped from the woods and waved her arms.

"Stop!" Mia cried.

He gripped foot to brake pedal and held on to the wheel of the heavy sedan. He pulled swiftly to a stop and jumped out of the car. "What kind of a fool thing was that to do?" Then he recognized the child as the worker from the Dew Drop Inn whose relative had been dumped in the creek.

"I'm sorry," she said, holding out one hand to him. In the other, she clutched a worn backpack. "But you looked nice and I wanted a ride into town."

"Ask her to get in the car," Mia said.

"Hop in," Quentin said.

"Oh, thank you," the girl said and opened the front passenger door.

Quentin noted the flurry of silk hanky. Mia must have climbed to the back seat. He'd have to watch his conversation with her; he didn't want the poor child to think he was crazy.

Quentin pulled back onto the highway in the wake of a tour bus. Forced to drive at a caterpillar's pace, he studied the girl. Her eyes were red and tear swollen, but not all the brightness in them had been watered away. She checked her surroundings with birdlike movements of her head, her pigtails bobbing as she did so.

"Nice car," she finally said. "My name's Susannah. What's yours?"

"Quentin."

She nodded, as if she was processing the name. "Are you the fifth son?"

Coming from the mouth of what he assumed to be a hillbilly, that question caught him off guard. "Only child."

"Hmm. It's funny, isn't it, why parents choose the names they do?" She crossed her skinny arms over her budding chest and a dark cloud shadowed her face.

"I'm named after a character in an old English novel," Quentin revealed. "My mother teaches literature." His mother held a chair in English at one of California's most prestigious universities, but he didn't think that would mean anything to Susannah.

"That must be nice," she murmured, uncrossing her arms and plucking at her skinny knees.

"And who are you named after?"

She scowled. "I named myself Susannah."

Quentin thought of the drunken granny, and figured it might be best not to inquire as to her parents. He was going to let the conversation die a natural death when Mia whispered in his ear, "Ask her why."

"I can't do that," he said without thinking.

"Oh, yes, you can," Susannah said. "Anyone can do it. If you want to change your name, you find out what the local law requires, then you do whatever it says. So if you wanted a cool name like Doggy Snoop-Snoop or Y-Max, that's all you'd have to do."

So his name wasn't cool, huh? He'd better watch out or he'd fall out of fashion with teen audiences and might find it hard to win a third Oscar. "How old are you?"

"What has that got to do with anything?" Her arms rose again over her chest. "I'm twelve, and I changed my name last year."

"What was your name before?" Quentin figured he'd better ask, or Mia would poke him in the ribs.

She stuck out her lower lip.

"Guess you didn't like it too much."

"You've been nice enough to give me a ride, so I'll tell you. You're not from around here, so you probably won't understand, but if you were one of the Gillmores, you'd change your name, too. Especially if your name was Pee-Wee Gillmore." Another scowl followed that pronouncement.

"Ah," Quentin said. His comfortable childhood and adolescence, spent in the buffered world of the upper middle class, clearly had nothing in common with Susannah's.

"That would be like being one of the Familianas," Mia said. "Bad seed of the neighborhood. It's pretty rare for anyone to come out as nicely as Susannah in those circumstances."

"Environment or heredity?" Quentin asked.

"Both," Susannah answered. "If you saw where I have to live, you'd say anyone in that environment would turn out like Queenie Gillmore. Or you'd say that if she's my grandmother, I might as well just curl up with a jug of moonshine and give up on life." She lifted her chin. "But I don't care that I don't have parents and she's my maternal grandmother. I'm smarter than any of them and I'll be different. Even if I have to run away, I won't be like any of them." Her chin had puckered, her lip quivered, but her voice was made of steel.

Quentin did not doubt her at all.

The bus braked and he followed suit.

"Take the left fork," Susannah said. "That goes to Dalton."

"So where's Eureka Springs?"

"It's just a mile the other way. I thought you might like to see where the real people live. Eureka Springs is tourista heaven."

She lay a hand on the car door and Quentin wondered whether she'd jump out as abruptly as she'd flagged him down. But she waited until he drove down the quiet main street and stopped the car before opening the door. Turning to him, she smiled and said, "Thank you for the ride, and for talking to me."

He sketched a salute and watched her walk away, backpack cradled in her arms. She entered a convenience store that appeared to be one of the few open businesses.

"What an amazing girl," Mia said, the hanky now back in the front seat. "I feel like crying and applauding at the same time."

"What do you suppose happened to her parents?" Quentin's first thought was he'd like to horsewhip them, but he knew he shouldn't jump to conclusions. She could simply be an orphan.

"Let's figure it out," Mia said. "Maybe Mr. G will give us credit for two jobs." The crimson square fashioned into a smile.

Quentin found himself smiling and wishing he could draw Mia to his side and kiss her until neither one of them could breathe. So many people messed up so much of their lives and he didn't want to be one of those schmucks, despite his poor track record.

"Mia," he said in a low voice.

"Yes?"

At least she didn't cut him off cold. Still stopped on the side of the road, he shifted the car into park and turned toward the passenger seat. The crimson hanky hovered a bit above the seat. He reached out a finger and touched the silk.

"I'm sorry I wouldn't talk things over last night. It was stubborn and wrong of me, like a lot of things I do." He ran his finger along the whispery cool silk. "If only I could see you, it would be so much easier to explain what happened and how sorry I am."

"Just say what you'd say to my face," Mia said, but at least she didn't sound as standoffish as she had last night.

Quentin thought about how different it would be if he could scoot across the seat and look into Mia's eyes, tilt her chin, and claim her lips. If only she could feel his kiss, she'd know he loved her and only her.

He cleared his throat. He felt almost like an actor going on stage and there was a reason he worked his magic from behind the camera. But with Mia an unseen presence, he couldn't shake the feeling anything he said or did was as stiff and artificial as an amateur at a cattle call audition.

"I'm listening," Mia said.

Quentin glanced out the car window. A few people strolled by on the sidewalk; little traffic seemed to come this way. Feeling a little bit silly, but determined to do whatever it took to prove to Mia the sincerity of his feelings, he lifted the silk to his lips.

He kissed the fabric, then lowered it to the seat between the driver and passenger's sides. He smoothed out the square and stroked it against the leather of the seat. "These fabrics are like you and me, in a way, Mia. You're smooth, I'm awkward. You're hemmed at the edges, I tend to unravel at the damnedest times. Your colors are true, mine run to muddy." He raised the silk and crushed it against his chest. "But so help me, Mia, there's one thing I'm not confused over. I love you. You've got to believe I didn't stand you up because I doubted that."

"Then why? Why, Quentin?" Mia whispered and she must have reached out to him because he felt a tug on the cloth, then it inched from his grasp.

Quentin snatched at the cloth, not to stop Mia from taking it, but in an attempt to touch her. His hand brushed the fabric but nothing else. No shape, no substance, could he feel.

"Goddammit," he cried. "I just want to see you. Touch you. Feel you in my arms again." He abandoned his side of the car and scooted to the middle of the front seat. Leaning forward, he encircled the air space where the hanky fluttered chest high.

"If only I could see you," he said, "I'd kiss that precious nose of yours that turns up just the tiniest bit on the tip." He reached out a finger and mimed tracing the outline of her nose. "And I'd kiss each and every one of your freckles." He pursed his lips, aching to taste her kisses. "If only I could see you, I'd pull you close and whisper sweet nothings in your ear."

"And then what would you do?" Mia's voice had lowered to the pitch he knew and loved as her "come and love me" voice. Quentin's hopes flamed. Surely she would forgive him, surely she loved him despite his stupidity.

He drew a small circle in the air. "I'd try to show you just how much I love you," he whispered. "And I'd try to get a good look at your latest lacey concoction." He continued circling a finger, imagining Mia's perfect breasts under his hand, remembering all too vividly how her nipples swelled above proudly puckered aureoles and full breasts that made his mouth water.

"Oh, God," he said, shifting to relieve the pleasurable discomfort overtaking his body. When he moved, he noticed that the windows had steamed over. "Mia, I want to make love to you, hold you heart to heart and show you you're the only woman I want."

Mia gripped the hanky. She was having a hard time remembering how badly Quentin had hurt her. Even in her state of invisibility, even though she sat within his embrace but couldn't feel his touch, her body reacted as wonderfully as always to Quentin. He looked so sincere, so very much in love with her. "And then what would you do?" she asked again, her lips within an inch of his.

He groaned and Mia couldn't help but smile. "You'd throw me down on this car seat and make mad passionate love, wouldn't you?"

"Yes!" Quentin fell forward on the seat, his arms wrapped around nothing but air. "I'd hold you close and never let you go."

Mia hated to break the mood, but she had to know, had to ask the question. She held the crimson hanky so that it almost touched her chest. Only if he waffled in his answer would she listen in to his thoughts. "If I'm the only woman you want, why didn't you come to our wedding?"

He lifted himself from the seat. Stroking the air with one hand, he said, "I was afraid."

Mia inched the hanky closer to her heart. She couldn't imagine being afraid without some concrete reason. Was there someone else in his life? She touched the silk to her shirt.

Rap! Rap! Rap!

"Jesus!" Quentin twisted around toward the steamy driver's window where the heavy knocking noises were coming from.

Mia dropped the hanky, unsure whether or not she was glad for the interruption. An official-looking man in a blue cap was pounding on the car window.

Quentin cracked open the door. "Yes?"

"All right, you, get out and spread 'em."

"Me?" Quentin looked around. "Do you think he means me?"

"Do ya see anyone else in that car?" The officer pulled the door open.

"I guess you won't have any trouble breaking me out of jail, Mia." He winked, then climbed from the car.

Mia hopped out too, ready to run interference. Quentin didn't react too well to authority. Sometimes he didn't know when to debate and when to keep his mouth zipped tighter than a Ziploc bag.

"Did I do something wrong?" Quentin was asking as the policeman patted him down.

"Wrong? Hah! No, nothing, of course not." The officer unwrapped two sticks of Juicy Fruit and stuck them in his mouth. Between chews, he said, "Now I want you to walk real nice and straight for me." He pointed down the sidewalk. "See if you can't do a little heel-toe-heel-toe."

Quentin turned around. He had about six inches on the officer. "And why should I do that?"

This was the part where Mia started to get nervous. Quentin always wanted to know why he was supposed to do something. Mia figured that trait came from growing up with such intellectual parents. Quentin had told her when they wanted him to do something, they always explained why. For instance, when he was five and hadn't wanted to return to kindergarten because he was bored after the first day, his mother had spent an hour discussing with him the positive benefits of socialization among one's peers. Mia smiled, remembering how amazed she'd been at the story. Her mother would have just swatted her on the behind and told her to scat to the school bus without giving her any back talk.

"Are you asking me why I told you to do something?" The officer bristled and smacked really hard on his gum. He also slapped his nightstick against the palm of his hand.

"Yes." Quentin had that dangerous set to his jaw. Mia walked over and whispered to him, "Just do it. We need to get back to work."

"Oh, I'll do it all right. Just as soon as this little guy tells me why."

That did it. The officer slammed the nightstick into the ground next to Quentin's feet. "Walk, dammit!"

"Please, Quentin."

He strolled forward, taking three or four long-legged steps.

"Oh, a wise guy. That's it, I'm taking you in." He pulled a pair of handcuffs from his leather gun belt.

Quentin's jaw dropped. "And the charge?"

"Public drunkenness. That ain't something we take lightly here and I don't know where you're from though I'll be finding out and checking your record, but we don't cater to it in Dalton. You can spend the day in the drunk tank and think about your sins. That ought to help set you straight."

"Mr. G," Quentin called. "Is this one of your jokes?" He leaned toward the officer. "You do look a little bit like him." He tweaked at the corner of a handkerchief in the officer's breast pocket. "Got another magic one in there?"

Despite her congenital respect for authority, Mia laughed, a sound that died quickly as the officer slapped the cuffs on Quentin's wrists.

"What makes you think I'm drunk?" he asked as the officer shoved him into the back of his patrol car.

"I've been sitting here watching you talk to yourself in that car for the past half an hour and if you ain't drunk, you're crazy."

Mia leapt for the car, but the officer slammed the door before she could slip in. He hopped into the driver's seat.

"Quentin!" Mia called his name and waved the hanky.

He didn't seem to hear her but neither did he seem too concerned over his arrest. He flashed a thumbs-up signal out the window as the car peeled away, the siren calling out to clear its path.

Mia leaned against the hood of the Town Car. Had she been the one hauled off to jail, she'd have been a wreck. But she was pretty sure Quentin was even this moment taking mental notes and pictures of his surroundings, considering how he might use the experience in his work.

Practical as ever, she decided to make the

most of the moment. She tamped down her uneasiness over him. Surely the officer would take him to the town's station, check his identity, ask for his autograph, then let him go. So she needed to figure out where the police station was and try to work in some sleuthing over Sharyn Stonebridge's mysterious connection to this part of the world.

Yet she couldn't help but suffer a fit of frustration at having their heart to heart interrupted, especially by Quentin getting himself hauled off to jail. For someone who thrived on order and purposeful activity, she sure found herself mixed up in the craziest situations!

Mia glanced around at the tiny main street of Dalton. The businesses consisted of a barber shop, a video rental shop, a convenience store, a lopsided building painted with the message "Get a Piece of Heaven with a Beaver Lake TimeShare," a hardware store, and, to her surprise, a newspaper office.

Having already visited Purgatory courtesy of Mr. G, she bypassed a "piece of heaven" and pushed through the door labeled in peeling letters "Ozark Echo." Starting with the press was usually good advice.

A cowbell hanging from the door knob clanged as Mia entered the office.

"May I help you?" asked a woman with a bun of gray hair without looking up from the paper she was reading.

Mia jumped, then as the lady continued

reading, she realized the woman had responded to the sound of the bell, not to her presence.

The woman put her finger on a line of text and glanced up. Seeing no one, she shrugged and continued on.

Mia passed the desk. If she slid open the drawers of the filing cabinets at the end of the room, perhaps she'd find the old copies of the paper. It was pretty much a wild goose chase, but she couldn't think where else to start.

Cocking an eye at the woman, Mia inched open a file drawer. Bingo! Row upon row of microfilm boxes, all neatly labeled. Now all she needed was a date and topic index. Working quietly, she checked each of the nine drawers, to no avail.

Going through the film one box at a time was pointless. She tapped one perfect finger nail against her front teeth. If only Quentin hadn't gotten himself arrested, things would have been so simple. He would have bestowed one smile on the gray-bunned lady and presto, she could have told them where to look, probably could have told them whether Mia was completely off-base.

She spotted a skinny magazine size book on the edge of the woman's desk. *Eureka Springs Directory*, including Dalton.

She edged it off the desk and, wondering what the woman was reading that held her attention so completely, carried the book out of the line of her peripheral vision. Mia turned to the S's.

No Stonebridge. No Stone. She flipped to the B's but found no Bridgestone. She frowned. She was positive Sharyn's thoughts had honed in on Eureka Springs. Sharyn might not have any relatives here, but if she'd ever been associated with the area, surely someone would know of her. She was, in her own way, fairly distinguished. Surely small towns like Dalton and Eureka Springs couldn't claim so many stand-out successes that they'd know nothing of her.

The phone rang.

It kept on ringing.

The woman finally reached a hand toward the receiver. "Echo," she said absentmindedly.

Then the woman perked up. "You don't say!" Her finger strayed from her place in the book and she picked up a pen and scratched on a note pad. Then she hung up, stood up, and raised her hands toward the ceiling. "Thank goodness, a story at last!"

She tugged on the front of her navy blue dress and collected a small pillbox hat from the coatrack by the door. Attaching it to the top of her bun, she squared her shoulders and marched out the door.

Mia wondered idly what small-town calamity had occurred, but she was more curious about the woman's all-engrossing reading material. She stepped behind the desk and picked up the book. "How to sell to the tabloids," she read aloud and, shaking her head at people's fascination with the rich, famous, and the bizarre, she put the book down.

And stopped short.

When she'd entered the office, she hadn't even noticed the computer. But the sight that met her eyes now made her mouth water. The backwater newspaper office held a state of the art system, complete with the fastest available modem. Mia settled in the woman's chair and with a quick dance of her fingers over the keyboard, she logged onto her favorite on-line service.

From there she skipped to the Web. Now she'd learn something. This was research they should have done before they'd even gone after A. G. Winston, but she and Quentin had argued over the best approach. Quentin had been in too much of a rush to stop at a library to do some on-line sleuthing. And since Quentin had drawn the long stick when they'd put it to their time-honored test of "long and short," they'd skipped the research at that point.

Hoping the woman didn't return too soon, Mia located the home page for Winston Enterprises and settled in to learn all she could about Sharyn Stonebridge and Alexander Graham Winston.

11 ∾

Jemi snatched her hand away from Alex's tender hold. "Goodness, look at the time!" She sailed off the bed.

He blinked and stared down at where her hand had been only seconds before. "Did I frighten you?"

"Me?" Jemi laughed, a nervous sound that she scarcely recognized. "Grizzly bears don't scare me."

"But a gentle man does?" He spoke softly and she knew he wasn't making fun of her.

Frankly flustered, she shook her head both yes and no. Clearly he wanted her and she felt the same. She was no stranger to sex, certainly not a prudish person, so why had she shied away from the simple biological fact of their mutual attraction? "Come on, we've got to make this bed and get on to the next cottage."

He nodded and rose. "Perhaps we can discuss this later."

And perhaps not. She had a scary feeling she might not be in control of her reactions. She

167

was used to being her own boss, of her property and of her emotions. With her worry over the possible sale of the inn and the total disruption of her existence, she didn't need this most unusual man stirring up feelings she was unprepared to handle.

Determined to stick to the job at hand and hurry through the chores, Jemi dropped the used sheets onto the floor and tossed the clean bottom sheet in Alex's direction. He reached for the edge, but she saw that funny lost look on his face again.

"We do the same thing in reverse," she said, tucking her side of the sheet in.

He followed suit, working with good coordination.

"You never did tell me who made your bed when you were a kid."

"No, I didn't."

"Is it a big secret?" Jemi snapped the top sheet open and let the cotton drift over the bed, enjoying the scent of fresh laundry. She sent all her linens to Dalton where she'd struck a deal with a laundry operator to use only environmentally friendly soap and add a special herb mixture she'd concocted to the rinse cycle.

Bent over the side of the bed where he was tucking in the sheet, he still didn't answer.

Jemi smiled. "I've got it. You're really a famous movie star hiding out here in the hills. Or a prince. And when you were a kid you were waited on hand and foot so of course you've no idea how to perform life's simpler tasks."

He straightened and looked at her with that wide blue gaze that made her feel as if he could read her mind.

"Am I right?" Jemi reached for the quilt.

"That's a very inventive story."

"But the truth is more boring?"

"I'm afraid I'm simply the product of a middle-class family with enough income to employ a housekeeper."

"Drop-in or live-in?"

He looked surprised at her question. Well, she may have been born in the boonies, but she'd heard the stories of her parents' child-hoods. Both Arabella and Ransford Dailey were the children of wealth and privilege. Ari always said it was too bad their grandparents all died young. Had Arabella and Ransford been more than eighteen when both ended up wealthy, perhaps there would have been money left for the Dailey children.

"Live-in." He smoothed his side of the quilt.

"Ah-ha." Jemi grabbed the dirty laundry. "That explains a lot."

"I don't see that it explains anything at all." He spread his legs like a sailor on a rolling ship and stared as if he wanted to argue the point. "It's simply a statement and doesn't lend itself to any conclusions without further supporting evidence."

Jemi headed out the door. "Come on,

Einstein," she said, "we can debate while we clean Queen Anne's Lace."

Alex followed her out of the cottage, thinking he could use a shot of fresh air. The red-haired wood elf had heated his blood that had no business boiling and gotten him to thinking things better left unthought.

At the next cottage, the one she called Queen Anne's Lace, he walked straight to the bed, removed the quilt, and began stripping the sheets. Jemi gave him a surprised but satisfied look and attacked the bathroom. Try as he might, though, he couldn't keep his resolution not to peek at her bottom as she leaned over the tub. As a consequence, he rushed on his duties and finished remaking the bed before she completed the bath.

"I'll move on to the next cottage," he said from the bathroom doorway.

She turned around from where she was scrubbing the toilet with that bristly brush. "You're a quick study, aren't you?"

He lifted his shoulders. He couldn't call the specifications for changing a bed complicated. "Thank you," he added belatedly.

"Oh, no." Jemi dropped the brush in the bucket. "The next cabin is Mr. Grandy's. He didn't go on the hike and I've no way of knowing whether he's going to stay or check out." She peeled off her rubber gloves. "Nuts." Wiping her face with the back of her sleeve, she said, "I should have delivered his breakfast myself."

"I didn't mean to drop the tray."

Her expression mingled shock and horror. "You dropped his breakfast tray? Tell me I didn't hear you say that."

Perhaps that information had been best kept to himself. After all, it had done no harm. "I'm afraid you did, but—"

"You're fired!" Jemi moved on him, pushing him from the bathroom, toward the door of the cottage. "How could you do such a stupid thing!"

She raised her hands and pushed against his chest, but when he'd backed as far as the front door, Alex halted. She was too tiny to move him if he didn't want to be moved. He studied her hands and thought he rather liked the picture they made reaching up straining against his chest. His heart thumped beneath them and he lay one of his hands over them. One of his covered both of hers.

"It's okay," he said. "Grandy didn't mind at all. He rather enjoyed the cinnamon rolls. And he did indicate he'd be staying for several days."

Her eyes widened. They looked even bluer. He noticed she hadn't tugged free of his hand. "Well, why didn't you say so earlier?" She looked at his hand, then freed hers slowly.

"I didn't think of it," he said, mentally

kicking himself. She'd told him how worried she was over the supposed California investor. But he was reluctant to lead her on about Quentin Grandy. Whatever the madcap director was up to, he surely wasn't here to purchase a hole-in-the-wall like the Dew Drop Inn. Why, the guests here didn't even have television or a VCR. He couldn't imagine who would want to buy this place, other than perhaps another overgrown hippie. It was pleasant enough in a rural way, but lacking in every modern convenience Alex regarded as a necessity.

If he owned a hotel, each room would be equipped with on-line access and laptops would be available at the concierge desk. Only a day away from the city, he knew he'd soon be itching to get back to work, something he could have done quite simply had this place been properly equipped.

Of course, he didn't know how much work he could get done if Jemi were anywhere within eye range.

Jemi lifted her hand and snapped her fingers. "Yoohoo," she said, "still with me?"

"Yes, quite."

"I apologize for firing you. It was wrong of me. It's bad karma to take my anxiety out on someone else." She extended a hand. "Forgive me?"

He shook, but kept the contact as brief as possible. He had to get his mind back on track and her slightest touch derailed him.

Looking up at him, she smiled. For the first time that morning, she looked at peace. The result was amazing. She looked even younger than she had before, and a light seemed to glow from within her. "Come on," she said, "last one to finish these chores gets to wash the lunch dishes."

Whistling, she retrieved her bucket.

Alex scooped up the dirty laundry. Pursing his lips, he blew out tentatively. He'd never been a whistler, but working with Jemi was making him want to learn a whole new universe of skills.

Quentin rubbed his wrists and checked out his surroundings. He was the only occupant of his cell, but through the bars, he saw a woman with orange hair watching him from the other luxury suite of the Dalton Police Station.

He knew the dialogue from all the bad movies he'd watched in his life. Leaning against the bars and affecting a squint, he said, "Whatcha in for?"

"What's it to you?"

"Just being neighborly." Then he looked closer. Sure enough, the woman Jemi Dailey had dumped in the creek only a short time ago occupied the other cell.

"You got anything to drink?" She blinked and hunched forward over sagging breasts not held back very well by the wrinkled plaid dress she wore.

"All out," he said, deciding she had to be the same woman. "My name's—"

"What's a matter, forget your own name?" She cackled.

Quentin didn't think his name fit the image of a tough guy thrown in the clinker. Thrusting back his shoulders, he said, "The name's Dutch. Dutch Moran."

"Is that so?" She cackled again. "Well, unlessen you've got something to drink under that silly shirt of yours, your name could be Harry S. Truman and I wouldn't care."

Quentin digested that bit of information. Then remembering how upset Susannah had been, he decided he'd better quit playing pretend and try to figure out what had happened in this old woman's life to make her turn out this way. The bright, inquisitive child he'd chauffeured into town deserved better than the town drunk for her family.

He glanced over his shoulder but the policeman who'd dumped him in the cell had disappeared. "I'd give you a drink if I had it," he lied, "but that guy with the badge took my bottle."

She nodded. "Sounds exactly like something Roddy Pelican would do. My name's Queenie. Queenie Gillmore." She rose and advanced on unsteady feet to where the two cells joined. Reaching through, she offered a gnarled hand. "Nice to meet ya, Dutch." She squeezed shut her watery eyes, then opened them. "That name sure sounds familiar."

Quentin shrugged. "I get around, if you know what I mean."

She laughed. "You mean you're as famous as I am, I reckon." She sighed and scratched at her carroty hair. "It's hard being someone everyone knows, ain't it?"

"What do you mean?"

"You know, you get thrown in jail and they don't even bother asking your name cause they remember you from last week. And when you go to the market, all the other people there shopping for their bacon and beans scoot out of the way. And the library won't even give you a card cause they figure you'll just lose the books when you're on a good ole five-day drunk."

Quentin doubted that the old woman had ever walked through the doors of a library, let alone tried to get a library card. Then, remembering the intelligence glowing so clearly in Susannah's eyes, he reprimanded himself for his mean-hearted conclusions. Who knew what turns in the road had led to Queenie Gillmore's current condition? "I guess I do know what you mean," he said, thinking that if he didn't succeed on this improbable mission, he'd never experience a moment's peace again. He'd forever be known as the guy who'd left his bride standing at the altar.

And the once-upon-a-time Oscar-winning

director who'd lost the producer who made his entire career make sense.

"Yeah, it sure is rough." Queenie sagged against the bars of the cell. "And nobody ever understands."

"So you come here a lot?" Quentin figured he might as well pump the woman for information, thinking whatever he learned he and Mia might be able to use to help Susannah. In his secret heart, he agreed with Mia: If they intervened in the child's life, as well as succeeded in their mission with A. G., Mr. G might smile upon them. And to Quentin that meant one thing and one thing only: Mia would return to him.

She scratched her head again, causing the outrageous orange hair to stand on end. "They bring me here for my own good, mostly. Blue brought me here today, cause he seen that I would have hurt myself otherwise." She shrugged. "I don't mind. I've nothing to go home to."

"No family?" Quentin prompted.

"I used to have a daughter and a son." She sniffed and started to turn away.

"What happened to them?"

"My son got kilt trying to rob a bank up near Fayetteville."

"And your daughter?" Quentin wondered which child had produced her precocious granddaughter.

"Oh, her." Queenie walked back to the single bed in her cell. "She was too good for this town. Took off early on, though she left her cradle droppings behind for me to raise."

"Susannah?"

Queenie nodded. "A good little girl, too, she is, but I don't know what to do with her. She's smarter even than her mother was, which was pretty smart, I gotta tell you. Why, if Janet hadn't been half as smart as she was, she never would have conned me into raising her lovechild." Queenie's eyes sharpened craftily and she half-laughed. "Course, I've fixed her good on that one, but she'll never know."

Quentin didn't understand that last reference, but clearly she meant Susannah had been born out of wedlock. These days that didn't mean so much. "What about her father?"

"Hummphh! You think he would have had anything to do with the brat? You don't know a lot about men, do you, Mr. Dutch Moran?" Queenie slapped at her cheek, as if she were chasing a mosquito. "For one thing, Janet wouldn't name the father, some rich guy passing through on vacation was all she'd say. What with the way Janet carried on, that smacked of the truth. So she went to school with her belly out to here, then a week after she dropped her litter, she skipped town.

"But at least she carried her to term. If she woulda had an abortion, that woulda been the end for me. But as her momma, I took in the child." She sniffed, and Quentin's heart was touched by the human tragedy she described.

"Does she come to visit you?"

"Her?" Queenie snorted and walked back to the bars. Leaning against them, she said, "Miss High and Mighty visit Dalton?" She slapped her thigh. "She does send money, though, I'll give her that much. Once a month I get a check in my P. O. box. She made it clear a long time ago the money would keep coming as long as the world never finds out she's got a daughter, and she sure doesn't want that same world to know she's got a mother who looks and acts like me!" Queenie went off on an extended cackle. "She'd rather admit to the child than to me!"

Quentin attributed Queenie's rambling explanation to her still toasted condition and merely asked, "Where does your daughter live now?"

"Off in California, land of golden dreams." Queenie sighed. "I think I'll be taking a nap now," she said, and staggered to the cot in her cell. Without another word, she fell onto the bunk and began snoring.

Quentin was left to process the information she'd given him, and to hope Mia showed up soon. Visiting jail to obtain background information for a story was one thing; spending the night, quite another. The cop who'd picked him up had refused to listen to him or look at his identification. Quentin wasn't one to shout "Hey I'm somebody important," but if the cavalry in the shape of Mia didn't arrive soon or a more intelligent officer appear, he'd start to rattle the cage.

Still, all in all, he had accomplished something. He'd discovered Susannah had a bright and capable, though heartless, mother. If he and Mia could find that person, maybe they could do a little more intervening.

He settled onto the edge of the hard bunk and had almost followed Queenie into slumber when the slap-slap of footsteps on the concrete floor jerked him to attention. Expecting the officer, he opened his eyes and leapt up.

A middle-aged woman in a navy blue dress patted the biggest wad of hair he'd ever seen perched on someone's head. In her other hand, she held a reporter's notebook.

Quentin groaned and backed away from the cell door. He'd rather face the cop and his nightstick than meet the press.

12 ⌣

Mia had scarcely had time to scan Winston Enterprise's home page when the office door opened and Susannah walked in. Looking very much at home, she deposited her backpack by the door, then rounded the desk and pulled back the chair where Mia had been sitting only seconds earlier. She read the screen, frowned, then glanced around the office, obviously seeking the person who had been logged on to the computer.

With a shrug, she scooted up to the desk and began paging down, studying the information Mia had called up on Winston Enterprises.

Mia debated what to do. If Susannah recognized A. G., would she tell Jemi? And would that derail her plan to draw him into Jemi's arms?

A photo began filling the screen. Susannah's mouth formed a satisfied smile as the image of A. G. Winston appeared.

Feeling foolish for having hesitated, Mia hit the Escape key on the keyboard several times.

The photo stopped scrolling onto the screen, and Susannah frowned.

Mia backed away. She had to spring Quentin from jail. He could talk to Susannah and convince her not to reveal what she'd discovered.

Mia slipped out the door of the newspaper office and walked quickly down the sidewalk of the main street, wondering where the other citizens of Dalton were keeping themselves and where to find the jail.

She turned a corner and came face to face with the full parking lot and brick edifice of the First Baptist Church. Of course, Sunday morning in a small country town, most of the people would be at church. The sign in front of the church proclaimed the subject of today's sermon as "Why Carry Nation Was Right."

Mia thought of the drunken scene she'd witnessed earlier and of innocent Su-Su growing up in the shadow of Queenie Gillmore. How had living in a town of teetotalers affected the older woman? Whatever her past, Queenie needed help.

Across the street from the church Mia found the police station and city hall. Beyond those two buildings, the town gave way quickly to trees and hillsides covered thickly with broad-leafed vines Mia didn't recognize. The vines obscured trees, fences, and telephone poles, choking out light and air and giving Mia the feeling that if she stood still for long, the vines would claim her too.

The sun shone from overhead now and Mia
appreciated the warmth on her shoulders. It
was funny, but even in her invisible state she
could feel the heat. This part of Arkansas didn't
seem to get as warm as the northwest corner
where she and Quentin had spent a month
orchestrating Chelsea Jordan's turnabout from
suicidal movie star to contented preacher's
wife.

On her way to the police station, she inhaled
the clean mountain air and wondered if the
country weren't creeping into her city heart
and wooing her affections.

No officer occupied the desk in the small
office of the Dalton police force. Mia walked
inside, the theme from Mayberry R.F.D. rising
in her mind. She spied two barred cells.

Quentin sat in one, sipping a cup of coffee
and chatting with the gray-bunned woman
from the newspaper office. So Quentin's arrest
was the story she'd raced out to cover. As for
her subject, he looked not the least concerned
to be sitting on the wrong side of the bars.

Mia fluttered the hanky.

"Ah, here she is now," Quentin said, rising
and strolling over to the door. He kissed the air.
"My dear, I've just been sharing with this
representative of the press the true reasons
behind my arrest."

Had he lost his mind? "She'll think you're
crazy. I think you're crazy."

The reporter held out her hand, 180 degrees

from where Mia stood. "I'm willing to investigate any story, no matter how bizarre." She dropped her hand. "If you were stuck in a town like Dalton, you'd leap at the chance to write something other than deaths and births." She sat back in a chair positioned next to Quentin's cell.

To test something she'd suspected since she'd become invisible, Mia walked in front of the reporter and waved the hanky. The woman didn't even blink.

Quentin pointed to a ring of keys hanging from the wall. "I've been trying to persuade Mrs. Page here that if she helped me escape from jail she'd have something interesting to write about. But if you would agree to assist me, she'd really have some good copy."

"That's not a very good idea, Quentin." Mia's sense of rules rose to the forefront. "If I let you out, they'll come looking for you and then they'll be justified in arresting you. And besides, if you encourage this lady to write a story about an invisible person, she'll probably get locked up in the local funny farm!"

He settled onto the bunk again. "I daresay they've run stranger stories in the *Ozark Echo*. And the police can't squabble when I've been unlawfully detained in the first place. How can it be wrong to escape from jail when I've done nothing to deserve being here? Mia, honey, prove to Mrs. Page you're real and that I'm not crazy."

Mrs. Page scribbled furiously in her notebook. Suddenly she looked up. "Did you say 'Mia'?"

Quentin nodded and chugged on his coffee. "This could use some sugar," he said with a grimace.

"As in Mia Tortelli?" The reporter's voice rose on the last name.

Quentin nodded again.

"Then you really are Quentin Grandy!"

"Isn't that what I said?"

"Yes, but—"

Groaning erupted in the other cell. Mia noticed a woman lay on the bunk. Her bleary eyes opened and she called, "Dutch, if you're my friend you'll get me out of here and give me a drink." She hiccupped, then added, "Or at least get me a drink."

"Who's Dutch?" Mia and Mrs. Page asked in unison.

Quentin tapped his chest. "My alias," he whispered. Louder, he said, "Just be patient, Queenie. All good things come to those who wait."

"D. T.'s come to those who wait too long for a drink," she grumbled.

"Why don't you do a story on her?" Quentin asked.

The brows on the reporter's forehead merged with the roots of her bun. "On the town drunk?"

"Hey, I got feelings, too," Queenie called,

punctuating the sentence with a belch so loud Mia cringed.

"Imagine, Quentin Grandy, right here in Dalton!" Mrs. Page's bun bobbed. "Where nothing exciting ever happens. Even the tourists don't stop here; they trot on in to Eureka Springs with their rich noses in the air."

Without pausing for a breath, the reporter poised her pen over her pad and said, "Are you here on vacation? Or are you scouting locations for a new movie? Ooh, now that would be terrific!" The pen raced across the page. "I just loved *DinoDaddy*. What are you working on now? Is it true you've renounced your playboy ways?"

Mia thought of using the silk scarf to gag the aging Lois Lane.

Mrs. Page wiggled her brows and crossed one leg over the other, swinging a plump ankle in his direction. "Aren't you getting married soon?" She cocked her head, as if consulting an interior map. Or calendar.

"You're on your honeymoon!" Mrs. Page jumped up and clapped her hands. "You wait right here. I'll be right back. I've got to get my camera! I've always wanted to scoop the tabloids." She ran from the room, all thoughts of invisible people clearly chased from her mind.

When she opened the door, she bumped smack into the short officer who'd arrested Quentin. Drawing up her bosom and in a strict schoolteacher's voice, Mrs. Page said, "You

idiot! That man you arrested is the famous
director Quentin Grandy. If he was talking to
himself, you can be sure he was creating some
wonderful scene for his next terrific new film.
You'll be lucky if he doesn't sue this city for all
the money it hasn't got. Now let him out—
no—wait till I get back with my camera. You
know how these people can be about making
life difficult for the press!" She sailed past the
dumbfounded officer.

"You really Quentin Grandy?" he asked.

Quentin produced his wallet and flashed his
California driver's license. Politely enough for
someone in his circumstances, Mia thought,
Quentin added, "I was wondering when you
were going to ask to see my identification."

"Oh, oh, well, I had to hurry to church." The
officer reached for the ring of keys and a
parking ticket book lying on the desk. He
winked, and said in a buddy-buddy way Mia
detested, "Give me your autograph for my kids
and we'll forget all about this arrest business,
okay? And I'll get you out of here before that
leech has time to grab her Polaroid."

"Deal." Quentin put his wallet up and accepted the pen and ticket book. The door
swung open.

"Dutch," Queenie croaked.

"Let her out, too," Quentin said, pen poised
over the page.

"Whaddya care about her for?"

"Cellmates make for soulmates, or hadn't you heard."

Mia smiled.

The officer unlocked the other door. "Up and at 'em, Queenie."

The woman sat up and rubbed her eyes. She rose and walked forward, her disheveled orange hair crushed like wheat after a hailstorm. Moving with a surprising amount of dignity, she paused beside Quentin and said, "You're a gentleman, Dutch, and don't let anyone else tell you different."

Quentin bowed, then signed his name.

To Mia's surprise, he handed the pen not back to the officer, but over his shoulder, along with the ticket book. Realizing what he was up to, she accepted the items and signed her name beside his.

They were a team.

She smiled and hurried with Quentin and Queenie out of the police station. At the door, she couldn't resist a look backward.

The officer was scratching his head and mouthing, "Mia Tortelli. Who the heck is that?"

Queenie Gillmore lived in what would be described politely as squalor. She directed them to the trailer that leaned at a haphazard angle in a clearing in the woods between Dalton and the Dew Drop Inn.

Both Mia and Quentin were used to location trailers. But even Mia, growing up in poor and crowded East Los Angeles, was unaccustomed to country poverty. The only thing Queenie's trailer had in common with the ones they had known was the spelling of the word.

Rusting auto parts decorated the front yard. Three protesting metal steps led to the door. Queenie hauled it open and said over her shoulder, "Come in if you're not too proud."

Quentin looked over his shoulder and the sadness on his face touched Mia's heart. She knew he was thinking not only of Susannah, but of Queenie, too. No one should have to live this way.

Their hostess swept a pile of clothing off the built-in red and gray vinyl table that separated a closet-sized kitchen from the living room area. A black and white kitten went flying and landed with a hissing spit.

"Family pet?" Quentin asked.

Queenie shrugged and scrabbled about in a sagging cupboard. "Pee-Wee, I mean Susannah, brings 'em home. I let 'em stay as long as they earn their keep."

"Oh?" Quentin wasn't much of a cat person, but Mia hoped he'd asked in what way the kittens earned their room and board.

"Ah-ha!" Queenie produced a bottle of Jack Daniels and cracked open the seal. "I knew we had some groceries around this place." She slapped two faded pink coffee cups on the table.

The kitten chose that moment to rub its tiny self against Queenie's ankle. "Ah, go catch a mouse," the woman said in a gruff voice, but bent over and scratched its head. The kitten climbed up Queenie's leg and kept going until it settled on her shoulder.

Queenie poured the whiskey into the cups. "Like I was saying, Dutch, here's to good times and new friends." She lifted the cup and slammed back the contents.

Mia stared at the old woman, then wondered what Quentin would do. She had only to wait a moment, as she watched her once-upon-a-time fiance mimic Queenie's drinking habits.

He choked and coughed. Setting the cup on the table, he said, "Queenie, that's top-quality moonshine and if there's anyone who knows good likker, it's Dutch Moran."

She cackled. "You must watch too many movies. We ain't drunk moonshine here in years."

"Oh, yeah?" Quentin settled into the crack-led red vinyl bench seat. Mia could see he was blinking watery eyes. To her horror, Queenie poured another round.

If the two cellmates were going to get good and toasted, Mia decided she'd better act sensibly and investigate the trailer for some clues to Susannah's parents. She frowned at Quentin and waved the hanky, but he didn't seem to notice.

The rest of the home consisted of two bedrooms and a bathroom. The smaller of the bedrooms obviously belonged to the girl. The bed was neatly made, no clothing littered the floor, and several heavy textbooks lined the desk wedged in between the bed and the built-in clothes chest.

She'd decorated the walls with travel posters of Los Angeles, New York, and Paris and glossy color photos of computers. The contrast between this dump lost in a forgotten neck of the woods and the pictures tugged at Mia's sentimentality. Susannah deserved a much better life and if Mia had her way, the child would get it.

Mia couldn't understand how such a bright girl had ended up in Queenie Gillmore's keeping. She looked around for personal pictures or a photo album. Sneaking through someone's possessions definitely made Mia uncomfortable. She'd take a peek in Queenie's room first.

She stepped into the narrow hallway leading past the bathroom and the end bedroom. From the kitchen, only a few feet away in the tiny trailer, she heard Queenie laughing and talking. Every so often Quentin would nod and make interested noises.

Mia sure hoped he was pumping her for her life story. The squalid surroundings were getting under her skin and reminding her of her own early years. Her parents had been kind and loving, but the poverty had breathed all around them, eating into their attitudes and wearing them down.

The condition of Queenie's bedroom stopped her cold. The stacks of junk made the pile of clothing she'd tossed off the table look like nothing. Thinking of the woman's reference to catching mice, Mia gingerly picked a path through to the dresser next to the bed.

There sat a framed photograph of a smiling red-haired woman with her arms around two young children. Queenie and a son and daughter? Mia lifted the imitation brass frame, brushed the dust off it with the back of her hand, and peered at the girl beside Queenie. She could have been a younger Susannah, except for the way her chin tilted out, announcing a defiance foreign to Susannah. Same long blonde hair, green eyes, and crooked front teeth.

The boy, maybe seven or eight, had red hair that stuck out a lot like Queenie's. He wore a Superman outfit. The trio stood in front of a frame house that could have been anywhere in suburbia.

Holding her breath, even though she certainly couldn't get caught as long as she was invisible, Mia slipped the photo out of the frame. The date had faded, but she could make out the words, "Janet and Jim, second and third grade."

Mia replaced the picture and sat it back in its place of honor on the relatively unlittered dresser. Closing her eyes to the unmade bed and the trash, she started to back from the room. Once upon a time, Queenie Gillmore had been a happy mother of two children, Janet and Jim.

And if Janet Gillmore wasn't Susannah's mother, Mia Tortelli would swallow her socks.

Still, she liked to be thorough. She glanced around, looking for letters or old photo albums. Under a laundry basket filled with empty Schlitz cans, she found a stack of envelopes tied with a red ribbon, all postmarked Los Angeles and addressed to Ms. Q. Gillmore care of a post office box in Dalton. Her fingers trembling with excitement and nervousness at poking in someone else's private business, Mia opened the first envelope.

Empty.

She checked others. All were empty. The most recent was postmarked two months ago.

She replaced the bundle under the beer cans wondering why someone would save empty envelopes. But given the mess in the trailer, that was a silly question. Queenie didn't throw anything away.

On the other hand, she didn't tie her beer cans with red ribbons.

The rest of Mia's poking and prodding revealed only more rumpled clothing and empty beverage containers. Saddened and feeling soiled, she returned to the front room.

The bottle of Jack Daniels sat nearly empty on the table.

Queenie glanced at it fondly, then patted Quentin's hand. "You're a good one, Dutch. It's not every man who would have gotten me out of jail like you did. Why, most folks around here would have insisted on keeping me there. For my own good, they would have said, with their prissy noses up in the air. If most people got what they needed for their own good, the world wouldn't be the place it is, but I always say that's not for nosey-Petes to say what's what." Her head slipped onto her hands. The kitten must have jumped down earlier, as it was nowhere to be seen.

Quentin rose quietly and glanced around. Mia fluttered the hanky and whispered, "Ready to go?"

He nodded. "But I hate to leave her like this. We could at least put her to bed."

Mia thought of the bed and wasn't sure it was much of an improvement. But she hated to think of Susannah coming home and finding her grandmother slumped over the table.

Quentin leaned over and said, "Queenie, it's Dutch and I'm taking you to bed."

The woman smiled and slapped his hand playfully. "Oh, Dutch, you're such a flirt." Her eyes closed again and Quentin lifted her and carried her to the back of the trailer.

He, too, paused in the doorway, but braved his way to the bed. Mia straightened the covers. Quentin slipped the worn shoes from Queenie's feet and tucked her under the grimy sheet.

Then he stood, looking down at the bed and around the room. "Goodnight, Queenie," he said and walked from the room.

Outside the trailer, Quentin held onto the side of the door and gulped deep lungfuls of air. "How does someone end up like that? My God, Mia, I can't stand it. I had no idea this sort of place even existed!" He stumbled to the car and leaned over the hood.

"Dizzy," he said, then slid to the ground.

Mia ran to his side. "You silly goose, you can't guzzle Jack Daniels and not feel dizzy."

He tried to focus his eyes. "Dutch could."

She stroked his hair. "You're not Dutch."

"Yes I am. Quentin's only my alias. Sometimes I pretend to be this famous director guy, but I'm really good old Dutch. Good old Dutch wouldn't do the stupid things Quentin does."

"Like what?" Mia continued stroking his hair.

"Like not show up for his wedding." Quentin hiccupped. "Dutch would have ridden up on a Harley and swept his bride off. And the two of them would right this minute be living happily ever after, making sweet passionate . . ."

"Yes?"

Quentin's chin tipped forward and he began to snore.

13 ~

Alex had always considered himself a high-energy person. He required little sleep; his mind whirred constantly at a high rate of activity, refreshing itself from the pleasures of computational and quantitative reasoning as much as from the few hours a night spent in slumber.

But a day spent with Jemi had given him new insights to the phrase "high energy." From cleaning the cottages, she'd turned to readying lunch for seventeen guests. He'd assisted, but hadn't proven to be of much aid. For one thing, he knew nothing about tofu and brown rice scramble. She finally ordered him to slice the bread and stay out of her way. He did so, admiring her grace and efficiency as she prepared the food, then flitted back and forth from the dining room, decorating the buffet and dining tables with fresh flowers.

During lunch she mingled and chatted with the diners, listening to the tales of the flora and fauna they'd discovered on their morning hike.

In sporadic attempts to gather data as to the people who chose to vacation in such a rustic environment, Alex hung back in the kitchen, peeking into the dining room only occasionally from the doorway.

Most of the guests congregated around two central tables. One couple, heads close together, occupied the table farthest from the kitchen. They giggled and kissed, and fed one another bites of the lunch Jemi had concocted. Alex tried to picture himself offering morsels to Sharyn, but quickly gave up.

One other guest sat alone from the others. As tall as Alex and strikingly thin, she wore her long blonde hair tied back and dark glasses perched on her nose. She pushed a fork around her plate and every so often lifted a nibble to her lips. Pain, Alex decided, and loneliness, kept her aloof.

Jemi bustled back into the kitchen, hands laden with dishes. He jumped to help her and couldn't help but ask, "Who's the blonde with the signs of anorexia?"

Jemi turned back from the sink where she was unloading the dishes. "Malinda," she said, "but you musn't tell anyone or try to talk to her. I promised her absolute privacy."

"Oh." The name meant nothing to Alex, but what did register was Jemi's protectiveness coming to the aid of yet another person in need.

"She's a model," Jemi said, then collected the coffeepot and a tray of cups. "I told you it's not necessary to hide in the kitchen."

"Hide?" Alex tried for a smile. He wanted to check out the rest of the guests before he left his kitchen retreat. "Who's hiding?"

She pinned him with that clear blue gaze of hers, a look that said far more than any words, then whisked off into the dining room.

He stuck to his position near the doorway.

A few minutes later, one of the guests who sat with his back to the kitchen turned. To his dismay, Alex recognized a software designer he'd employed occasionally as a consultant when he started Winston Enterprises.

The man and his companion, glowing with good health, chowed down on the tofu and rice. Alex remembered the man as a party animal who'd loved nothing better than a rare steak and a six-pack of Lowenbrau, but he was coming to see there was a reason people were drawn to the Dew Drop Inn, and gentle exposure to healthy new habits had something to do with the attraction of the place. To his relief, Alex overheard the man tell Jemi how sorry they were to have to leave that day.

After lunch, while Alex did the dishes and cleaned off the tables, the Rickie the Ranger character led a bird watching subgroup off toward the back of the property. Jemi herded a more active group down to where she said the creek opened into a swimming hole deep enough for diving. With a smile and a wave, she invited Alex to join them when he'd finished in the kitchen.

For reasons he didn't want to admit to himself, Alex took his time over his chores. He wiped and polished the tables, feeling a certain sense of satisfaction in returning order to the room.

He would have joined the group at the creek, had he known how to swim.

According to Sharyn, a man of his accomplishments could have hired a private swimming coach at any point in his life. She swam every day in the Winston Enterprises pool, using the exercise to keep her body aerobically fit. But even though Alex had been instrumental in building the employee gym and pool facilities, he avoided them. He worked out in private, embarrassed by his gangly and awkward body. He was strong and fit, but he never had achieved his image of the ideal male. Too skinny, too tall, too uncoordinated.

His mother, having thrown him in the pool at age five, hadn't helped his fear of the water either.

Alex understood why his strong-willed mother had done that. To her, the evolutionarily correct response of a young child thus threatened would be to thrash about and swim to survive.

Alex, though, had gulped in half of the water in the family pool and been rushed to the hospital by paramedics.

He squeezed the water from the dishcloth and hung it from the peg as Jemi had instructed. He glanced down at his dress slacks and shirt, then began to smile. Of course! He'd be safe from entreaties to enter the water. He had no swim trunks.

Leaving his sleeves rolled up, his walked down the back steps behind the kitchen and followed the creek in its round about course through the grounds of the Dew Drop Inn.

The first thing Alex saw was Jemi sunning on a rock between two male bathing beauties. The guys wore Speedos smaller than Band-Aids. One guy was smoothing suntan lotion on Jemi's shoulders.

She glanced up and waved from the far side of the swimming hole. "Come on over, Alex."

He managed an active enough wave in return, then looked around for a way to cross the creek. But in order to do that, he'd have to walk back the way he'd come and cross on a little footbridge made from a log. That would sure make him look like a sissy.

So he stretched and yawned and looked around as if taking in the scenery.

Several of the guests were playing water polo, splashing and laughing and every so often dunking one another under. At the sight of that, Alex's stomach clenched. Malinda lay on a blanket under a tree, unmoving, eyes hidden by those dark glasses. The honeymooners were nowhere to be seen and Alex, struck by longing, figured they'd retreated to their cabin.

Then he noticed some of the guests swimming in the buff. Jemi, though, wore a suit, but as wet as it was, glistening in the sun the way it did, she looked almost naked. Alex swallowed and wished himself beside her and those two other guys hanging on her every word a million miles away.

"Aren't you coming over?" Jemi called.

He shook his head and dropped to the grass. He'd pretend to take a nap and let his mind work on that chip design problem. He'd spent too long away from work. Today was the first day in as long as he could remember that he hadn't begun the day by turning on his computer and his stock ticker first thing in the morning. He cradled his head under one of his arms and let the sun warm his face. One day away from the market could cost him part of his fortune.

A day away could also make him not want to go back.

Alex shot up, chasing that foreign thought from his mind. Not go back? Don't be silly, Alexander Graham Winston, he told himself firmly, then settled down again in the fragrant, springy grass, feeling overdressed in his long pants and white shirt. He wished he could strip off his clothes and dive in the water, Adonis and Neptune combined in one mighty god.

He laughed at his silly image and commanded the chip design to enter his mind.

What he saw instead, against his sunwarmed eyelids, was the image of Jemi leaning over him. Her breasts filled the tank swimsuit and threatened to spill over the low scoop neckline. For someone who dressed in manly overalls, Jemi sure wore sexy swimwear.

A splash of water dripped on his nose.

He willed his mind to behave.

A second droplet fell.

He opened his eyes and saw Jemi leaning over him.

Not just a vision, but the real thing.

Pure woman.

"Hey," she said softly, "I thought maybe you felt uncomfortable around the guests so I swam over to invite you. Personally." She smiled and straightened.

Standing, even as short as she was, she looked a long way away. Alex wished she'd bend back over. He assured himself that desire had nothing to do with the vision of her sumptuous body so close to his eyes. His lips. His tongue.

He licked his lips and jumped up. "I couldn't possibly party with the guests, you're right about that. I'm the hired help and that's what I have to remember. If you tell me what to do next, I'll go and do whatever it is." He said all that in one long, rushed sentence.

She gazed up at him, a water goddess temporarily on the shore. "Hmmm," she said.

"And that means?"

"My brother Ari is coming for dinner tonight. He doesn't care for my food so he always brings dinner. But you can set the table." She smiled and chased a water droplet from her nose. "As long as you set it for three and agree to join us."

If that was the price he had to pay for not being coaxed into the water, he'd pay it gladly. "I'll do that." He glanced over to the frolicking guests. "What about their dinner?"

"Oh, they're on their own for dinner. The price includes breakfast and lunch and I arrange for Rickie the Ranger's sister to pick them up in her tour bus. They go into town."

"Where they're tempted to eat beef and pork and all manner of things to ruin them?"

"Oh, most of the fine dining places run Dew Drop Inn specials." She smiled again. "They know me and they understand my guests. Who, by the way, usually tip really well." She patted him on the arm, and Alex stiffened. She was making him feel like some charity case.

"Ari will be here around eight," she said, then walked to the edge of the grassy plateau where Alex had paused. Without looking back, she dove into the water, eventually rising to the surface and breaking free, shaking her red braid and joining in the water polo game.

Alex watched for a few more minutes, then edged away. For someone used to dominating an internationally renowned corporation, for someone who'd been *WorldView* magazine's Person of the Year, for someone used to being hailed as a genius, at this moment he could describe himself only as feeling sadly inept.

He trudged back to the office cottage, wondering which dishes to use for dinner.

Ari arrived for dinner at the same time Mrs. Page drove up to the Dew Drop Inn.

Disregarding the sign that instructed visitors to park in the circle outside the main grounds, she stirred up the dust in front of the office cottage and leapt out. Ari was just strolling up from the parking area, his arms loaded with groceries.

"Oh, no!" Jemi jumped up from the chair in front of the broad window. She and Alex had been reading in companionable silence, waiting for Ari's arrival. Other than his growling stomach, Alex was quite content. He'd found a book on the history of the Roman Empire. Aware of his woeful lack of knowledge outside the sciences, he'd determined to speed read the book, only to find himself enjoying the panoramic pageantry and slowing down to savor the characters and their stories.

He marked his place and looked up when Jemi cried out. "What's the matter?"

"Mrs. Page. She's a snoopy reporter and I've told her and told her she's not to bother my guests." Jemi drew herself up to her full five feet four inches and frowned fiercely.

The guest in the Bluebell Cottage chose that moment to walk out on her porch. Mrs. Page paused, a hunting dog sniffing her quarry. Jemi lay her book on the chair and dashed for the door. "You derail Mrs. Page and I'll head off Malinda. I'm not letting that nosy woman ruin the promise I made."

Thinking of how unhappy the model seemed made Alex even more determined to help. He approached the door, grasped the knob in his hand, then stopped. Jemi had motioned Mrs. Page into the office so she now headed his way, a headful of gray bun bouncing with each step she took.

He spotted a man carrying two overflowing grocery sacks, an overnight bag slung over one shoulder. The man had the same red hair as Jemi and whistled a complicated tune.

That had to be Ari.

Mrs. Page crossed the broad porch.

Alex ran a hand over the growth on his face and wondered whether the reporter would recognize him. But that was a chance he didn't want to take. The last thing he wanted was the press announcing his presence at the Dew Drop Inn.

That would no doubt lead to Sharyn's arrival, and for some reason, he felt quite reluctant to see his intended.

"Good evening, Mrs. Page," called the red-haired man.

The reporter halted at the door. "Oh, Ari. Hello."

"What a surprise to see you here."

"Now, don't get snippy. You know I wouldn't bother your sister if the situation weren't extremely er—extreme." She practically bounced on her toes. "But guess who's in town?!"

Alex shrank back from the door, contemplating flight.

"Marilyn Monroe?" Ari looked down at the reporter through hooded lids. He had the face of the Roman gods Alex had been reading about and the same cropped hair that would have been curly had it been allowed to grow. Her brother had gotten a good six inches more height than Jemi and despite his manicured appearance, he exuded an air of tough competence.

"Quentin Grandy!"

"You don't say." Ari shifted the sacks but remained on the porch. "Have you seen my sister?"

"She ran out on an errand. And the most

exciting thing is that Quentin is here on his honeymoon." She patted the camera she carried. "And I'm here to capture the event."

"Wouldn't you call that rather kinky, Mrs. Page?" Alex could tell Ari was laughing at the woman and she didn't even understand that subtlety.

"Oh, I won't follow them into the bedroom."

"Why not? If you've followed them this far, why not invade their privacy the rest of the way, check out what they wear to bed?" He wiggled his brows. "And what they do in bed, too, Mrs. P."

"I do believe you're teasing me." Mrs. Page paced across the porch and back. "The job of the press is a difficult one and people like you don't make it any easier."

Alex wondered in just what category of people she included Ari.

"You mean because I protect my clients? Because I don't whisper in your ears what so and so picked up on her last buying trip?" Ari set the bags on the porch and dropped the overnight bag off his broad shoulders.

"Sleeping over?"

"Want to take pictures?"

It took Alex only a few minutes to figure out these two obviously had a history of dislike of one another. He never would have spoken to a member of the press in such a fashion, but then, he didn't have to put up with sneaky people trying to take private pictures. Sharyn handled the press, and the only people who interviewed him were professionals involved in money, economics, science, and computing. They all shared a common language with him.

Jemi crossed back to the porch. She greeted Ari, then said to Mrs. Page, "Did Alex take care of whatever you want?"

"Alex?"

Jemi shook her head, obviously exasperated. "If you want something done, do it yourself. What do you want, Mrs. Page?"

The reporter shook a playful finger. "You naughty girl. Quentin Grandy's here on his honeymoon and you didn't squeak a peep."

"He's what?"

"On his honeymoon. All I want is one picture. One teensy-weensy picture."

"Even if it was true, Mrs. Page, I wouldn't let you take a picture."

"You're saying he's not here or he's not here on his honeymoon? Which?" Her ears had perked up.

Jemi must have realized she'd given some tidbit away. "Neither." She rose and pointed to the car. "Please go away, Mrs. Page. You know I guarantee privacy to my guests and I'd think it would bother you that you're interfering with my attempts to run a successful business by showing up here and worrying my guests."

"Which cottage is he in?"

Jemi shook her head.

"Is it the Sunrise? Oh, you can tell me, Jemi."

Ari turned to the reporter. Very gently, he took her arm and began walking her off the porch. Maintaining his hold, he opened her car door. She got in without protest. He slammed the door and waved his hand.

Bye-bye, Mrs. Page.

Alex had turned to sneak into the kitchen when Jemi caught him. Her silky soft skin belied the strength of her viselike grip. "What is with you, hiding behind the door?"

He shifted from foot to foot. If he told her the truth, she would laugh. Alex, you're such a wit, she'd say. Of course you're the country's richest bachelor. Ha. Ha. That's why you're homeless and working for board and keep.

"I declare you are the oddest man I've ever met."

And Jemi was the most unusual woman he'd ever encountered.

Ari walked in, loaded with his goods once more. "So this is your latest stray," he said to Jemi, turning a searching look in Alex's direction.

"I'm Ari, Jemi's big brother," he said, extending a hand around one of the grocery bags.

"Alex. My name is Alex."

"Got a last name, Alex?" Ari headed toward the kitchen, but waited for the answer to his question.

"Last name?" Jemi hadn't bothered to ask, so

he hadn't thought up a name. But he couldn't use Winston. Or maybe he could. Jemi hadn't even heard of Quentin Grandy. For a woman who catered to rich people seeking shelter from the fast lane, she was remarkably ignorant of who's-who. But perhaps that only added to the charm of the Dew Drop Inn.

"Winston," he said at last.

"Winston," Ari repeated, then nodded and went on into the kitchen.

"All you had to do was stall Mrs. Page. What was so difficult about that? Alex, you have to understand the last thing any of my guests want is a reporter poking around. That's one of the things they come here to escape." She sighed and a dreamy look waltzed into her eyes. "Can you imagine what it must be like being so famous you have to hide?"

Alex thought of the around-the-clock guards at the Winston Enterprises building, of the high-tech security cameras and alarm system installed to secure his Newport Beach estate. Feeling as awkward as he knew he sounded, he said, "I imagine one would have to make allowances in one's lifestyle."

Jemi giggled. "Yeah, allowances like getting used to being chauffeured everywhere, even to McDonald's!" Then stroked her long braid then flipped it back over her shoulder. "Oh, well, it's fun to dream."

"I've got Chinese," Ari called from the kitchen.

"My favorite!" Jemi pulled Alex by the hand. "Never mind about Mrs. Page. Just try not to be so shy next time."

Not knowing what to say, Alex silently followed Jemi to the kitchen. For someone who had never completed the task before, he thought he'd done a fair job on the table. Assuming they'd dine in the kitchen *en famille*, he'd dressed the large pine work table with a checkered blue and white cloth he'd noticed when he pulled all of Jemi's kitchen things out the night before. Only the night before?! Then he'd gathered bits and pieces of a rambling vine covered with red berries and fashioned a centerpiece, using an old milk jug for a vase. White porcelain plates gleamed atop the table-cloth.

Jemi's brother was unpacking white take-out cartons. "Table looks nice tonight, Jemi," he said, managing to sound pleasant while directing a fierce glare straight in Alex's direction.

Alex wondered whether the brother were this protective of Jemi all the time. Then he remembered the picture he must make: homeless, destitute, his chin sprouting a scraggly beard, his clothes bearing the brunt of twenty-four hours without a change or a shower. Alex needed to think of a way to reassure the concerned brother he was neither scoundrel, rapist, nor thief.

"Alex did it," Jemi said, setting chopsticks by each plate.

He jumped guiltily.

"Nice job, Alex. Are you into design?"

"He's an engineer," Jemi said. "Only he's out of work right now. Maybe you know someone who needs an engineer?"

Ari raised his brows. Alex opened his mouth to protest.

"That's why he's staying here," Jemi continued. "He needs a job and I need a replacement for Casey for the next few weeks."

"Did her mother go and drop another foal?" Jemi nodded.

Ari made a face. "Well, there's no need to explain Alex's presence to me, Jemi darling. I'm not your keeper." But his glance towards Alex said otherwise. "I brought the clothes you asked for in the note you sent with Blue. Which reminds me, you really ought to get a phone."

"You don't have any telephone?" Alex couldn't help his outburst. "Not even a cell?"

"No." Jemi stuck a platter of Chinese food in the microwave. "And Ari, I'll thank you not to bring me one for Christmas the way you delivered this contraption." She smiled, but Alex felt the force in the words.

"But you're using it." Alex couldn't help but point out that fact.

"Yes, because it's here. Don't you see, if I had a phone I'd use it too, and pretty soon I'd feel as if I couldn't survive without a fax and a Xerox copier and a computer with a modem."

"I don't think I understand your point," Alex

said politely. He used those devices every day and as a result, found life to be much simpler and more efficient.

"Then I'd be dashing about like everyone else. Zip. Hurry. Rush, rush, rush. I'm striving for an ideal here and I think that's what's so special about the Dew Drop Inn. People plan ahead to come here. They write letters asking when they may stay and I write letters in response. When they're here, they know they're not going to settle into an afternoon of fishing and be interrupted by some pesky telephone call."

Ari took the platter of cashew shrimp from the microwave. "It's okay, Jemi. Those of us who keep trying to drag you into the twenty-first century respect you. But you're my baby sister and all I want to do is make your life a little easier."

Jemi jutted out her jaw. "Easier isn't necessarily better."

"If you sell the inn will you continue to live here, follow that ideal?" The question slipped from Alex's mouth before his brain could censor it as "none of his business."

"Oh, if I sell, that will be different." Jemi popped in the next platter, a beef and broccoli blend that caused Alex's mouth to water. "Ari's promised I can stay at his apartment in Manhattan. There it's perfectly okay to rush about. The city inspires it, thrives on it." Her eyes glowed. "I don't know if you've ever been there, Alex, but Manhattan is the most amazing place. So many beautiful people. Furs and jewels and the streets are seas of yellow taxis. I'll never forget the first time I saw these two women in Bloomingdale's, each with a tiny dog, and the dogs wore coats that matched the women's!" She laughed. "I thought about doing that for Sugar, but I didn't think she'd stand for it!"

Alex smiled, but his smile faded as he thought of his condominium in Trump Tower. Sharyn had already pronounced it hopelessly outdated and declared redoing it would be one of her first projects. Now that he thought about it, she'd talked more about that the night he'd proposed than she had of her feelings for him, something that had pricked his secretly romantic heart.

Before he could formulate any comment about Manhattan, she'd switched platters yet again and told them to sit. Instead of sitting, though, Ari scooped rice into a large bowl and fluffed it with two forks.

"So you have or have not been to New York, Mr. Winston?" Ari asked as he placed the rice bowl on the table and pulled out his chair. He emphasized the "mister" just enough to tell Alex he'd been found out. Jemi might live in the backwaters of society, but Ari clearly recognized him as A. G. Winston.

Alex stalled, pulling out Jemi's chair, then

slowly seating himself. "I've traveled there on business before," he finally said.

"Oh then you must know what I mean!" Jemi dug into the food. "You can eat different take-out every night for oh—at least a month and never have the same thing twice. All those cute corner markets and delis with so many mouth-watering aromas filling the air. And the food is great!"

As starved as he was, Alex ate less than usual. Ari kept pinning him with that "touch my sister and I'll kill you" look, and Alex wanted to get the coming confrontation over and done with. He had no rational explanation for having deceived Jemi, so no matter what he said, Ari would have no reason to believe him.

But he knew he didn't want Ari to reveal his identity to Jemi. Not yet. He wanted a little more time, a little more time as plain old Alex, working, living, and playing side-by-side with Jemi.

A little more time away from his real life.

14 ⌒

"**Y**ou may not care who I am," Ari said as soon as Jemi left to conduct the nightly yoga session, "but I sure as hell know who you are."

"You're Jemi's brother and you want to know why I haven't told her who I am." Alex faced the other man, meeting his gaze squarely.

"You've got that right." Looking slightly surprised at Alex's forthright statement, he pushed back from the table and crossed one leg over the other. "I wasn't born under a pumpkin leaf. What's the deal here, Winston? What's America's richest nerd doing scamming on my sister?"

"It's not like that at all." Alex pondered the best way to explain how he'd gotten into this situation.

"Look, Jemi is too kindhearted for her own good, and I don't want to see her hurt. So why don't you tell me how she came to think of A. G. Winston as a homeless, out-of-work engineer?"

Alex took a deep breath and decided to recount the events exactly as they'd taken place. "Someone kidnapped me from California, flew me here in a private plane, then the next thing I know, I get hit over the head and knocked out."

Ari stared at him in a most unbelieving fashion, but Alex continued. "When I came to, I had a sign on my jacket that said 'Will work for food' and Jemi found me on her back steps." Even as he said the words, Alex wasn't sure he would have believed them.

"Huh-huh," Ari said, drumming on his knee with a spare chopstick. "Where are your kidnappers now?"

"Singular. He's staying here at the inn."

"And holding a gun on you so you can't tell Jemi who you really are?" Ari shook his head. "Maybe my parents were right. Maybe too much money does make people nuts."

"I'm quite sane, thank you," Alex said. He ran a finger over his sprouting beard. "But I can't tell you why I wish to remain incognito."

"Can't or won't?"

"I don't know," Alex said, but he did know.

Ari stood. "I think you should know that I am acquainted with your fiancée."

"Sharyn?" Alex knew his surprise showed. "She's been here?"

"Oh, not here." Ari laughed. "I couldn't

imagine that lady setting foot in Arkansas. She
came to my shop in New York."

A bell went off in Alex's head. "You're that
Aries."

Ari nodded.

"The designer Sharyn just has to have redo
my Trump Tower apartment?"

He nodded again. "I spend most of each
month in New York, but I fly out here for a few
days every couple of weeks. I keep a shop in
Eureka Springs and frankly, I miss the fresh air.
Even if I weren't coming to check on Jemi, I've
enough of the hills in my blood to bring me
back."

Alex digested this information slowly. Then
he too stood and held out his hand. "I want you
to understand I will not harm Jemi in any way.
I'll only stay a few more days." Alex hesitated,
then said, "It's strangely refreshing not to be
me."

Ari accepted his hand. "Hurt her and I'll
make your apartment the laughingstock of
Manhattan. And I'll personally thrash you," he
added.

"Fair enough."

Ari began collecting the dishes and carrying
them to the sink. He tied an apron over his
black cotton slacks and T-shirt and started to
wash. Alex found a clean dishcloth. "I'll dry,"
he said.

Ari smiled and Alex was pleased to see

Jemi's brother had lessened his hostility toward him. Their talk turned to more neutral topics and as they were finishing the dishes, Ari said out of the blue, "Jemi's prettier, you know."

"Excuse me?"

"She's prettier than Sharyn." He winked. "And nicer, too."

Alex opened and closed his mouth. He should object, defend his fiancée as the most perfect woman in the world. But somehow he couldn't call her face to mind. The image of a red-haired urchin, her pert golden face kissed by the sunshine, overtook his mind.

"I'm back," Jemi announced as she sashayed into the kitchen. Stretching her arms over her head, then swooping low to her ankles, she said, "Did you bring dessert, Ari? Yoga makes me hungry."

Alex folded his dish towel, feeling suddenly very hungry, too.

But not for food.

For love.

"I'll let you two catch up," Alex said, heading for the door. "I'm going to take a walk."

Ari winked and said goodnight. Jemi waved a casual hand, her attention centered on a box of cookies Ari had handed to her.

"Fool," Alex said to himself as he marched down the back steps, "dreaming about a woman who prefers cookies to you when you've got a perfect woman waiting at home."

*   *   *

One of the convenient things about being invisible was it made it easy to curl up just about anywhere for a nap. So while Quentin slept off his Jack Daniels in the back seat of the Lincoln, Mia dozed in the sun in a dilapidated lawn chair.

The cooler air of evening awakened Mia about the same time Quentin sat up holding his head. "Where am I?"

Mia smiled, though a bit grimly. Quentin was going to feel lousy, no more so than he deserved, having egged Queenie on the way he had. She didn't know what had gotten into him; normally he hardly drank at all.

"Mia?"

She stretched and abandoned the rickety lawn chair. "Right here," she said, peering into the car through the open door. "Ready to go?"

He grabbed his head. "Go? I don't even want to breathe."

"Come on, it can't be that bad. You only drank half of a fifth. We need to get moving. I think we should talk to Susannah, see what she remembers about her mother, then check the records of the local high school. I can slip through the window tonight to do that. Then tomorrow—"

"Stop!" Quentin struggled to sit up. "Can't we just go home?"

"Home?"

"Back to the Dew Drop Inn."

"Do you think Mr. G would want us wasting time?"

"I haven't wasted any time." Quentin rubbed his eyes.

"Drinking away half the afternoon and then sleeping it off? Oh, no. In the meantime, I discovered that Susannah's mother probably lives in California and her name is Janet. And once upon a time, Queenie led a fairly normal life." Mia looked smugly at Quentin, pleased with her sleuthing.

Only he didn't look so impressed.

"And did you also discover that Queenie used to run her own seamstress business in Eureka Springs? And that her husband died in a forestry accident and the company refused to pay any benefits to her or the kids?"

Quentin licked his lips like a desert wanderer in search of an oasis. "And that her son got killed in an armed robbery when he was only sixteen? And that Janet got pregnant at fifteen and ran away from home the week after she gave birth?"

"I—" Mia started, but Quentin held up a hand.

"And when Janet wouldn't tell Queenie the name of the baby's father, Queenie confronted the man she thought had fathered the child, and he got so insulted he made sure no one sent her business anymore, and she's been struggling to get by and raise the kid ever since?"

Mia knew her mouth hung open. "How'd you find out so much?"

"You don't think I *like* Jack Daniels, do you?" He leaned forward, reaching out blindly. "Mia, I want to help Susannah, too, and letting Queenie drink and talk seemed the most direct way to figure out what had happened in their lives."

Mia felt foolish. She'd been so taken with the idea of playing detective she'd overlooked the human element. She stroked the silk over his hand. "I'm impressed," she said. "So now what do we do?"

He gave a gentle tug on the hanky. "How about a shower and another nap? And then we'd better check on A. G. After all, he's the man we're supposed to be helping."

Mia climbed into the front seat. "I have a feeling by helping Susannah we're also working on A. G."

Quentin groaned his way behind the wheel. "What makes you say that? The two don't have anything to do with one another."

Mia fluttered the crimson square and supplied the answer guaranteed to drive Quentin crazy, the answer that was usually correct. "Women's intuition."

Walking without seeing, Alex halted on the brink of the swimming hole. One more step and he would have fallen in.

Forced to stop, he left his hands crammed in his pants pockets and looked up at the night sky. The Big Dipper glowed crisp and clear overhead. More stars than were ever visible in Southern California had come to life above him.

Most of their names he knew. Astronomy had been one of the subjects that hadn't bored him in college. But for the moment, given the simplicity of his surroundings, he let go of that knowledge and tried to experience the sight as an ancient might have done, for their beauty and majesty, and for the sheer awe the untouchable lights invoked.

Jemi found him like that, gazing up at the sky like the village idiot.

He sensed her presence even before she called his name softly. Turning, he sought her face in the starlight.

"It's a nice night, isn't it?" she asked, stepping close to him then dropping to the ground, hanging her feet over the bank.

Alex felt even more gangly standing once she sat down. He could walk away, steer clear of the attraction he felt toward this sprite, or he could sit beside her.

The crescent moon winked down at him. He considered the resolution he'd been trying to form: that he would return to California first thing tomorrow.

He sat down beside her and hung his feet over the side of the bank, too.

"It's better if you take your shoes off," Jemi said.

He nodded and followed her advice.

She breathed deeply and tilted her head backward. "I love watching the constellations. The sky in early summer feels friendly, like a big family with a lot of children at the table."

He smiled. "That's a nice analogy."

"Do you have a big family?"

"I'm an only child."

"Oh." She swung her feet gently. "An only child and the housekeeper made your bed. You must have been lonely."

He shrugged. "Maybe I was, but I didn't have much time to notice." He'd repressed the nights he'd cried himself to sleep as a very young child. He'd wanted a brother or sister and his mother had told him sharply that only women with nothing to contribute to the world spawned children. That comment had left him wondering whether that made him a contribution or merely a fish.

"Don't be silly. Children know when they're lonely. Look at Susannah. She grew up in the most awful conditions, but she's not lonely. She works here and also at the Dalton newspaper. And she has a boyfriend, I mean a good friend who is a boy."

"Do you think there is such a thing?"

"Is this a *When Harry Met Sally* question?"

"No. It's simply a question."

She laughed and patted his hand. "I may live in the boonies, but I have seen the movie. Okay, do I believe a girl and a guy can be friends?"

"That is the question."

She cocked her head to one side. Alex found himself itching to explore her delicate earlobe, preferably with his tongue.

"Sure. Don't you?"

"I'm not sure," he managed to say, his mind not at all on the discussion.

"Since I say it's possible and you're not sure, I guess the answer is yes, men and women can be just friends. Though the premise that they can't sure made for a good movie." She kicked back on the grass and gazed at the sky. "Sometimes I come down here at night and swim in the moonlight."

Alex's heart stilled. "You do?"

"It's lovely. Want to take a swim?"

He stiffened. "I—er—no, thank you."

She sat up and took him gently by the shoulders. Turning his face to hers, she said, "You can't swim, can you?"

"Why do you say that?"

She ticked off on her fingers. "You turned blue earlier today when you got too close to the edge. When I asked if you were coming in, you froze over. And now, just look at you, there's fear oozing from every pore."

He'd never impress a woman who could see

through him so clearly. Resigned to the unveiling of his secret, he said, "No, I cannot swim. Yes, I am afraid of the water."

She patted his hand again. Alex was beginning to feel a little bit like Sugar. "My sister Pio used to be afraid, too, but I helped her overcome the fear of drowning. I can help you, if you'd like."

He squirmed, but he wanted desperately to take her up on her offer. If there was any human being he'd ever met whom he would trust to teach him to swim, it was Jemi. But he wanted her to admire him, not pity him.

"Oh, that's all right," he finally said. "Maybe tomorrow."

"Hmmm." She lay back on the grass. "Susannah should be back tomorrow, so we shouldn't have as much work to do. Ari said he might come again for dinner. That surprised me, cause I thought he had to be back in New York."

Alex figured big brother was sticking around to keep an eye on him. "When you mentioned your brother, you didn't say anything about him being a big-time New York decorator."

Jemi plucked a blade of grass and whistled through it softly. "I didn't figure it would mean anything to you. Besides, I don't like people who claim to be Mr. or Ms. Somebody Important. I see some of that with the guests, but it really turns me off. You are who you are and that's that. My brother is very successful and I'm happy for him. But if he weren't a good person, I wouldn't care how much money he made or who he was, he still wouldn't be my friend."

"You have some pretty good rules."

Jemi smiled. "Oh, they're not rules. I've just been picking my way through life, like an ant trying to cross this grass, up one stalk, down one stalk. You sure you don't want to go swimming?"

"You go ahead. I'll watch."

"That's never as much fun."

"Well . . ."

"Come on!" She rose in one fluid movement and before Alex knew it he stood beside her. "If you don't want to go in nude," she said, "leave your underwear on."

Then she stripped off her overalls and T-shirt. Alex gaped, but then he saw she wore a tank suit underneath. His heart raced, but he knew it was the sight of her near-naked body that was a greater stimulant than his own fear of the water.

"I—uh," he stammered, quite unable to say he wore no underwear.

Her body formed a perfect arc, splitting the night and slicing into the water below with a neat splash. After a few seconds, in which he knew his heart stopped beating, she reappeared, smiling and working her arms against the surface of the water. "If you come in," she called, "I promise to help you learn to like the water."

He swallowed. He thought of the expensive private coaches Sharyn had urged on him, of the way he'd always found an excuse to avoid them.

"I—uh," he repeated, then slammed his lips shut. Hey, Alex, he said to himself, you're the guy who walked out of college at nineteen because they had nothing left to teach you. You're the guy who started your own company. You're the guy who woke up one day to find himself on the cover of *WorldView*. Who says you can't learn to swim?

He rose. Closing his eyes for a brief moment, he uttered what might have come close to a prayer, had his mother and father let him believe in a supreme being. He unbuttoned his shirt with hasty, stumbling fingers and stepped free of his shoes, socks, and trousers. It was dark, and Jemi didn't seem to mind, so he'd simply pretend to disregard his nudity.

That would be easier than learning how to swim.

He walked along the bank until it dipped toward the water. He could face easing into the water, but not leaping in. He wished he could, as gracefully as Jemi had done, like a fish, but he knew he was not capable of such a feat.

He'd already walked up to his waist in the water when she swam over to him and held out a hand. "It's nice and warm, especially for June," she said.

Alex took her hand. His teeth wanted to chatter but he refused to give in to such weakness.

"Sometimes," she said, "the mountain water stays cold clear up till July. But it's been hotter than usual."

He suspected she kept up her chatter to put him at ease, and he was grateful. He smiled at her and tightened the elastic that held his unruly hair back. "I'm all yours," he said, grinning to lighten his own mood.

Jemi almost swooned when he said that. If only you were, she said to herself, I know what I'd do. I'd hide you away and never let the world steal you from me.

Aloud, she said, "Okay, lesson number one. Getting the feel of the water. That's all we'll do for now."

Jemi coaxed him toward her, leading him into the deeper end of the swimming hole.

Somehow, the thought of teaching Alex thrilled her. Perhaps it was because he seemed so accomplished in other ways, because even though he was down on his luck at the moment, Jemi sensed in him a man who knew how to make things happen. And one day, she predicted, he again would be on top of the world.

She felt in the way his hand relaxed in hers that he'd decided to trust her. She smiled and wiped droplets of water from her face. For her, as comfortable in the water as on land, the fear of swimming was completely foreign; but she had other fears, and a great capacity for empathy.

"Can you feel the bottom? Squeeze your toes against the clay. Say to yourself 'I'm safe, Jemi is with me.'"

Alex murmured, "I am safe, Jemi is with me."

"Good. Good. Now I want you to relax and let your body drift against my arms. I'm going to hold them under your back and let you feel what it's like to float. I bet no one has ever showed you just how good it feels to float before, right?"

Alex, his face a study in concentration, nodded.

Jemi smiled again. "Now let your muscles go limp and let your legs float, float, float up to the surface of the water. Your feet are seeking the moon, and you are feeling calm. Let your head tip back and your body lay as if upon a table. Picture the table you set for dinner tonight, with that beautiful centerpiece, picture it resting on your belly. Let your feet rise, your chest relax, your shoulders sink against my hands."

Alex was amazed to feel his body let go of the tension, to feel himself respond to Jemi's soothing instructions. His feet did indeed drift upwards and he found himself lying back, looking up into a sky filled with stars. "Wow," he said.

"Wow," she murmured, her arms firm beneath his back, her eyes riveted to his lower body. "It feels good, doesn't it?"

Surprised, Alex nodded. "It does. I feel as if my body has reached some peaceful accord with a formerly foreign territory."

Jemi smiled. "Trust you to express it in a unique way."

"Trust you to be the one to bring me to this state," Alex said, and reached up to trail a finger along her cheek. "What's next?"

"You just keep floating like this, soaking up the feel of the water," she said, trying to keep her mind on the lesson rather than on the mounting desire she felt as she watched his lean, muscular and oh-so-masculine body drifting in the moonlit water.

"You're amazing."

Jemi shrugged, unsure of what she should say. Part of her wanted to scream at him, drag him from the water, and throw herself on top of him. Didn't he realize what he did to Jemi the woman? She wasn't just the child of hippies who ran a funny sort of resort and could be a guy's friend. She was a woman and right now she needed a man.

But not any man.

She wanted Alex.

But she wanted him to want *her*, Gemini

Dailey. Even though she wasn't a blonde California beach bimbo, even though she dressed in violet overalls, even though she didn't know foundation from eye shadow.

He'd caught her off-guard that morning, making the bed in the Bluebell Cottage. But no matter how much the strength of her desire frightened her, she wanted more from this man called Alex.

No matter the risk to her heart.

15 ⁓

At home in the cool waters of the creek, Jemi shifted her arms, slipping one closer to Alex's shoulders, the other nearer his buttocks.

That's when she confirmed he wore not even the tiniest scrap of a bathing suit.

"Oh, my," she whispered.

"What's the matter?" Alex sounded very relaxed.

"Nothing." Jemi let her lower hand creep back to his waist. "Let me know if you want to float on your own."

"I feel as if I already am." He fanned his arms out. "The water feels less threatening than it ever has before."

"The water can be your friend, your element." Jemi tried to keep her mind on the lesson at hand, rather than on her own wayward desires. She was reacting like a woman starved for affection.

Face it, Jemi, she told herself, that's what you are. She'd been stuck out here in the woods far too long. If Mr. Grandy didn't seek her out first thing tomorrow, she'd go to him, ask him to make his offer.

And she'd take it, no matter what his offering price was. If she swallowed her pride, she could work for Ari. He'd already assured her of a place to live in New York City and a job in his shop. She might appear a bumpkin, but she was a swift learner and Ari trusted her.

"I think I can float on my own now," Alex said softly.

"Good." Jemi continued standing next to him. "Feel your body buoyant in the water, drifting like a rubber yellow duckie in a bathtub of your childhood. Picture yourself as a float, bobbing and bobbing. You're weightless, you're comfortable."

While she spoke, she eased her arms out from under his body, without moving from the spot where she'd sunk her toes into the muddy bottom of the creek. If Alex didn't make a move on her tonight, she knew she'd throw herself at him, pride be damned.

Alex's face was screwed into the very picture of concentration. With one hand, she tapped his forehead lightly. "Let go, Alex, enjoy the caress of the water."

He gave her a smile, tight at first, then slowly softening. She wondered again about his sideways nose so strangely awkward against his otherwise perfect face.

"What happened to your nose?" she murmured, reaching out to touch it with the tip of one finger.

"I've never told anyone," he said, floating naturally and wonderfully on his own, "how I broke it."

"Oh?"

"But I've never felt so good in the water. Or so natural with a pretty woman." He winked, continuing to fan his arms and flutter his feet. "As a child, I wanted to be an astronaut. I read everything I could on the topic, trained diligently. My parents, ever aspiring to rear an overachiever, arranged an interview for me with the NASA people when I was only twelve."

"Twelve?" Jemi was amazed. "Why would they talk to anyone so young?"

He managed to shrug, floating there in the still waters of the creek. She wondered whether he realized he floated on his own. "I was overeducated from day one," he said. "Anyway, my parents took me to Houston and we toured the Space Center. It was awesome. They let me try out one of the training capsules, experience 5 G's. Then they broke the news very gently to me that I'd never be an astronaut."

"Why ever not?" Without even knowing the circumstances, Jemi felt indignant for the twelve-year-old Alex.

He glanced up toward the glittering stars in the June night sky. "My eyesight was too weak."

"But you don't even wear glasses!"

"Not now, but I did then. Since that time I've had corrective surgery, for severe nearsightedness, but, well, by then my life had gone down another path and I'd pretty much given up on walking on the moon or traveling to Mars."

"So what does this have to do with your nose?" Jemi usually managed to stay on track, no matter how far someone else strayed from the point.

He laughed. "Oh, when I got home from Houston I climbed up to my parents' attic and leapt out, determined to fly. At least once."

"And you broke your nose?" she asked softly.

He nodded.

"And that's all?"

"Yes."

"Well, you're damn lucky." Jemi smacked the water with an emphatic fist. "What were you trying to do, kill yourself?"

Alex lifted his shoulders and immediately lost his balance. He began flailing and choking.

Jemi supported his back. "Relax, Alex. I'm right here. Feel your feet? They can touch bottom. Let them sink into the mud. Feel that? You're okay. Now slowly arch again, let yourself go free."

He quit fighting. Looking embarrassed, he

said, "Sorry. My apologies. And no, I was not trying to kill myself. But I think I did try to punish my parents. They'd pushed me so hard and I felt like such a disgrace."

"Hmmm." Jemi would like to teach his parents a thing or two about the nurturing and loving all children needed. For a little boy who dreamed of being an astronaut, to be told by all the powerful authorities his dream was over had to be a terrible blow. "What do you do now, to take the place of flying?"

He stared at her blankly, then stroked his arms against the surface of the water, floating free of her supporting hands. With a grin, he said, "I conquer the impossible!"

"I'm impressed," Jemi said, admiring his tenaciousness and his muscled thighs as they cleared the surface of the water.

"It's the teacher," he said. "Tonight I learn how to float. Tomorrow, will you teach me to swim?"

"You got it."

Alex slowly settled to his feet and began walking toward the bank. "It's getting late," he said, "and I'm sure your guests will be up early in the morning, clamoring for your attention. Thank you for the lesson. It means more to me than I can say."

Jemi waded beside him, toward the bank, embarrassed by the fact that all she could think of was that when he cleared the water, she'd get to see him naked. What had gotten into her? For the last few years she'd lived a quiet and complacent existence, not mourning her lot in life. The minute Alex had appeared, though, she'd felt every ounce of stored restlessness tugging at her.

Alex pushed his way toward the bank, amazed that he'd actually relaxed while lying on his back in a body of water. He cast a glance sideways at Jemi, thinking very unscientifically that his meeting her had been a miracle. Two more strides and he'd be at the edge of the creek. He stopped, wanting the night to go on and on, savoring the moment. Registering the surge of his pulse and the heat inflaming his body, he knew that tonight anything might happen.

Jemi hopped onto the bank, moving effortlessly as always. Caught in the moonlight, her body gleamed with a light of its own. She twirled her arms slowly, raining droplets of water down on the grassy bank. The effect of the moonlight and shadows on her figure, combined with her body's response to the cooling air against the wet fabric of her maillot, set Alex on fire.

He acknowledged his own arousal and desire. Boldly, he prepared to rise naked from the water, engorged and aching with desire for his very special water nymph.

He wanted Jemi and he wanted her to want him, simple Alex the kitchen helper.

Now, tonight.

Feeling like some new man baptized in the water, a being completely foreign to A. G. Winston, Alex strode from the water. Naked, triumphant, and feeling freer than he could ever remember, he stood on the bank, savoring the sight of Jemi standing before him.

He took a step towards her. He couldn't swear to it, but he thought he heard her catch her breath. A man of science, not given to prayer, he almost uttered one now for guidance.

Jemi saved him from having to come up with an appropriately sexy line by saying, "You've got a marvelous body."

"Really?"

"Absolutely." She reached out a hand and trailed it down his chest to his waist. "Long and lean and thankfully not mean."

Alex wanted to take her hand in his. He stood there, staring at her, knowing himself for the geek he'd always been.

Suddenly, something jabbed him in the back and he jumped forward.

The next thing he knew, Jemi's tiny self was crushed against his lanky, awkward frame. "Not mean," he whispered, "but starved."

"Starved?" She sounded almost disappointed as she untangled her chin from his chest and looked upward.

"Not for food," he said, and found her lips with his.

Her lips were hot and seeking, and answered

his own need in kind. He tasted, he plundered, he offered himself.

After the longest moment he'd ever lived, Jemi broke off the kiss. "Wow," she said.

"Wow," he echoed, smiling and hugging her close.

On tiptoe, she sketched the outline of his lips and brushed her hips across his aroused penis. "You are a most unusual man," she whispered.

Alex swallowed. He wanted to hear himself described as sexy, commanding, masculine. Unusual reminded him of his nerdiness and called to mind his other life, his real-world responsibilities.

In the back of his mind, he heard an uninvited voice whisper, "What about Sharyn? Remember her?" But in truth, no image appeared in his mind. Jemi's vibrance and zest and sweet curves overshadowed everything else. And even though she'd kissed him back, he didn't know whether he should proceed. "Thank you," he finally said. "I suppose I am unusual." He began, one agonizing inch at a time, to pull away from her warmth.

The next moment, Jemi flung herself back into his arms. Surprised but definitely pleased, he kissed her again before reluctantly letting her go.

Jemi gave him a lopsided smile. "You'd better put your pants on," she said, "in case we run into any of the guests."

"Oh, yes, of course." He reached for his

pants. They held firm, as if caught on a bush. He tugged, and to his amazement, his trousers broke free of his grasp and began slithering away on the grass.

He stared. He really ought to have his vision checked.

"Alex?"

Jemi would think him not only romantically retarded, but crazy too if he told her his pants had just walked off. "Uh, I can't seem to find my pants."

"Where did you leave them?"

"Right here. I think," he added.

Jemi joined him in his search, unable to believe his clothing had disappeared. Some prankster must have nabbed them while they'd been engrossed in Alex's swimming lesson. At least it broke the tension of the moment, the two of them on hands and knees hunting for his pants.

"Wear my towel," she finally said.

As they trudged in silence back toward the cottages, Jemi could have cried from frustration. She'd seen and felt how much he desired her. She'd lost herself to his touch.

And then he'd pulled away.

Yet she sensed he hadn't wanted to let her go.

What was it with her and men?

More importantly, with her and Alex?

Distressed, and incredibly frustrated, she tried to think of the encounter in terms other than personal rejection, but even her sunny nature couldn't recast the scene.

He'd wanted her.

He'd stopped.

Breathing hard, all her juices flowing, Jemi forced one foot ahead of the other up the path, wondering just what she'd done to turn him from her side?

She wanted to ask him, but she didn't know how. Jemi Dailey, who could rescue almost any creature, didn't know how to save herself.

Mia always took her responsibilities seriously, and she most certainly considered it her duty to check on A. G. and Jemi once she and Quentin made it back to the Dew Drop Inn. Quentin, holding his head, had begged the reprieve of another nap, which after another long look at his sorry bloodshot eyes, she'd agreed to let him have. Then she'd set off, wafting across the grounds, in search of A. G. and Jemi.

Quentin sure had dozed a long time out at Queenie's trailer, because the sun had long since set. Mia couldn't find either of her quarry at the office cottage. She systematically began covering the grounds, appreciating that in her invisible state, she really didn't tire.

When she emerged into the grassy clearing overlooking the inn's swimming area, she halted abruptly. Jemi was standing on the bank, drip-drying. A. G. was about to exit from the water. She tiptoed up, to gain a better view. That's when she saw Alexander Graham Winston emerge stark naked from the creek.

"Oh, my," she murmured. Quite the specimen of aroused manhood. Mia sure hoped Gemini Dailey appreciated the figure he cut. Mia couldn't help but peek, but she knew the only man she longed for lay asleep in the Sunrise Cottage.

Her plan to throw the two of them together appeared to be working, but Mia grew concerned when Alex, clear of the water, hadn't yet approached Jemi. Hurrying up behind Alex, she shoved him into Jemi's arms.

With quite satisfactory results.

But honestly, A. G., for all his brains and money, was slow on the uptake with women. Mia had turned to leave when the genius broke the kiss and practically apologized! That time, she pushed Jemi into his arms. That embrace ended, too, and Mia did the only sensible thing.

She stole Alex's pants.

Then, grinning, and feeling sure she'd solved the problem, she hurried back to Quentin, Alex's trousers tucked under her arm.

Matchmaking made her amorous.

She hoped Quentin had awakened by the time she made it back to the cottage. Even though they couldn't make love, and even though she still hadn't technically forgiven him for what he'd done, she needed him.

She needed to love him.

A. G., rising from the creek in all his aroused glory, hadn't pushed her buttons one bit. And yet, as drunk as a skunk as Quentin was this afternoon, she'd had to sit on her hands to keep from throwing her invisible self on him and her pride to the winds when they'd gotten back to the cabin.

Quentin had left the door open to the cooling night air, and she waltzed through. He lay on the top of the quilt covering the heart-shaped bed, one arm wrapped around one of the pillows. Mia slipped onto the edge of the bed and reached out, tracing the outline of his mouth with the crimson silk.

He stirred, and smiled, eyes still closed.

Feeling very daring, Mia leaned over Quentin and unbuttoned his shirt, spreading the fabric to reveal the curly dark brown hairs and muscled chest she missed drastically. For almost a year now, she'd slept wrapped in his arms. For almost a year, they'd made love every night. For almost a year, she'd claimed the man of her dreams as the man of her heart.

She drew the outline of a heart on his chest, then leaned to kiss the center, stroking lightly with the silk as she did so.

Quentin stirred, and to Mia's pleasure, he murmured her name.

"I'm right here," she said, touching his chest lightly with the hanky.

"And I thought you were only in my dream," he said, his smile widening. "Kiss me, Mia."

She leaned over him, lowering her lips to his. She put every ounce of intensity, urgency, and desire she felt into that kiss. Her body flamed, her senses reeled.

"I can't feel you," he cried.

Mia tickled his lips with the silk. "Use your imagination, sweetheart," she murmured, caught up in the swirling sensations shooting through her body. Just thinking of making love to Quentin drove her wild. "I'm yours, here to command."

Quentin didn't seem at all sleepy anymore. He'd pushed up on one elbow. "Are you sitting beside me?"

She nodded, then realized how ineffectual that gesture was. "Yes, right beside you."

"Straddle me," he said, and she climbed across his hips.

"I'm here," Mia said, "and your wish is my command."

"Right, right here," Quentin said with a tortured-looking grin. "You know, Mia, that I love you and want you and kick myself one thousand times a day for ruining our wedding. And at this moment in time, all I can think of is how much I want to make love to you."

"Me, too," Mia said, a daring idea scooting into her mind. She'd always been so practical and such a good girl. But invisibility freed her

in oh so many ways. Wiggling her hips against
Quentin's groin, she said, "Pretend you can see
me, sitting here, leaning over you. Pretend you
can see me as I start ever so slowly to lift my
blouse."

"I like this idea," Quentin murmured.

Quentin always slept in the buff. Mia could
feel his erection jutting against her inner
thighs, even though she knew he couldn't
sense her there. That idea sent an even naugh-
tier idea flitting through her mind.

Could she? Did she dare?

Lifting forward on her hips, she shrugged out
of her cotton top and tossed it over her shoulder. "I'm oh-so-slowly lifting my blouse over
my breasts, over my shoulders, above my head.
Whoosh, it's gone, tossed to the floor." Mia
cupped her lace encircled breasts with her
hands. "Would you like to see my breasts,
Quentin? Would you like to kiss them until I
squirm with pleasure?" Before she knew it, she
was breathing awfully hard and fast.

And so was Quentin, and panting and
thrashing a bit on the bed. "Oh, God, Mia, I
didn't want you to torture me!"

She leaned forward and let her breasts tease
his chest. "Oh, didn't you? I think that's exactly
what you wanted."

He laughed, a strangled sort of sound.

"You deserve a bit of torture, you know,
Quentin." Mia unhooked the front of her bra
and cupped her flesh in her own hands. "You

could be the one touching me right now," she said, lifting one of his hands toward her and filling it with the silk hanky. "My breasts are aching from wanting you." She touched her own pebbled nipple and shivered at the feeling the touch set off in her.

"I said I was sorry," he cried. "I love only you. I want only you!"

Mia leaned back, then slipped her panties off her legs. She kicked them off the bed. "I'm naked, now," she said. "Completely naked." She stood on the bed, one foot on each side of Quentin's hips, feeling strangely powerful and completely unlike her normal demure and practical self.

"Come for me," Quentin said in a voice that had lowered to somewhere between a growl and a pant.

Never, not even in the love they'd shared in the past year, had Mia ever put on such a show. In many ways, she remained the sheltered Catholic schoolgirl.

"What do you mean?" she asked, pretty sure she knew exactly what he meant.

"Lean over me, stand over me, lie by me. Think of me kissing you with my lips and make yourself come. I want to hear you cry out."

Her breath was coming in what she could only describe as heated gulps. "You want me to do that?"

He nodded.

She did, too, a sexy smile crossing her lips.

"First," she said, drawing back the sheet, "you have to do something for me." Oh, yes, she could be this wild and free!

"What's that?" Quentin asked, breathing heavily and staring upwards from the bed.

She fashioned the silk scarf in a loop and caught Quentin's wrist in the fabric. Then, still straddling his hips and nuzzling her naked body against him, she guided his hand until it wrapped around his penis.

"Together," Mia said, "even though we're apart."

"My little minx," he whispered, "what would I do without you?"

Even as he asked the question, she allowed her fingers to drift to the demanding, seeking, heated center of her body.

"Put one hand on your breast," Quentin said, his eyes glazing and his erection gripped in his hand. "Pretend your fingers are my lips. Feel my lips kissing your nipple, my mouth sucking at your breast." He groaned and his hand moved quickly on his body. "Mia, I can't live without you," he said.

Mia was already moving over the edge, but his directions, and the incredibly sexy sight of his hand cradling his penis urged her along helter-skelter. Before she could gather her senses, she cried out, and sank onto the bed. "Oh, Quentin," she said, "I love you too, too much."

16 ~

When Quentin drifted to sleep again, with a whisper of a smile on his lips, Mia slipped outside, both pleased and saddened by his smile. Yes, indeed, she did love him too, too much.

She also loved brownies, the rich chewy kind, and she'd learned at an early age not to stick her finger in the pan and scoop out the fudgy dough when the pan was still hot from the oven.

Eight-year-old Mia had burned herself badly doing that.

Her mother had tended to the wound, and when the stinging finger had blistered, her mother told her to look at that finger, all ugly and swollen, and remember not to be in such a hurry to grab things before they were ready.

Mia tucked her feet under her in the hammock on the porch of the Sunrise Cottage and thought how much more painful an injured heart was than a burned finger.

Looking up at the stars gleaming in the dark

country sky, she made a promise to herself. As much as she wanted Quentin, as long as she'd waited for him to fall in love with her, she'd not get in a rush now. Patience, Mia, patience. Quentin had to know in his heart he was ready for her.

A German shepherd approached the porch, tail wagging. Mia glanced around, but the dog, who walked straight to her and lifted a paw, seemed unaccompanied.

Mia took his paw and they shook. The dog then sat back on her haunches and appeared to study her.

"So you can see me, girl?" Mia murmured. "Just like last time."

"Woof!"

Mia smiled, remembering only a year ago when she and Quentin had slipped from their workaday world into Mr. G's unlikely scheme of life, death, and the in-between. She and Quentin had both been invisible, except to animals and five-year-old Timmy. And the amazing octagenarian Ely Van Ness, of course.

She stroked the dog's silky ears, mulling over the events since that trip to Arkansas and this one. Threatened with the prospect of death, Quentin had realized he loved her. They'd met the challenge set to them by Mr. G and recovered from their near-death experience. Miraculously, the doctors had said, which had made Mia smile.

She and Quentin had spent the next six

months working together day and night to complete Quentin's film *DinoDaddy* in time to get it into distribution for Oscar consideration. They'd met that deadline, going home each night to fall in bed together, exhausted, but never too exhausted to make sweet, generous love.

The film broke box office records. Mia and Quentin celebrated, then dove into negotiations and preproduction on *Permutation*, the film waiting for their return from their honeymoon to begin principal photography.

Their honeymoon.

Where they should be right this minute.

The dog gave a low whimper and Mia accepted it as sympathy. "Thank you," she said, patting her head.

"Wurr-woof!"

"Shush," Mia whispered. "People are sleeping."

The dog lay down, her paws covering her nose.

"Doing penance, are you?" Mia asked, thinking, as always, of Quentin.

She looked again to the heavens, wishing for an answer to her question. Did Quentin love her enough to make their marriage work?

Or had the weirdness of near-death only made him cling to her? Had she loved him so much she'd talked him into believing he loved her? Had his failure to show for the wedding been caused by his subconscious telling him the truth: Mia best fulfilled the roles of friend, partner, sidekick.

But wife?

She sighed, unable to think of a better definition for wife or husband than a combination of all those roles. But she knew she had to be strong and prepare herself for the possibility that for Quentin she'd been just another one in his string of girlfriends.

Suddenly the dog leapt up and padded to the edge of the porch, nose pointed toward the back of the Dew Drop Inn's grounds. Mia wondered who or what was coming, but as soon as she saw the dog's tail began to wag, she relaxed. The dog, so much at home, probably belonged to Jemi.

And sure enough, Jemi, with A. G. walking stiffly beside her and wearing his dress shirt and a beach towel, came into view.

The dog barked.

"It's okay, Sugar, it's just me," Jemi called in a low voice.

The dog barked again, twice.

"Oh, and Alex, too," Jemi said.

The dog sat back on its haunches. Mia couldn't help but smile. She appreciated any creature who insisted on accuracy. But as the couple drew nearer, Mia knew something had gone wrong. They'd returned much too soon. And the way they walked at a distance from one another, not looking into each other's faces, painted a picture that Mia knew needed some touch-up work.

Jemi called the dog again, but the shepherd remained planted next to Mia's feet.

"She's usually such a good dog," Jemi said without looking at A. G. She whistled; the dog barked but didn't budge.

"Oh, no, that's the Sunrise Cottage!" Jemi clapped her hands. "Off that porch this instant! All I need to do is annoy Mr. Grandy. Talk about a perfect finish!"

Mia edged toward the porch steps, figuring the dog would follow her. She did, but barked an accompaniment to her prancing steps. Then a better idea struck her and she opened the door to the cottage and ran inside to wake Quentin.

Of course the dog followed her into the cottage.

Jemi dashed to the porch. Quentin met her in the doorway, wearing only his hastily donned jeans. "What's it take to get some sleep around here?"

Standing behind Quentin, Mia said, "Give her a hard time, Quentin. You can ask questions later, but I need some help here."

"Just go with the flow?" Quentin muttered under his breath, then said to Jemi, "Who wants to stay at a place where you get attacked by wild animals? Nature's one thing, but I don't want it in my bedroom."

Mia sat down on the foot of the heart-shaped

bed and patted the space beside her. Sugar jumped onto the bed and cocked her head. Her tail began to thump against the quilt.

"Mr. Grandy, I promise you my dog has never disturbed a guest. Never once." She raised her chin in a way that made Mia like her even more. She didn't give in easily. "Now, if you'll just let me in, I'll get my dog and you can get back to sleep."

Footsteps sounded on the porch.

About time, Mia thought, having been waiting for A. G. to join the fray. From what she'd seen of their kiss beside the creek, his protective instincts should be well-stirred.

"Give him a hard time, too," Mia said to Quentin.

"What do *you* want?" Quentin said in a rough voice that reminded Mia of his Dutch Moran routine at the jail.

"I've been listening to you shout at Jemi, and I don't think there's any reason to act in such an uncivilized fashion." As he delivered this sentence, A. G. kept one hand gripped on the towel he wore.

Mia shook her head. Sugar lowered her nose onto her paws.

"What's it to you, anyway?"

Quentin had moved to the side of the doorway just enough so that Mia could see past him. Jemi stood almost nose to chest with Quentin, and A. G. loomed beside her. The genius had a good two inches on Quentin.

"This woman is my—uh, friend and what happens to her concerns me."

A. G. sounded like a character from a nineteenth-century novel but Mia could see fire flashing in his eyes. He'd clenched his jaw and doubled his free hand into a fist.

"I thought she was your boss," Quentin said, wiggling his eyebrows.

"That's none of your business," Jemi said. "Sugar, come. Alex, let's let Mr. Grandy calm down."

"I don't think," A. G. said very slowly, "Mr. Grandy wants to calm down."

"That's right. I don't!"

"Poke him in the chest," Mia said.

With one wild, quick glance over his shoulder, Quentin whipped back and shoved A. G. Jemi jumped out of the way.

And before Mia could think of the next move, A. G. drew back his fist and cold-cocked Quentin.

He hit the floor with a resounding thump.

"Woof!" Sugar jumped down, but no faster than Mia, who ran to his side and fanned him with the hanky. Sugar licked his face. Jemi ran to the bathroom and came back with a washcloth and a cup of water.

A. G. stood in the doorway, staring back and forth from his hand to the prone man at his feet.

He looked quite satisfied with himself.

Quentin's eyelids began to flutter. Jemi leapt

up, hands on her hips, and said to A. G., "Look what you've done!"

He nodded, as if accepting a compliment.

"He'll never buy the inn now," Jemi cried.

Oh, oh. Mia realized the whole scenario had backfired. Instead of Alex the hero, she'd created Alex the skunk. She bent over Quentin, who continued to come around.

"If you can hear me," she barely whispered, "blink your eyelids twice but don't say anything yet."

He blinked once, twice.

"When you sit up," Mia said, "act like you can't remember anything that just happened. You have no idea A. G. slugged you and you love German shepherds, especially ones that visit your cabin at night."

Quentin blinked his eyes again, then stretched his arms over his head and yawned. Then he looked around, and said, "What am I doing sleeping on the floor?"

"Mr. Grandy?" Jemi still kneeled beside him.

"Did I drink Jack Daniels again?" Quentin demanded, then sat up holding his head. "I ought to know better. Twice in one day. I suppose I've made a scene and you've all come to put me to bed?"

After tonight, Mia would award Quentin her own personal Oscar for Best Actor.

"Would you like that?" Jemi asked eagerly.

"Be a good idea," Quentin said, with a wink,

then circled her ankle with one hand. "You keep me company?"

Mia bristled, but she knew Quentin only said it to tease her. He'd gone along without balking and now he wanted to have a little fun at her expense. Well, it had cost him a good knock on the jaw plus a thump on the head, so she guessed he could have a little fun.

But only a little.

Jemi, in a damp tank suit, created a picture to make any man smile. Watching them, Mia forced herself to answer whether the picture made her jealous.

Nah. She'd handled those doubts. Only Quentin's indecision stood in the way of their happiness now.

A. G. moved into the room. He bent down and plucked Quentin's hand off Jemi's leg.

This time Quentin winked at A. G. "So that's the way the wind blows? Couldn't happen to a better man. You two put me to bed and I'll try not to cause any more trouble tonight."

"Bravo," Mia said.

"I think I'm hearing things," Quentin said, holding his head as A. G. lifted him up and carried him to bed in one effortless sweep.

Jemi chewed at her lip. "I hope you're not hurt. I can go get some ice."

"No, no. I'm seeing things, too. Is that a dog? In my cottage?"

"Oh, Mr. Grandy, it won't happen again."

Jemi held onto Sugar's collar before she could leap onto the bed.

"I think it's a nice touch," Quentin said. "I just might buy this place after all."

Jemi looked very puzzled. A. G. leaned over and whispered to her, "Partial amnesia."

Jemi nodded, and said beneath her breath, "Thank the universe!" Louder, she said, "We'll let you sleep now."

"Oh, don't go," Quentin said. "Isn't that your kitchen help who carried me to bed?"

A. G., who had stepped back toward the door, cleared his throat. Mia wondered how *WorldView*'s Man of the Year felt about being referred to as "kitchen help."

But he stepped forward, still girded by the towel. "Ah, Mr. Grandy," he said, "good evening."

Lying against his pillows, his head throbbing, Quentin figured he might as well make use of this interlude. He felt pretty damn good about the information he'd gained from Queenie that afternoon, even if it had cost him the world's worst hangover. His tongue might as well have been a dirty sock and his head threatened to shut down from pain.

Mia had just orchestrated a fairly clever scene, and now he wanted to get in on the action, too. He didn't want her to have to carry all the creative burden when it had been his screwup that landed them this assignment.

Quentin motioned to the two easy chairs.

"Got a minute? I thought we could discuss a little business."

"Business?" Jemi answered in a voice that squeaked, darting an excited glance toward A. G. "After all this?" She let go of Sugar's collar and the dog bounded onto the bed.

"Sure, business." Quentin ran a hand over the dog's coat, then glanced around, checking for, but not finding, the crimson hanky. Had she gone? He assumed from the dog's contented presence that Mia lingered nearby, but if she'd drifted off, he hoped she'd be impressed with the progress he intended to make.

"I'll just go back to the kitchen and start the bread," A. G. said, turning away.

"Oh, no, I want you to stay too." Quentin waved him back. "When I investigate a potential investment, I like to get the workers' point of view, too." He threw a wink at A. G., but he wasn't sure the man caught it. What the hell; this little charade could do double duty: get to know Jemi and A. G. and let them each see the other's dreams and goals. Yes, Mia would be proud of him.

Maybe even forgive him.

He pictured her straddling him, her face lit with surprise and pleasure as she climaxed, wishing for the day he could see that performance in person. But that thought derailed him, so he wrapped it up and saved it for later.

Jemi pulled one of the chairs closer to the bed and sat down. A. G. remained standing.

"So you want to talk business?" Jemi said, leaning toward him, fixing those big eyes on him. When she did that cozying-up gesture, her breasts threatened to push over the limits of her maillot. Quentin registered that he made only a clinical observation of this bounty; he also hoped that Mia understood he'd only tugged on Jemi's ankle to spur A. G. into action.

Right now, staring hard at Jemi's breasts, A. G. didn't look like a man who needed any encouragement. The man ran his tongue over his lips hungrily.

Good start, Quentin thought.

"This business, in particular. What makes you want to sell the Dew Drop Inn?"

Jemi puckered her lips. Quentin thought of Mia's habit of running a fingertip across her lips while concentrating and found himself wishing she was snuggled by his side during this discussion.

"The letter informing me of a possible buy-out offer took me completely by surprise," Jemi said. "I really didn't want to sell, but then I hadn't thought of it. I've lived here most of my life, Mr. Grandy, and I love the inn."

She sighed and smiled. "But part of my heart longs for the city. I'd really like to turn the inn over to someone who loves it as much as I do, so I can explore life elsewhere."

"So you wouldn't sell to just anybody?"

"Oh, no. Not even for big bucks."

A. G. stirred against the wall where he

leaned. Quentin suppressed a laugh, assuming Jemi had shocked Winston's entrepreneurial nature by such a disclosure. Not exactly the thing to state to a potential investor, truly.

"And if I offered you a decent, but low price, and promised to remain true to the spirit of the inn, you'd consider my offer?"

Jemi caught her breath, then said softly, "Yes. Yes, I would."

"What about you?" Quentin turned toward A. G. "Would you remain here without Ms. Dailey as owner?"

"Er . . ."

"Let me rephrase my question. Do you like working here?"

A. G. studied his hands, then lifted his head. "As a matter of fact, I do like it." He nodded, in a satisfied sort of way, as if he'd just answered some question important to himself.

"And what did you do before you came here?" Quentin wanted to hear A. G.'s description of his life, discover why A. G. had believed himself happy. That question lay at the crux of Mr. G's assignment, and until he and Mia understood that truth, they couldn't be sure of succeeding in their mission. He knew Mia thought Jemi represented the solution, but he wanted to be sure. Too much hinged on the outcome to risk assuming the answer.

"He was an—"

"I asked him," Quentin said gently.

"You could describe me as an engineer.

That's what Jemi was about to say." A. G. nodded. "I made it possible for computers to function faster and more efficiently."

"Computers," Quentin said, as if that answered everything.

"Yes, the force of today, tomorrow, and beyond," A. G. said. "Before computers, we were like man without the knowledge of fire. Now, all things are possible, all accomplishments lie within our grasp."

"All?" Quentin asked, though not sharply, thinking Mia would correct A. G. right off. Accomplishments of the heart and soul would certainly not fit under that umbrella.

"Yes, most certainly." A. G. leaned forward, his eyes shining. "The entire world is interconnected, joined by the World Wide Web. With the exchange of ideas and information made possible, man has at his fingertips the stepping stone to all inventions and improvements. We continue daily to invent faster and better computer technology, and as it becomes more accessible, everyone can join in the productivity of tomorrow."

"Everyone?" Quentin thought of Queenie, of her squalid living conditions. But even in that cramped trailer, Susannah had connected with the technology of today, so maybe A. G. did have a point.

"Everyone who wants to be involved can be involved."

Jemi puckered her lips again. "Is faster and more efficient necessarily better? For instance, if someone wanted to buy the inn and turn it into a computer camp, I'm not sure I'd like that idea. What's the point of staying indoors glued to a computer when you can be hiking in the woods, communing with nature? Or swimming?" She looked directly at A. G. when she asked her last question.

"Those activities have value," A. G. said, "but they don't produce or create."

Jemi's face had taken on a stubborn look. "I don't see what difference that makes."

Quentin's goal had not been to get the two of them into an argument. "Time out," he said. "Does producing and creating, then, make you happy?" He addressed his question to A. G.

As usual, the genius took his time responding. He pleated the knees of his trousers, then said, "Yes."

"And is that all you need for happiness?"

A troubled look flitted across A. G.'s face. Quentin registered A. G.'s glance toward Jemi and smiled when he finally answered, "Perhaps not."

"What else, then?"

"Is this question related to your potential investment in the Dew Drop Inn?" A. G. asked politely enough, but Quentin heard the steel in his voice.

"Possibly," he answered.

"Well, then, I can state that happiness is not a simple equation. I have not as of this date arrived at anything so brilliantly simplistic as the Pythagorean theory to define that evasive state." He swept his hair back over his shoulder. "But I would suggest to the interested observer that happiness may require a desire to please another which creates a desire greater than the simple statement of its existence."

Jemi blinked. Quentin did, too. "Come again?"

A. G. shrugged. "All that is to say I'm not sure what happiness is. Up until twenty-four hours ago, I thought myself content, thought that my life contained every element needed to please me from now until the moment of my death. But now I'm not so sure." He stared down at his feet when he finished this speech.

A. G. had it bad for Jemi, which pleased Quentin to no end, because he knew Mia would be jumping up and down with joy at her matchmaking skills. Summoning a businesslike smile rather than the silly grin he wanted to sport, he said, "I don't know about you two, but I'm thinking this place will be an excellent investment. And I would keep everything exactly the way it is."

"You would?!" Jemi jumped up and skipped a step toward the bed. Then she seemed to recover her sensibilities. She stretched out a hand toward him and they shook formally enough. "I do hope you feel strongly enough to follow through with a formal offer," she said.

Quentin nodded. "I would need a manager, of course."

"Oh." Jemi puckered her lip again. "Would you want me to remain?"

"Oh, no, you'll be off to the big city, won't you?"

She rubbed one foot against her opposite calf. "I would like to."

"Well, then, perhaps you could make recommendations?"

"Sure. Absolutely. I am sorry Sugar woke you up," she said, "but if this is what's come of it, I guess I can't be too apologetic."

Quentin grinned. "No, Sugar was only doing what a good dog should do."

The shepherd raised her head. "Come on, girl," Jemi said. "Off Mr. Grandy's bed."

The dog obeyed and padded across the floor and out the door beside Jemi.

A. G. hesitated. "A word with you," he said in a low voice to Quentin.

"Certainly." Louder, Quentin said, "Let me detain you just a moment longer to clarify the workers' point of view."

Jemi waved from the doorway and Quentin heard her whistling her way toward the office cottage.

"Just what do you think you're trying to pull?" A. G. demanded in a voice that reminded Quentin the gawky genius was a dominant force who controlled a Fortune 500 company.

"Happiness?"

"That may serve as hippie talk, but it doesn't answer in this situation, Grandy. What do you mean, leading Jemi on like this? You know you're not the investor she thinks you are. You'll break her heart when you disappear and she's left to carry on, her dreams up in smoke."

Quentin nodded. "Maybe, maybe not," he said, but before he could figure out how to explain his actions, A. G. spoke again.

"I don't understand you. You go to the extreme of kidnapping me supposedly to interview me so you can make a movie of my life. Yet, you really don't seem to care about that at all. Now you're off on this tangent of buying this place. What gives, Grandy?"

Quentin gave A. G. an assessing look. He didn't see any harm in telling Winston a little bit of the truth. "It's like this," he said, "things aren't always what they seem. I no more want to make a movie of your life than I want to buy the inn. But there are other forces at work here that are pretty damn hard to explain to a person as rational as yourself."

Alex grinned wryly. "I'm beginning to think I could believe almost anything."

Considering what Mia had put the guy through, Quentin found that easy to accept. "Sometimes life is like love. The 'why' isn't important at all. You know what you want, you know what you have to do to make it happen, and yet, you still screw it up."

"I'll say!" A. G. dropped into one of the easy chairs. "Once you know who you want and you've messed it up a few times, do you suppose things can still work out?"

"I most certainly hope so!" Quentin said. "Now, get up and go after Jemi."

A. G. sprang up. "Right!" At the doorway, he paused. "Watch yourself with Jemi. I don't want her getting her hopes up and having them dashed."

Quentin gave him a thumbs-up, feeling pretty optimistic himself. Wanting the best for Jemi was a darn good start on the road to A. G. finding true happiness for himself.

17 ~

On feet lighter than air, Jemi danced from the Sunrise Cottage to her kitchen. "What if?" she asked the walls she'd painted herself. "What if?" she asked the herbs she'd planted in the kitchen window boxes. "What if," she whispered as she crossed her fingers, "I were free to go?"

Alex marched into the kitchen on that note, looking extremely cross.

"What did Mr. Grandy want to know?"

His only answer was a shrug.

Jemi studied his dark expression, realizing celebrating the prospective sale of the Dew Drop Inn in front of a man who had recently lost his job could only be called thoughtless. Thanks to her, he probably thought he would lose this port in a storm.

She stepped toward him, a hand outstretched. "Oh, Alex, here I am all excited and you're probably thinking you're facing yet another layoff!" She grasped his hands. "But you mustn't worry about that. I would never sell to anyone who wouldn't hire Casey and Susannah, and now you, too."

He gave her a crooked smile. Squeezing his hand, her subconscious kicked in the thought that this hand did not belong to a man frightened about the unemployment line. Neither too cold, too hot, or too clammy.

His hand, warm and tender, carried strength in his long, tapered fingers. That hand made her want to offer more than her own small one for his embrace. That hand, too, had knocked Mr. Grandy out cold. No one had ever protected her in that manner. She licked her lips and glanced into his eyes. There, rather than anxiety, she saw what looked a lot more like . . . concern? . . . sympathy?

"Hey, be happy for me, okay?" She gave his hand a gentle tug then let go. She circled the kitchen, pirouetting around the pine table. "I really don't feel like baking bread right now."

"What do you feel like?" Alex's voice carried more than a hint of interest, and he watched her with a hungry gaze that rekindled the flame he'd ignited, then doused, beside the creek.

"Maybe taking a walk?" She circled the table again. "I've got to move around or I'll simply burst." All the passion and tension at the swimming hole coupled with the prospect of the most exciting change ever to come over her life was too much for Jemi to absorb in peace and quiet.

"I noticed," Alex said slowly, "a brochure in the office that described a natural hot spring on your property. Would you like to show me that spring?"

The image of Alex naked and aroused as he climbed from the creek flashed in the forefront of her mind. She knew her cheeks colored. "That would be nice," she said in a slightly breathless voice. "Let me get you another fresh towel."

He nodded and Jemi walked over to the linen closet, yanked out a towel, and then paused. "I'll be right back," she said and raced out of the kitchen.

Alex heard her running lightly up the stairs. He hoped Quentin Grandy, Hollywood wonder boy, looked forward to becoming the proud owner of the Dew Drop Inn, because Alexander Graham Winston meant to hold him to his words.

Flexing his fingers, Alex studied his hand. He'd never hit anyone, hadn't even known he had it in him. But if Grandy messed with Jemi's hopes, he'd pop him again.

Jemi's spirit deserved far better than to be crushed by some dilettante's whimsy. Of course, Alex thought, wondering what kept her upstairs for so long, there were times when Grandy seemed like a straightforward enough guy. Somehow he didn't think that kidnapping billionaires counted as one of Grandy's every day pastimes.

He heard Jemi moving around upstairs. He puckered up his lips and blew lightly; to his surprise, he generated a scratchy tune. He thought of Jemi beside him in the water, giving him the confidence to overcome his most secretly shameful fear.

He pictured the wet bathing suit clinging like Saran wrap to her breasts, the nipples jutting out like gumdrops on the type of bakery confection he'd never been permitted as a child.

His whistling took shape and he shifted from foot to foot, willing her to hurry back.

From her post in the kitchen doorway, Mia lowered the square of silk from her heart and fluttered it in front of her face. "Oh, my, he's hot," she murmured.

But this time she wasn't slacking off on the job. She'd stick with the two of them until she knew, proof positive, they'd dared to claim the happiness she knew they'd find in each other's arms.

Footsteps sounded on the stairs. Still dressed in only his shirt and towel, he walked to the front room to meet her. She seemed a little flustered, and he hoped she hadn't changed her mind.

"Everything okay?"

She blushed a little, but nodded yes as she tucked her own towel around her waist. Holding out a hand, she said, "Let's go be wonderfully irresponsible and in the morning I'll drive into Dalton and pick up some cinnamon buns at the bakery there."

Alex joined his hand with hers, savoring the ease with which she accepted contact. Sharyn scarcely like to be touched at all. Sharyn—

Alex cut off the thought. Tonight belonged to Jemi.

And to him.

Alex whistled softly.

"Hey, you've got it."

He grinned and the whistling stopped. "Practice," he said, "and a good teacher is all it takes."

"And you'll find learning to swim will be exactly the same thing."

For the first time in his life, he believed those words. They started across the grounds, following the creek that gurgled gently over smooth rocks. The water played an accompaniment more musical than the many Los Angeles Philharmonic performances he'd sat through. The night insects provided the woodwinds, an occasional call of a bird the tympani. Alex smiled down at Jemi and wondered what confluence of factors he had to thank for this night.

Then, before he even knew he'd shifted his arm, he'd taken Jemi's hand in his. She squeezed his fingers and smiled up at him.

Amazing, Alex thought. It was as if his hand had moved of its own accord. Jemi's smile, her touch, her presence by his side warmed him in a way he'd never before experienced. Tonight was truly theirs.

But in the morning, he knew he had to leave.

He had to return to his life of responsibility. Not once in hours had his mind turned to an invention, not once during the day had he checked the foreign markets. Not once had he even had the decency to feel guilty over disappearing from his fiancée.

No, he had to return tomorrow before he learned too many new habits that interfered with his well-ordered, happily structured existence.

Jemi breathed in deeply. "Doesn't the night smell alive?" She inhaled again, dropped his hand and raised her hands to the sky.

Alex sniffed the air, then breathed more boldly, though he missed her touch. Living in Southern California, he never thought too much about the fragrance of the air. Inland, the air smelled only of smog; by the beach where he lived, salt air freshened the city odors, but he spent so much time indoors he scarcely thought about his outdoor environment.

Jemi danced around, waving her hands slowly and gracefully. The movements eased the loose knot in her towel, and the covering slipped from her waist to her hips, then pooled on the ground. She laughed and bent to retrieve it with that fluidity Alex admired so much.

"After you teach me to swim," he said, "perhaps you could show me how to be half as graceful as you are."

Jemi gazed up at him but he couldn't read her expression. "That's a pretty compliment, but there's no secret. It comes from years of yoga and a bit of ballet. You could learn, and after practice, you'll find yourself moving differently, your body will be freer of its own accord."

"That sounds rather mystical," Alex murmured, wishing Jemi would take his hand again. And then, even as he slowed his pace and gazed at the few inches separating their bodies, he found his hand once again placed in hers, exactly where it belonged.

"Much of life is mystical," Jemi said, "if you allow yourself to be open to its magic."

Glancing at their joined hands, Alex smiled. "I do think I see what you mean."

They'd reached the swimming hole. Jemi led him around it and pointed to a log lying across the creek. "Footbridge to the hot springs," she said, stepping lightly onto the log and running across it like a circus tightrope performer.

Alex placed one foot on the log and glanced

up to see Jemi watching him from the other bank. Well, tonight was a night unlike all the others in his life. Rather than treading one careful step at a time, Alex mimicked Jemi and ran across the log.

Her smile rewarded him. She reached for his hand again, and said, "Better watch out or I'll turn you into a country boy."

He laughed, feeling free and very unlike Alexander Graham Winston.

In a thicket to the right of Jemi and A. G., Mia prepared her sound effects. She rustled a leafy branch against a shrub.

Jemi paused and placed a finger to her lips. Mia added the snapping of twigs.

"Oh, my," Jemi whispered.

"What is it?" Alex peered into the darkness.

Mia intensified the volume of her production, cracking two large branches together and stirring the underbrush.

"A b-b-bear?" Jemi backed into Alex's chest.

To Mia's satisfaction, Alex shielded Jemi with his arms, hugging her waist. She doubted he'd ever seen a bear outside of a zoo, and stifled a giggle when Alex vowed, "Don't worry. I'll protect you." Then he turned Jemi to face him and kissed her.

"Bravo," Mia whispered.

Jemi clung to him.

Mia smiled and lay the stick she still held

quietly on the ground. Some work was so satisfying! Watching the lovers made her long to return to Quentin and brought to mind her own sensual boldness earlier in the evening. She blushed, but in a pleased way.

Jemi and Alex were breaking for air, stepping back and gazing at one another in a way that gave Mia cause for concern. She'd rarely seen two people more in love, yet in need of such help to let their hearts rule them.

They moved forward on the path.

Mia, still on duty, followed.

Jemi led the way up a path along a hillside, her pulse racing from their kiss. She'd never seen a bear anywhere near the Dew Drop Inn, but she didn't regret for one moment having flung herself into Alex's arms.

She alternated between feeling incredibly bold and unusually shy. She paused at the hewn rock steps that descended to the frothing and fragrant natural hot spring. Alex stopped right behind her, so near she felt his breath on her hair. But even though she knew how close he stood, when he rested his hands on her shoulders, she reacted to his touch with a sudden start.

"Did I frighten you?" he asked, his breath whispering past her ear.

She shook her head and dropped her towel on a bush.

Alex trailed a finger across her bare shoulders. Still standing behind her, he whispered, "I hope this doesn't sound too corny, but I want you to know I've never met anyone like you."

It not only sounded corny, it sounded like a pickup line. Jemi's heart increased its pace. If he covered her breast with his hand, he'd feel her heart thumping against her chest. *Kiss me again. Now!*

But his hands remained on her shoulders. Guessing his uncertainty, sensing he wanted to say more, she held still, wanting to encourage him without appearing pushy.

He didn't move or say anything for the longest time. Oh, bother, Jemi thought, why do we make these things so complicated?

Something rustled, a noise similar to ones they'd heard before. Alex chuckled, which surprised her a little. "Do you think," he said after a long pause, "if I kiss you again, that old bear will vamoose?"

In answer, she held her breath and turned and lifted her lips to his. Alex slipped a finger under the strap of her tank suit and eased it off her shoulder.

Then he lowered his head and kissed the spot where the strap had covered. In a voice that had lowered and roughened, he said, "Ready to get in?"

She nodded.

He lowered the other strap and paused. Her heart thumping, Jemi smiled up at him, and let him continue to peel the suit from her body.

Alex turned her around, more carefully even than he would have handled a prototype of a computer chip. She gazed up at him, slightly parted lips fashioned in a half-smile that warmed him and encouraged his desire. He swallowed, hard, and drank in her beauty.

He feasted on the sight of her full breasts, tipped with nipples that fulfilled every promise of the outline of her wet bathing suit. Her waist curved in and out over narrow hips and legs that proclaimed gloriously the discipline of her athletic lifestyle. He couldn't tell by the moonlight whether her thatch of hair that held the power to excite him so wildly matched the red of her braid.

"You too," Jemi said and reached for the buttons of his shirt.

Alex rushed at the buttons of his shirt, suddenly in an incredible hurry despite his knowledge that he needed to ease his way into this experience. He might be the only virgin billionaire he'd ever heard of, but he'd read every book on the subject of lovemaking he could find.

And rushing did not equate with pleasure.

He slowed his hands, letting a moment pass before he shed his shirt and towel. Jemi gazed at him, a hungry and wondering expression in her eyes that made him feel both protective and incredibly horny. He waited a moment, letting their hunger build. She ran her tongue over her top lip. He counted to five.

"Turn around," he said, and she obeyed.

Jemi felt his fingers caressing her hair, loosening the braids and spreading her hair like a veil over her shoulders. From behind her, he leaned over her shoulder and cupped her breasts. "I never realized what a hindrance clothing can be," he said.

She smiled, thinking she had begun to like the funny way he spoke. And speaking of funny, what he was doing with his fingers, warm, heated, and seeking, as he explored her breasts, sent shrieks of desire through her very being. She tipped her head back against his shoulders, seeking his lips with hers.

He gave her the kiss she craved, leaning over her to crush her mouth with his, all the while working his fingers in sensual whispers across her tormented breasts, dancing and teasing her nipples until she thought she'd either cry out or bite him in the throes of excitement. Smothering a cry, she broke off the kiss.

"You too," she said, facing him and reaching up on tiptoe to loosen his ponytail. Naughtily, she rubbed her breasts against his chest, but wouldn't let him suck on her nipple. Two could play the game of sensual torture, she thought with a smile and a shiver of desire. Gently she worked the band off and spread the silky length of his hair down his back and over his shoulders. She wanted him to drape it across her breasts, she wanted to drown in the weight of it.

Again, she licked her lips, savoring the sight of Alex aroused, trembling with wanting him, and with the feelings that complicated the simplicity of sex. She knew herself well enough to know it wasn't merely the act of love she wanted to share with him. Jemi gazed into his eyes, so dark in the moonlit night. Reaching up, she traced the bumpy outline of his broken nose, the nose he'd broken when his dreams of becoming an astronaut had died.

"I barely know you," she said, "but I like everything about you."

He tilted her chin and kissed the tip of her nose. "Thank you, Jemi." Then he smiled, a mysterious crook to his lips, and motioned toward the water. "After you."

She waded into the bubbling water of the spring. She'd been coming to this private pool since her childhood, and had always thought of it as a special place, warmed by the earth's power, kissed by the forces of nature.

It had never seemed more special than it did tonight.

Alex followed her into the pool. She motioned him to join her on a natural rock ledge that formed a perfect seat. Dipping her neck and shoulders beneath the surface, she welcomed the warm swirling waters and breathed in the vapors hailed by the area's nineteenth-century settlers as healing spirits.

"Do you believe in karma?" she asked.

A long silence followed, but Jemi was getting used to the idea that Alex never answered any query immediately.

"Would you define that?" He spoke formally, but at the same time as he asked the question, she felt him circling his hand with a torturing slowness over the inside of her thigh.

"Well, karma is the universe keeping itself in balance."

"That's not a theory I studied in school."

"But you said you dropped out of college."

"Yes, yes I did." His face was scrunched in concentration, and as delicious chills traveled up the thigh he continued to stroke, Jemi wondered whether he was deliberating over karma or on other ways to drive her to slow, sensual repletion.

"Perhaps you should go back to school now."

He shook his head.

"I'm going to, you know," she said, determined to talk more before giving into the heat melting the core of her body. She'd only met him the night before, but gazing at his dark eyes and hawkish brows, Jemi knew she wanted to know everything there was to learn about this man.

"Mmm-mmm," was all he said.

"When I go to New York, why don't you come, too?"

That got his attention. He stilled his hand. Then he lifted it from the water and placed his fingers gently across her lips. "Tomorrow," he said, "we'll talk about all that. Tonight"—he spread his arms wide, embracing the moon and stars and the world that held them in its spell—"let me answer your questions without words."

"That's beautiful," she whispered, and forgot all about the many questions she'd intended to ask him.

Alex smiled down at Jemi, but he made no more move to touch her, wrestling with a question very much on his mind.

Why now?

Why Jemi?

He'd not remained celibate out of choice or some moral imperative. His high school and college years, surrounded by other overly brainy and insecure boys, hadn't lent themselves to meeting girls. They'd all been obsessed with sex, of course, but few of them, even in the coed dorms at college, had managed to do anything about the obsession.

Then he'd dropped out of CalTech and started Winston Enterprises. He'd worked around the clock. All the friends he'd asked to join him in his business were males. One of them, the luckiest and most normal of their crew, had been married to a sweet young woman who doted on him and soon produced a child, a daughter who looked exactly like her father.

But the rest of them had satisfied themselves with fantasies.

Then his company had taken off, gone public, hit the big time, as the saying went. Suddenly a wealthy man, he'd become the target of many interested women.

But he soon learned they were interested in the image, not the man hidden beneath the success stories.

Not until he'd met Sharyn had he found a successful woman who regarded him as a colleague and not a pocketbook to be cracked open.

Lonely and desperately desiring to explore the pleasures of the flesh, he'd begun to fantasize over Sharyn soon after she started consulting with Winston Enterprises.

After almost a year of working closely together, she'd finally agreed to become his wife. But even then, she wouldn't go to bed with him. Not until we're married, she'd insisted.

And then on the day they were to announce their engagement to the media, good old Quentin Grandy had come along and kidnapped him.

"You're awfully quiet," Jemi said, "even for you." She smiled up at him and he regarded her solemnly.

"You're a very special woman," he said, knowing he wanted her, for better or for worse, realizing that he'd wanted the idea of a woman to call his own far more than the person of Sharyn Stonebridge. He sighed, but knew that problem would be one for him to solve to-morrow.

Tonight only Jemi existed for him.

She'd tipped her head back to gaze up at the stars. The water ebbed and flowed about her breasts, one moment covering, then with the next swirl, offering her satiny flesh to the moonlight and magic of the night.

He let his hand float with the water, hugging the curve of her breast. She stirred against him and he shifted in the water, moving about on the ledge until they sat face to face.

Then he stretched out his legs and, wrapping them around her hips, cradled her body.

"This is quite the nicest hot springs I've ever seen," he said, leaning forward and lifting a tendril of her hair back from her cheek. "I particularly like the water sprite."

"Do you?" She smiled impishly and before he knew she'd moved, she climbed onto his thighs and straddled his lap.

He groaned and felt himself seeking immediate, greedy entrance to her. "Jemi, Jemi, you don't know what you're doing to me!"

"Oh, but I do." She nibbled on his ear and lowered her hand to where their bodies joined beneath the steaming water.

When she wrapped her hand around him he

shuddered with pleasure. He caught her mouth and tasted her lips, her tongue, the recesses of her mouth like a man starved.

Which described him most accurately.

Breaking away from the kiss but not from her hands that now stroked him until he could see blood behind his eyelids, he said, "I'm not sure how one says this, but—"

"Oh, don't worry." Jemi laughed, sounding unusually nervous. "I took care of things."

"Things?" The echo made him sound as foolish as he felt. He'd not given a moment's thought to birth control, clearly what she referred to. "Actually, that wasn't what I was going to say, but I'm pleased that one of us thought to be practical."

"Practical?" Jemi had caught the echo habit. She stroked faster and buried herself against his chest, nuzzling her breasts to his skin. "I haven't put this diaphram-a-bob in place in almost two years. I almost gave up on it."

He thought of her dashing up the stairs back at the office cottage, taking forever. "So that's what you were doing?"

She nodded.

Between the heat of the water and its sensuous caresses and the miracles Jemi's hands were working on his body, Alex felt like a boiler about to bust. Or a hot air balloon soaring to the heavens, destined to explode and crash to earth.

"What I meant to say," he managed to say before he broke to tease a nipple with his tongue, "is despite my air of being a man of the world, I am a stranger to sexual adventuring."

Jemi blinked. "Are you telling me you don't play around much?"

"Not exactly."

"That it's been a long time?" Her hands slowed, but continued to envelope his shaft in a wonderful warm vise of pleasure.

"Not exactly."

"I see." She bit her lip, and Alex thought maybe she did see. "Are you telling me it's okay I couldn't find any condoms cause there's no way you've ever been exposed to any sexually related diseases?"

"That's it."

She stared at him as if he'd sprouted six heads.

"So I'm your first woman?"

He nodded.

She wrinkled her nose. "Men?"

"Oh, no." He outlined her jaw with his finger, then tipped her chin so their gazes met. "Jemi," he said softly but deliberately, "I'm a virgin."

It was her turn to nod. He thought her eyes glittered a bit, as if a hint of tears lurked there. "Why me?" she said in a low voice, her hands completely still.

He thought about his answer, aching to go on, knowing he must respond accurately and truthfully for his sake as well as hers. "You are the first woman who ever wanted me for me."

Jemi looked deep into Alex's eyes. She still sat on his thighs, her legs circled around his hips, her hands claiming his penis, which certainly knew what it wanted.

Alex a virgin? She raised one hand to capture a handful of his silky hair and crushed it between her fingertips. Then she ran a finger over his craggy brows, down the masterful angle of his jaw, to his broad and powerful shoulders.

"I don't know what kind of women you hang around with, Alex, but they're fools." With that, she fitted her hips to his and there in the steamy waters of her favorite hot springs, she opened herself to him. Whispering into his ear, she said, "Love me, Alex."

Wanting to shout and beat his chest, Alex filled her slowly, teasing her and reaping sweet torture on himself. He crushed her to him, then tried to regain his senses. Placing his hands on her firm and tiny bottom, he lifted her oh so slowly off him, then lowered her, letting her womanhood devour, one slow inch at a time, the fire of his desire.

He heard her breath come faster and faster as he rose and lowered her, savoring first one breast, teasing then the other nipple. She weighed so little he could move her as easily as a feather.

Reveling in the excitement she displayed so

freely, he lifted her again, then tipped her over his lap and trailed a devishly slow finger across the shadowed crevice between her buttocks.

She gasped and he nestled his fingers more deeply. She squirmed against him and he slipped his hand around her body between her legs, joining with the water to lap at her heated, pulsing sex, to bring her to the gasping, panting, screaming pleasure of release.

He knew he would explode soon. Senses he hadn't known he possessed filled his body, overtaking any formerly rational aspects of his mind. He lifted Jemi onto his lap, kissed her once more on the lips, and buried himself in her gently throbbing warmth.

They moved together, faster and faster. Greedily, he plundered her heat until his eyes glazed and he could no longer tell the stars in the sky from the ones in his blood.

He felt her shudder. The waves of her release drove him over the edge, and he cried out and gave himself up to Jemi.

She clung to him, her arms and legs wrapped so tightly around him he thought she'd cut off what was left of his circulation.

Not that he cared. He'd die happily in her arms.

"Oh, my," she whispered, kissing the side of his head. "Oh, my."

Pleased with her night's work, Mia strolled back to the Sunrise Cottage. Not a voyeur by nature, she'd departed the hot spring as soon as Jemi climbed onto A. G.'s lap. She had no doubt even those two couldn't mess things up from a point that romantic.

It was odd, she reflected, settling into her lonesome hammock, how much simpler other people's love lives were to fix than her own.

18 ~

Mia saw her first.

Mia alone expected Sharyn Stonebridge, yet she'd let the woman's impending arrival slip from her mind. She'd been dwelling on her feelings towards Quentin, and trying to rescue Susannah, and matchmaking between A. G. and Jemi.

She ran inside the cottage to warn Quentin, and, finding him in the shower, dashed back outside.

Sharyn emerged from a black limousine pulled up on the grass by the steps of the office cottage.

The woman's white-blonde hair glinted in the sunlight, looking terribly artificial above the svelte line of the black and white suit that Mia guessed to be a Dior. Looking every inch the conqueror, Sharyn glanced around, her lips curled in scorn. She tapped the toe of her black patent leather pump for a few seconds, then leaned in the car, reached around the driver, and laid on the horn.

Jemi dashed out the front door, wiping her hands on a dish towel. This morning she wore blue and white striped overalls that made her look like a railroad engineer who'd strayed from the tracks. Rather than her usual braid, though, her hair hung free, swirling around her shoulders attractively. Mia smiled, knowing as she did with her feminine intuition that A. G. had inspired the change in hairstyles.

Sharyn advanced up the stairs, a portfolio briefcase under one arm. Jemi was all eyes, taking in the outfit, the power walk, the diamonds that winked on her ears and most notably on her left ring finger.

"Hello," Jemi said, fingering the pockets of her overalls. "Welcome to the Dew Drop Inn."

Sharyn raised her brows as if to suggest the place was no great shakes. Mia had to restrain herself from delivering some unseen punishment; this scene needed to play out on its own.

Then she thought of the crimson square. She'd felt it wrong to use it with Quentin, but with Sharyn the hanky counted as fair play. Mia yanked it from her skirt pocket and lowered it gingerly to her heart.

"How can I help you?" *Look at her! No matter how long I live in New York, I'll never look like that! What's the use? I should stay buried in the country.*

"I have a reservation." Sharyn managed to produce a smile. *What a dolt! What hand-me-down bin does she get those rags from?*

Jemi bit her lip. *No one's checking in today. Surely I haven't made a mistake. The California investor was the only new guest for this weekend.* "Your name?"

"Smith." Sharyn adjusted her sunglasses. "Gloria Smith. But I don't believe I gave my name in my letter."

Jemi stared at the woman. "You aren't from California, are you?" *Sinking feeling, too overwhelming to put into words.*

"Yes I am as a matter of fact. And if you'll just show me to my room, I'd like to freshen up. Then you may send the owner to see me." *Halfwit child. Barefoot, too!*

"I see." Jemi ran one bare foot up and down the opposite calf. *What have I done? If this is the California investor, then who's Mr. Grandy? Oh, if only Alex would wake up and come downstairs, he'd be able to handle this woman. But I'm not sure I want him to see anyone this gorgeous!*

"Let's not take all day about it, hmm?" Sharyn stalked off the porch. *Typically incompetent hillbilly.*

For someone so pretty, she acted awfully sour, like a peach not ripe enough to eat. Jemi backed into the office cottage, flicking the dish towel against her thigh.

Mia, whose head hurt from listening on two channels, pulled the hanky from her chest and followed Jemi inside, more than curious to know the whereabouts of A. G. Winston.

Jemi walked toward her desk, but she knew darn well the only cottage available, the Wildflower, had been taken over by the mockingbird family. They'd even taken to calling it the Mockingbird Cottage. While some guests might find the noisy birds a charming aspect of country life, she'd bet Ms. Smith would pitch a fit. Well, it would have to do. She stepped into the kitchen to gather clean towels and a pitcher of ice water.

"Hey, Jemi!"

"Susannah." Jemi gave her a hug. "I'm glad to see you're back."

The girl nodded. "Sorry I ran off. I won't do it again."

Jemi ruffled her hair. "Don't worry about it. But now that you're here, run these over to the Mockingbird Cottage for me."

"That blonde lady outside is checking in?"

"You saw her?"

"I left my bike in the back, but I couldn't help but notice her. And her car is parked on the clover! City people sure are rude." Then a sad look crossed over her face. "But I guess country folks can be too."

"Plenty of people everywhere are good, and don't let that slip your mind," Jemi said. "The guest's name is Gloria Smith. When she asks to see the owner, don't tell her it's me, okay?"

Susannah grinned. "Gonna show up Miss FastStuff?" She offered her hands for a high-five, then collected the towels and pitcher. "I shall be at my most dignified!" With that, she headed out of the kitchen, her bare feet slapping on the floor, her faded, oversized cotton shirt hanging off one shoulder.

No sooner had Susannah left the room than Alex walked in. Jemi stood where she was, feeling in the bright light of morning incredibly shy.

"Hey," he said, walking toward her in a pair of cutoffs Ari had left for him, looking so sexy she almost lost her breath. He opened his arms for an embrace.

Jemi ran forward and wound her arms around his waist.

"Still like me this morning?" Alex said into her ear.

"You bet!" Jemi colored a little, thinking of how little sleep they'd gotten during the night.

"I missed you when I woke up in your bed to find Sugar guarding the bedspread and you gone."

Jemi grinned. "At least she let you in the bed. Last night I wasn't so sure she was going to go along with our plan. But I had to get up to fix breakfast."

"Have I been fired?"

She stroked his long hair, smoothing a tangle. "No, but I thought you might want to sleep in."

"So I can gather my strength for tonight?" He leaned down and kissed her, a sweet and gentle kiss that soon gathered heat like a summer thunderstorm.

Jemi let the sensations roll over her, surrendering herself to this most unusual man who'd managed to amuse, tantalize, and comfort her.

Alex slipped his hands under her overall straps and began to free her shoulders.

"My silent tiger," she said, firmly replacing the straps. "As much as I'd love to play, a new guest has only just arrived and I'm afraid there's been some confusion."

Alex let go of her, but she could tell he wished he didn't have to. "What's the problem?"

The kitchen door richocheted open. Susannah stalked in and stopped, hands on her skinny hips. "Of all the nerve! That woman gives the term bitch a brand new meaning!"

Jemi had to agree, but she didn't think it right for Susannah to sink to the woman's level. "Let's watch our language, kiddo."

Susannah shook her head. "I'm sorry, but she takes the cake."

Alex cleared his throat. "Of whom are we speaking?"

Susannah stared at him. "So you stuck around? Well, the next time Miss Too-Good-To-Wipe-Her-Shoes-In-Arkansas summons the hired help, you can go."

"This is the problem I was about to describe," Jemi said. "This woman, Ms. Smith, says she's the California investor, but if that's so, then who's Mr. Grandy?"

The kitchen door opened again, but this time with much less force. Quentin Grandy stuck his head around. "May I come in?"

Jemi laughed, trying to soften the hysterical edge to the sound. "Sure. Everyone else is here."

He cleared the door and glanced around. "I thought I'd see if you had any of those cinnamon buns left. Oh, hello again, Susannah."

The girl nodded and watched him with what Jemi thought smacked of hero-worship. Well, whoever Mr. Grandy might be, he was good-looking and kind, too. But did he want to buy the inn?

"There seems to be some confusion," Alex said, looking at Grandy, "over your identity. A woman has arrived, claiming to be the person who wrote a letter describing her intentions to purchase this place. Jemi here assumed you were that investor. I think you need to clarify the situation."

"I see." Grandy rubbed his chin and looked around the room, again as if he searched for something he couldn't find.

"There aren't any buns this morning," Jemi said, almost blushing, "but I can cut you a slice of bread and put some preserves on it."

"Fine." Grandy went from stroking his chin to rubbing his belly. He watched Alex intently and when Jemi turned back around from the refrigerator, she could have sworn Alex had just finished making hand motions at Grandy.

Grandy took the bread and thanked her. "Well, let's see if I can't straighten out this mystery. I am from California, and I am interested in purchasing the Dew Drop Inn."

Jemi rolled her eyes. "But when did you decide to come here and why did you come here and when did you hit upon the idea of offering to buy my place?"

"Now *that's* a compound sentence," Susannah said, and cut herself a slice of bread.

"Some things just happen and you know they're right." Grandy jammed the bread in his mouth and took his time chewing.

Jemi thought of Mrs. Pace. She thought of Grandy speaking of a broken heart the night he checked in. "Did you follow your sweetheart here?"

"You might say that. Yes, yes, that's it! Hmm, excellent bread."

Susannah spoke around a mouthful. "Oh, Jemi, I forgot to tell you. Ms. Smith said she wanted to see the owner without a moment's delay. Said she had to get back where she belonged pronto."

Jemi sighed and looked down at her overalls and bare feet. She started out of habit to braid her hair and was surprised when Alex stepped over and caught her hand gently. "Leave it down? For me?"

She smiled up at him and suddenly all the

bitchy women in the world didn't amount to any problem at all. She knew too, watching him watch her, that he had done much more than amuse, tantalize, and comfort her.

He'd stolen her heart.

"Yes," she whispered. "For you."

"I have an idea," Grandy said.

Susannah offered him the bread knife. "More?"

"No, thanks. You say this woman is some stuck up cutie. Let me pretend to be the owner."

"Why?" Alex asked.

"Oh, would you?" Jemi said.

"I certainly hope you don't fall for her!" Susannah said, sticking out her tongue. "Even if she is knock-dead gorgeous!"

"She'll ride roughshod over you, Jemi, and try to offer you peanuts. And you might take an offer you'll regret. I'll simply act as your agent and get the best price possible."

Jemi chewed on her lip. Finally, she said, "You never did want to buy the inn, did you, Mr. Grandy?"

Quentin scratched his head. "Not when I said it, but if that's what it takes to make a happy ending, I'd buy it in a snap."

"Oh, you don't have to worry about me," Jemi said, smiling at him. "I won't sell the inn to this woman if she continues to give off bad vibes. But whatever happens, I'll be okay."

"I wasn't thinking only of you," he said.

Then sketching a quick salute, he said, "I'll just go find my shoes and have a word with this paragon of nonvirtue."

With that, he strode from the room.

"I don't know if I should have accepted his help or not," Jemi said.

Alex stared at the kitchen door. "Things," he said slowly, "aren't always what they seem to be."

And Mia, from her front row seat on the kitchen counter next to the window boxes overflowing with fragrant herbs, retrieved the crimson square from behind the canister where she'd hidden it when Quentin appeared on the scene. Perhaps things weren't what they seemed. Perhaps Quentin had offered so quickly to help due to his generous spirit; perhaps it had nothing at all to do with hearing the woman described as knock-dead gorgeous.

Consoled that at least A. G. and Jemi's love life appeared in good shape, Mia slipped out the back door, wishing her own love life weren't still in limbo. Then, her practical mind kicked into gear and instead of moping about, she headed at a trot toward the Mockingbird Cottage.

Time to put Quentin to the test.

Today, Quentin thought striding from cottage to cottage seeking the Mockingbird, all things were possible. Last night he'd made progress with Mia, of that he felt confident. In the kitchen, in that scene worthy of a "Beverly Hillbillies" rerun, he'd seen no sight of her hanky. Quick and resourceful Mia had probably already sought out this mystery investor.

He picked up his pace, eager to do his duty by Jemi and get back to what mattered most: winning Mia back.

He checked each of the cottages but none carried the name Mockingbird. Puzzled, he surveyed the cottages from the path beside the creek, wondering where to find his quarry.

Then he heard the cry.

"Qu-ent! Qu-ent!"

A strong sense of deja vu sent the hairs on the back of his neck prickling to attention. He'd heard that bird call before, the last time he and Mia had been embroiled in a Mr. G mission in Arkansas. He could still picture the bird that had seemed to cry his name the afternoon he'd discovered Mia skinny dipping, that special day they'd first made love.

This gray and white bird soared over his head, then swooped into a bush beside the closest cottage.

Quentin knew Mia would tell him the bird served as a sign, and that he should take the hint from the heavens and follow the creature. His rational nature continued to balk at such a concept, but what with dealing with ageless guys who wore red velvet robes and appeared at will, and invisible brides, and magic crimson hankies, he was beginning to deal on easier terms with what he once would have dismissed as complete foolishness.

"Qu-ent!" The bird hopped onto an outer branch of the bush and cocked its head. Quentin took a step toward the cottage.

He heard tiny chirps, echoes of the larger bird.

"Que! Que! Que!"

He edged forward. Three open-beaked baby birds jostled one another in a nest of twigs and grasses. Just then another gray and white bird swooped in, a plump worm dangling from its beak. This treat was divided among the offspring, resulting in momentary quiet.

Standing there watching the tableau, Quentin's heart stirred in a way it had never done before. Even the first time he'd realized how much he loved Mia, how his life would never be complete without her, he'd never experienced quite the emotions he felt now, watching the bird family and imagining Mia lying beside him in their bed, their child suckling at her breast.

Such a feeling of awe overtook him that he had to dab at his eyes. Humble wasn't a word he associated with his feelings, but right at that moment, watching the mockingbird family and thinking of the family he wanted to create and nurture with Mia, humble was the word uppermost in his mind.

"Please, God," he said aloud, "please let Mia take me back."

And with that prayer, Quentin, stalwart agnostic for so many years, knew he'd crossed a point in his life from which he could not double back.

"Qu-ent!"

The birds started their cries again, even louder and more raucous than before.

The door to the cottage slammed open. "Goddamn birds! Country quiet, now that's an oxymoron!" The blonde beauty in the doorway stopped, one hand to her heart. "Oh, my, but aren't you a welcome sight!"

Quentin moved up the porch steps, hiding his shock. "Ms. Stonebridge," he said, "what a surprise!" But even as he said these words, he realized Mia must have expected Sharyn to appear upon the scene, perhaps had even gotten the idea to bring A. G. to the Dew Drop Inn from something she had overheard at Winston Enterprises.

"Doing a bit of rusticating?" Sharyn shrugged her jacket off, revealing the flimsiest of camisoles and absolutely no hint of a bra.

Quentin swallowed. The woman did make a pretty picture. Yes, and pretty is as pretty does, Mia would say. "I'm here for a few days. You?"

"I *was* in a hurry to leave." She showed her teeth in a man-eating smile that put Quentin in mind of Mia's nickname for the woman, Sharyn the Shark.

"Didn't you just arrive?"

She looked at him with eyes that, while still

wide with a show of innocence, watched him closely. "Did I?"

"Did you register under the name Smith?"

"Taking up detective work? As a matter of fact, that's a name I often use when I travel."

Quentin lounged against the porch railing, sensing discordance in the scene. Had he been directing it, he would have let it play out to discover what the characters were about, so he figured he'd do the same in this instance. And he would act the role of the gumshoe. Fixing Sharyn with his best smile, he said, "Is A. G. with you?"

She managed to look both lonesome for her lover and come-hither in the same instant as she smiled and shook her head. It struck Quentin that this woman could indeed be good onscreen. Maybe even great. Chelsea Jordan came to mind and for only a second, he allowed himself to consider whether he'd found the woman he needed to film *Kriss-Kross*. Chelsea had no intentions of ever returning to Hollywood, and Quentin had vowed not to do the film he and Mia had written together in college until he found the perfect actress.

Quentin studied the woman closely, knowing she'd take it as a compliment. And in an instant, he knew Sharyn Stonebridge could never fill the *Kriss-Kross* role. She lacked Chelsea's vulnerability, her underlying goodness.

"A. G. couldn't get away from work, so I'm

here all alone," Sharyn said, emphasizing the last word. "How 'bout you?"

"Same here." Quentin smiled down at her, asking himself two important questions: One, why did he find it so difficult to throw himself into a role he used to play automatically and two, why had she lied about A. G.?

In the old days, in less time than he'd been lollygagging on this porch, he would have had Sharyn Stonebridge naked and begging for more. Now, he no longer wanted to play those games, so he'd pretend to play along until he'd figured out the answers to both questions.

Sharyn patted the creamy flesh above her camisole. "It's so hot. Why don't you come inside?"

Quentin produced his best woman-slaying grin and thrust himself hip-first toward the door.

19 ⌒

From behind a bush occupied by a family of mockingbirds, Mia watched Quentin saunter into Sharyn's cottage and shut the door firmly behind them.

Mia stared at the door, her idea taking full shape. Quickly, she scanned the ground nearby, seeking something to block the door. Nothing. She put her hands on her waist, thinking hard. She wanted Quentin locked up in that room with Sharyn for a good long time.

Then she felt the narrow belt of her skirt.

Thankful for the suppleness of the expensive leather, she whipped it off and tied one end to the door handle, another to the first spoke of the porch railing, leaving no slack. Try as they might, they wouldn't be able to open the door from within.

Then she dashed around to the side and found an open window. For better or for worse, she felt certain she'd soon know the truth of Quentin's feelings for her. Her mother had always said actions spoke louder than words. And her mother had a knack for being right about things.

"Why don't you turn up the air conditioner while I slip into something more comfortable?" Sharyn fingered the zipper on her leather garment bag. "I think it's going to get a whole lot hotter in here."

Quentin nodded, but didn't move.

Mia smiled. Wait until Sharyn realized there was no a.c!

"Does A. G. know you're planning to buy this place?" As he spoke, Quentin dropped onto the side of the bed. Mia frowned. He could have chosen one of the chairs.

"Back to playing detective?" Sharyn opened her garment bag and pulled out a black negligee. She draped it across her body, then cast it onto the bed before unpacking a silk pants and top outfit.

"Maybe I like to know a little bit about the women I sleep with," Quentin said, reaching over and fingering the negligee. "Nice, very nice."

Mia gritted her teeth and lectured herself to remember things weren't always as they appeared on the surface. And anyway, she'd started watching this one-act play, so she'd force herself to stay to the end. Well, not necessarily to the end, but she had to remain long enough to discover if Quentin would fall for the first bimbo to throw herself at him.

Would his fear that he couldn't be faithful prove to be true?

Sharyn unbuttoned her skirt, taking her time about it. "A. G. and I have a business relationship. He needs a wife and I find that a husband can prove to be a useful commodity. Whatever else I do is my own business."

Quentin lay back on the bed, his hands clasped behind his head. "And he feels the same way?"

Sharyn shrugged. "He may as well."

Quentin nodded, but didn't quibble. Mia wanted to throw herself through the window and ask the woman to consider the relationship she'd just described.

Poor A. G.; no wonder Mr. G had wanted them to intervene in his life. Here was the smartest, richest single guy in America about to marry a woman who cared more about cast-off ticker tape than she did for her husband-to-be.

Just to think what a man like A. G. could do if he were truly happy made Mia realize just why Mr. G had targeted him. And of course that made her wonder if Quentin had been late for the wedding for some mysterious reason having nothing to do with his own fears of faithfulness.

Her intended had turned on his side and lay watching Sharyn shimmy her skirt down her hips.

"When did you decide to go into the inn-keeping business?" Quentin asked.

She stopped in mid-striptease. "I don't think that's any of your business."

"No, but I've gotten to be friends with the owner and she asked me to act on her behalf in working out a deal."

"Oh." Sharyn pulled her skirt back on, all business. "That's different, then." She smiled that smile that made her look mean rather than pleased. Reaching into a briefcase, she pulled out a sheaf of papers. "Business first, then pleasure."

Mia wondered whether the woman even cared about seducing Quentin. The only spark of sincere interest she'd shown related to the business of buying the inn. But if she didn't want him, why go through the motions? Mia furrowed her brow, unable to understand such actions.

She'd been in love with Quentin since they'd met in college; she'd been a virgin when they finally made love last year. She could not comprehend toying with men the way a cat tormented a lizard, a creature it didn't want to eat but batted about only because it strayed across its path.

Quentin sat up and accepted the papers. He didn't take long to scan them. "These look to be in order," he said, "but I'm sure the owner will want her attorney to check them."

"There's not much chance some little pea-brain in this neck of the woods will think to do that." Sharyn laughed. "I know what the people are like around here, and darling, they're not too bright."

Quentin looked at Sharyn as if she had spinach stuck between her teeth, a move on his part that greatly pleased Mia. But she figured it would go right over Sharyn's self-centered head. "You travel here a lot?" Quentin asked idly enough.

"This is my first time. And my last." Sharyn held out her hand and Quentin returned the papers. "Does the owner live on the premises?"

Quentin nodded. "If you've never been here before, how do you know the people are ignorant?"

Sharyn shrugged. "Hillbillies are hillbillies."

"There's a little girl who works here. She's only twelve, but she's quite bright and certainly defies your stereotype."

"Not that girl who brought me the towels?" Sharyn shuddered. "Dirty and barefooted and when I asked which cabinet housed the TV she said, 'Ain't no tellyvision.'"

Mia thought Sharyn mimicked the local accent remarkably well, but she'd certainly never heard Susannah speak that way.

"So who will you hire to run the inn?"

"I only want to buy the place, I don't intend to keep it open."

"Buy and sell to the next highest bidder? A little real estate churning?"

Sharyn opened her mouth, then snapped it shut. Mia would have given a lot to know what she'd intended to say. Then she realized she could know! She popped the crimson hanky against her heart and almost fell back on the ground from the intense hostility she absorbed from Sharyn's innermost thoughts.

Run this dump? Step foot in the miserable town of Dalton ever again? Not this woman. Oh, no, I'll be Mrs. A. G. Winston and the only reason I'm wasting my precious money on this place is so no more of my friends will take it into their heads to come here on retreat.

"Penny for your thoughts," Quentin said.

Sharyn tossed the papers back in her briefcase.

Feeling sick, Mia crumpled the hanky in her hand. She knew enough and didn't want to hear any more.

Sharyn dropped her skirt and let it lay on the floor. She wore a lacy black garter belt and stockings, one of Quentin's favorite things. Mia held onto the windowsill, praying Sharyn would leave her camisole on.

She did, slinking over to the bed and slithering her arms around Quentin's shoulders. "Time to celebrate, don't you think?"

"I'm not really in the mood," Quentin said, pulling Sharyn's tentacles off him.

"I can do something about that," Sharyn said, smiling naughtily.

Quentin studied her, then rose from the bed. "When I want to get in the mood," he said, "I find the woman I love."

"What ever happened to love the one you're with? I've heard you're quite the playboy." Sharyn pouted her lips and managed to look a lot more peeved than sexy.

"I used to be," Quentin said, stepping back as Sharyn pursued him, "but something happened to me. I fell in love and this kind of cheap sex isn't what I want. Not anymore."

Mia hung over the windowsill, her head stuck into the room. She wasn't one to cry, but she felt definite dampness in the corners of her eyes. Quentin loved her, that she hadn't doubted. But whether he knew how much he loved her he'd just proven to himself.

Mia heard voices and footsteps. She jumped down from the window and looked around the corner. Alex and Jemi approached, Jemi moving like a filly on opening day, with Alex easily matching her pace.

"I'm not sure we should interrupt," Alex said.

"Please, for me." Jemi's anxiety showed in her face. "Just knock on the door and find out whether she's made an offer or not."

"I don't think it's wise, but for you I'll do it." Alex stopped at the steps to the Mockingbird Cottage. "Wait here."

Mia zipped around to the open window. Quentin had retreated to the door and was tugging on the handle. Of course it wouldn't open. She climbed through the window and flashing the hanky, whispered in his ear,

"A. G. is on his way in. Give him a show and let him know what kind of woman he's engaged to."

"Wait!" Quentin looked around but Mia was already scrambling out the window, racing around to untie the door knob so A. G. could enter the cottage.

Sharyn had Quentin cornered now. Looking into her green eyes so lovely on the surface and hiding such a hardened soul, Quentin felt sorry for her.

But not so sorry that he wanted to see A. G.'s happiness sacrificed.

He trailed a finger along her jawline. "Well, maybe one little kiss wouldn't hurt," he said, and lowered his mouth to hers.

She opened wide and kissed him greedily. That surprised Quentin; he'd expected greater finesse. He heard a knock on the door, and waltzed her, still letting her suck on his tongue, to the bed. He lowered himself first, and Sharyn climbed on top of him, breaking the kiss long enough to tug at his belt.

The knock sounded again.

"Go away," Sharyn called, finishing with the belt and starting on the button of his pants. "When I need something, I'll call for you."

Quentin hoped Mia had been eavesdropping long enough to know he wouldn't be in this situation if she hadn't ordered him to let himself be mauled by Sharyn.

He also hoped A. G. opened the damn door before Sharyn got his pants unfastened.

The door swung open. A. G. stood there, staring at the two of them. Quentin groaned, knowing what he'd feel like were he in the man's shoes. Sharyn straddled him, her lips puffy, her arms raised to lift her camisole.

"Sharyn?" A. G.'s voice didn't sound at all like him.

"A. G.!" Sharyn lowered the camisole and looked back and forth between the two men. Then, pulling her hand back, she cracked Quentin a nasty left to the head. She leapt from the bed and ran to A. G., throwing herself in his arms. "Darling, you got here just in time!"

A. G. looked from her to the bed and back again. "So I see," he said, and stepped free of her arms. He stood there, staring for the longest time, then finally said, "Not even a kiss, Sharyn. That's what you said until we were engaged. Being the innocent and trusting fool that I guess I am, I believed you."

He shook his head, and rubbed his hand across the growth of his beard.

"A. G.," Sharyn said, yanking on her skirt, "things aren't always the way they seem—"

He laughed, a short barking sound. "That's for damn sure," he said. Turning to Quentin, he added, "Mr. Grandy, my sympathies," and turned on his heel.

Sharyn followed him to the door. "A. G., it really isn't what you think."

A. G. paused on the top step. "Maybe it's not, Sharyn, but even though I'm a trifle slow and I've accurately been described as a sheltered nerd, I'm not a sucker." He stared down at her. "Not anymore, anyway." He pointed to her left hand. "Our engagement's off, but you may as well keep the ring."

Jemi jumped up from the porch rocker. "You two are engaged?"

Sharyn caught A. G. by the arm and smiled up at him. "Of course we are. And who are you?"

Jemi stuck her nose up in the air. "I am the owner of this establishment."

Sharyn laughed.

A. G. shook off Sharyn's hand. To Jemi, he said, "I think we should leave. Ms. Stonebridge has some unfinished business with Mr. Grandy."

Quentin loomed in the doorway. "Oh, no she doesn't. I've played my role," he said, with a wink to A. G. "And now I've some important personal business to take care of," he said, and vaulted off the porch and loped toward the Sunrise Cottage.

A. G. stared after Quentin.

"Are you or are you not engaged to this woman?" Jemi asked.

"No."

"Yes!" Sharyn howled.

A. G. held out a hand to Jemi. "We were engaged to be married but I just called it off."

"But, last night, you were engaged?" Her chin quivered slightly, but she kept it at a defiant angle.

"Last night?" Sharyn looked arrows at A. G. "So my little nerd's not so innocent anymore?"

"Is that how you think of me?" A. G. spoke quietly, but Mia, still unable to drag herself from the scene, heard the iron in his voice.

Sharyn shrugged.

A. G. shook his head. "I really have been a fool."

Jemi stalked past A. G. without looking at him. Then she paused and said over her shoulder, "The Dew Drop Inn is no longer for sale." Then in a flash she was gone, racing up the path toward the office cottage.

"I really can explain," Sharyn said to A. G., reaching out to him. "You saw an audition. I've always wanted to be in the movies, and you walked in just when I was showing Quentin Grandy how good an actress I can be."

"Give it up, Sharyn. Quentin Grandy doesn't produce pornographic films. You know it and I know it so let's quit fooling ourselves." A. G.'s jaw worked. "I almost married you," he said, shaking his head as if he couldn't believe the words were true. "I fell for you, hook, line, and sinker. How many other men have you played around with?"

Sharyn's face had gone white. She backed to the doorway of the cottage. "What I do is nobody's business but my own. And don't think you can fire me from Winston Enterprises or you'll hear from my lawyers faster than you can spell lawsuit."

Sadness showed in A. G.'s eyes. "Don't worry about that, Sharyn. You're very good at what you do, but somehow I think you'll soon want to find another job."

"And why is that?"

"Because you'll want to find another sucker," he said, and walked away.

Mia followed, surprised and pleased to hear A. G., after covering twenty or so yards, break into a cheerful whistle.

Quentin waited for Mia in the hammock on the porch of the Sunrise Cottage, straining anxiously for a sight of the crimson silk square. He had a lot to say and he wanted to be done with the talking fast and get to showing her how he felt.

And the only way to do that was get her visible again, or take the plunge and join her in her altered state.

Just when he'd decided to scour the grounds for her, the hanky fluttered in front of him.

"Join me?" He patted the hammock.

"Thanks."

"That was quite a denouement you orchestrated back there."

"Thank you."

For someone as talkative as Mia, her brief

responses bothered Quentin, and he worried whether she'd witnessed him fending off Sharyn's advances or not. "Mia, sweetheart," he said, touching the silk gently, "I love you and you alone. I want to marry you and make babies with you and grow old and gray together." He stroked the silk, wondering how he could prove his words. "I would do anything to convince you of how I feel."

He looked down at the hanky. Took a deep breath. "Anything," he repeated.

If only he could hold her in his arms, look into her eyes, she'd know. She'd have no doubts left.

"Quentin, it's okay, I—"

Before she could finish the sentence, not really concentrating on her words as he thought only of how to convince her, he said all at once in a rush, grasping the hanky, "Please let me be invisible too!"

"—really do believe you love me," Mia finished her sentence.

"Mia!" Quentin stared at the face of his beloved. With a hand that shook, he traced her perky nose, brushed the top of her spiky hair, and outlined her kissable lips. "I never want to be parted from you ever again."

He lowered his lips towards hers, then halted. What had she said as he'd made his wish to become invisible? He looked her in the eye. "What did you just say?"

She dimpled and caught one of his hands in hers. "I believe you, Quentin. I watched you in that room with Sharyn. But most importantly, I watched you understand that you want to be faithful to me."

She scrunched up her face the way she did when she concentrated really hard. "And that's the most important issue here. You know you love me and I know you love me, but does your heart know just how much that means to you?" She tapped him lightly on the chest. "If you'd waited another second, you wouldn't have had to become invisible, but it is nice to have company."

"You mean I don't have to beg for forgiveness anymore or prove my love to you?"

Mia grinned and puckered up her kissable lips. "I didn't say anything about letting you off easy." She wound her hands around his neck. "You can start with a nice, slow kiss."

Trying for a penitent look and succeeding only in grinning from ear to ear, he complied.

And then she whispered in his ear what else he might do to win her complete forgiveness.

"Here?" Quentin pointed to the other cottages. "This isn't exactly a deserted hayfield."

"But we're invisible," Mia said, fluttering her lashes at him.

"Are you sure?" He stroked the curve of one breast, teasing her flesh through the soft cotton of her top.

"If you can see me now and you couldn't

before, then we both must be invisible, because I haven't changed."

"My lovely, logical Mia," Quentin murmured, lowering her onto the hammock so they lay arm in arm. "You've grown to be quite the daredevil, haven't you," he said, easing her shirt over her head and tossing it onto the porch.

"It's possible," Mia said with an impish smile, as she reached for the zipper of his pants, "that I'm becoming an exhibitionist."

She freed him from his pants and he groaned with pleasure and relief. "As long as you're my exhibitionist, I don't care!"

He fingered the white lace and satin of her bra and felt a surge of regret when he realized she'd chosen this finery for her wedding day. He placed a gentle kiss on each breast, then pulled back till he could watch her eyes. "Will you marry me?"

She gazed into his eyes and very slowly, nodded her head. "Yes, Quentin, I will." She kissed him, then said, "Just as soon as we wrap up our business here, that is."

Kissing his way to her navel, Quentin cocked an ear. "I think we've accomplished our mission."

"Then you didn't see the look on Jemi's face when she realized A. G. had been engaged to Sharyn the Shark."

"Oh!" Quentin nuzzled her flat tummy that curved inwards against her pelvic bones. "I have a feeling those two will work things out for themselves, but if they don't, of course we'll help them out before we leave."

He couldn't help but glance around before he began to edge Mia's skirt from her slender hips. No one stirred, for which he was thankful. Making love in a deserted hayfield, as they'd done, or started to do, in their last Arkansas adventure, had thrilled him. A porch in broad daylight just didn't seem the same at all, even in a hammock half-hidden from view.

But maybe, Quentin thought, a light bulb going off in his head, that was because a year ago, that first time he'd made a move on Mia, it hadn't been all that different from so many of his other exploits.

Now, he thought, smoothly switching sides on the hammock to shield her from passersby, he wanted to cherish and protect her, as well as make love to her.

"Mia," he said, before he continued his path of kisses, "I don't deserve you."

She smiled and tugged at his waistband. "Shhh," she said. "Weren't you the man who taught me not to talk nonstop when making love?"

In answer, Quentin kissed her mouth, then slipping the wispy scrap of lace she called panties from her hips, he proceeded to forget all about words.

He also forgot about passersby.

Or regrets.

Or other women.

Only Mia his love existed for him.

When she cried out and pulsed against his lips, he smiled and held her close. Then, as she tugged again at his pants, he stripped them off and joined with her in their invisible reunion, a very happy smile on his face, a smile created by Mia, visible only to Mia.

He clung to her long afterwards, moved by the intensity of his completion. Sex with Mia was so much more, and he'd almost shut her out of his life. Whispering in her ear, he said, "I'm the one who's been a fool."

"Oh?" She said it teasingly.

"I don't know what got into me, I really don't. How I could have thought for one second I might not be faithful to you I can't understand."

Mia smoothed his hair back from his face. "Perhaps it was meant to be."

"Oh, no, none of your predestination theory." He shook his head. "You're about to suggest I stood you up just so Mr. G could appear on the scene and we could show A. G. the emptiness of his existence."

Mia nodded, slowly. "It's not beyond reason."

"Oh, yes it is, and beyond logic, too."

"Quentin Grandy, are you or are you not invisible at this very moment?"

Glancing at his naked legs and butt, Quentin said, "I sure as hell hope I am!"

"Then how can you say anything is beyond reason or logic?"

Well, she had him there. "I don't know, Mia, but I do know I won't shrug off the responsibility for my own shilly-shallying on that theory. I screwed up and I hope to God I'm making amends right now."

Mia tickled him on his most ticklish spot, where his hipbone met his side. "You're getting a good start on your penance."

He caught her hands in his. "We don't want to keep our wedding guests waiting forever. What do you say we hop up and check on A. G. and Jemi?"

Mia sat up. "And Susannah, too. We have to do something to help her before we can go back."

Quentin nodded. "But we can come back in person and take care of her, if we need to."

Mia pulled her blouse back on. "Oh, it wouldn't be the same, Quentin. You know how easy it is to put off good deeds and we'll be on our honeymoon, and then into principal photography and the next thing you know Susannah will be half grown."

He tweaked her on the nose and scooted into his pants. "You're right, as always."

Mia smiled. "May I quote you on that?"

Suddenly Quentin paused and dropped back

into the hammock. "Did you think, when you saw me go into Sharyn's cottage, that I intended to make a move on her?"

Mia bit her lip.

"The truth?" he asked in a gentle voice.

"I don't know." As she looked at him, a shadow of the anguish he had caused her returned to her eyes and he wondered that she could forgive him. "I wish I could say absolutely not, but a part of me did worry. Most of me," she said emphatically, "believed you'd have nothing to do with her. But I had to know."

Quentin nodded. "Fair enough." She had given him forgiveness; he alone would continue to remind himself what his indecision had caused her to suffer. And that, Quentin figured, would serve him in good stead.

Mia lifted the hanky from the hammock. "We'd better not lose this."

"Or we'll stay invisible for the rest of our lives?" Quentin thought about it for a minute, then said, "Nah, Mr. G would bring us around. If for nothing else, to give us another job to do! The old scoundrel."

He got out of the hammock, then turned and held out a hand for Mia. She smoothed the silk but made no move to rise.

"Something else on your mind?" Quentin knew that look, knew her mannerisms even better than he understood his own.

"This hanky has magical powers." She offered him the crimson cloth. "If you hold this against your heart, you can hear people's thoughts. Even if they're speaking, if they're thinking something else, it comes through."

"Whoa!" Quentin caught the hanky in his hand. "This would be really useful in a pitch meeting. Think about it, sitting in a deal meeting at MegaFilms, wouldn't you love to know what the studio is really willing to ante up?" He fingered the cloth. "Think Mr. G will let us keep it?"

Mia smiled, but said in a stern voice, "I sincerely doubt whether it works under normal circumstances. What I want to tell you is I've been very tempted to listen in on your thoughts, but I decided it would be wrong."

"Why?" He asked the question quietly, but he thought he understood.

"Because we have to be able to share with each other what we're really thinking and feeling in order for our marriage to work."

"And using this would be cheating."

She nodded.

He leaned over and kissed her. "I do understand," he said, "especially because if I had once sat down and shared with you my fears before our wedding day, we wouldn't have ended up in this pickle."

Mia jumped up from the hammock, smiling as he hadn't seen her since he'd joined her in invisibility. "Oh, Quentin," she said, throwing her arms around him, "I love you so much! Now let's take care of business so we can go home and get married!"

20 ⤴

When Alex walked away from Sharyn, he realized he felt more relief than anger, more freedom than loss.

All along, Sharyn had played him for a fool.

All along, he'd been only a means to an end.

He should be furious, but instead he thought only of Jemi, a woman who had given herself lovingly to a down-on-his-luck engineer.

And because Alex didn't understand women, he smiled and picked up his pace.

He even began to whistle.

Alex found Jemi in the room where she stored the housekeeping cart, and much to his surprise, she didn't want to talk to him.

"Go away," she said, glancing up from where she stood sorting towels only long enough for him to catch a glimpse of red-rimmed eyes. "Scram."

"Don't you want me to help with the chores?" he asked in a quiet voice. Working alongside her he'd be able to explain whatever she wanted to know.

She turned on him, fire in her eyes. "Look, Mr. Alex with no last name. Susannah finally told me who you are, how rich and famous you are."

Jemi sniffed and tugged at the end of her braid. "You must have been laughing yourself silly over my not recognizing you." She raised her brows and gave him a sarcastic look that tugged at his conscience and his honor. "A. G. Winston the billionaire make my beds? What would people say?"

He said nothing, thinking she'd realize the flaw in her logic. He'd done the work before, so why not today? He, Alex, hadn't changed; he remained the same person he'd been yesterday. And, too, he didn't know how to deal with her anger.

"Jemi—"

"I don't want to hear any excuses. If you insist on sticking around playing your make-believe games, you can drive Susannah into town for supplies." Then she turned her back on him and bumped the laundry cart out of the kitchen and down the stairs of the office cottage.

He followed her to the back door, and had enough sense to squelch any offer to help with the cart.

He had lied to her and she had a right to be mad.

He hadn't wanted to hear Sharyn's explanation; hadn't believed it when she'd forced it on him.

And Jemi, pure and honorable and straight-forward, had every reason to be hurt that he'd made love to her when he belonged to another woman.

Alex sighed and dropped onto the top step of the back porch, the same step where Jemi had found him such a short time ago.

A short time.

A lifetime.

Then he gazed up at the sky, the vivid blue crown of the mountain day. He listened to the twitters and cries of the birds thick in the trees around the inn. He glanced down at his hands that, until this weekend, had never touched a woman the way he'd touched Jemi.

And Alex knew he and Jemi would make their peace.

What did Grandy like to say? Things aren't always the way they seem? Well, maybe not, but some things were meant to be.

Alex rose from the steps and walked through the back door of the office cottage. He'd find Susannah, drive into town, give Jemi time to calm down.

Then he'd tell her, in no uncertain terms, that he couldn't live without her.

Susannah sat on the floor in the pantry off the kitchen, keying entries into a high-end notebook computer, from time to time eye-balling the contents of a shelf.

He stared with great interest at the sight of the pig-tailed twelve-year-old breaking one of her employer's strictest rules. Suddenly, Jemi's comment that Susannah had known his identity made sense.

"Importing a little high technology to the Dew Drop Inn?"

The girl didn't even look up. "You of all people should understand."

She had him there.

Susannah's fingers flew over the keyboard. Alex envied her dexterity; his fingers were so large he usually linked a full-size keyboard to his laptop. "Jemi is a saint," Susannah said in a stern voice, "but just because she doesn't appreciate modern inventions doesn't mean I have to keep inventory with pencil and paper."

That made sense to Alex. "What program are you running?"

Susannah shrugged. "One I wrote myself."

He looked at her with even more interest, and wondered where she'd found the money for her expensive computer. The glimpse he'd had of her drunken grandmother didn't promote thoughts of ready cash.

She powered off the computer, closed it up, and said, "That's done."

"Jemi asked me to drive you into town for supplies. Is this a good time?"

"I'd like to, but I'd better help Jemi with the rooms first."

"She said she wanted to do that herself today."

"Oh." Susannah looked wiser than her years. He studied her eyes, emerald green and looking more knowing than was good for a twelve-year-old. "I saw that hoity-toity woman drive off. Lucky for her that limo driver had decided to take a nap in the car before heading out. I reckon that means Jemi's not selling the inn." As she spoke, she stuffed her laptop into a scruffy backpack.

"Do you think that's a good thing for Jemi?" Alex asked as they left the kitchen by the back door and walked to where Jemi parked her little Toyota truck.

"Do you?"

"Yes and no," he answered, thinking aloud. "She wants to live in a big city and experience life, but this patch of earth claims a piece of her soul, and I think it would kill a part of her to sell it off."

"Especially to someone as mean as that Smith woman!"

"What did she say to you?"

Susannah shrugged. "She said I was a dirty, barefooted, good-for-nothing hillbilly and she'd thank me to wear shoes the next time I came to her room." Susannah sniffed. "Like she was better than me or something because she had on pretty clothes and smelled like the perfume counter in the Dalton Five and Dime and carried a purse that must have cost a hundred dollars!"

Alex smiled, not without some bitterness. Sharyn would have considered a hundred-dollar purse far beneath her.

"It doesn't matter what shows on the surface if what's underneath is rotten, is what I say!" Susannah climbed into the pickup, cradling her computer on her lap.

Alex slipped behind the wheel. He'd had a chauffeur for so long he'd almost forgotten how to drive. When he returned to California, he'd find another job for his driver and buy a car instead of that silly limousine Sharyn had selected. He'd lived hidden behind the sheltering screen of wealth long enough.

They drove into town in companionable silence. Susannah directed him to the Piggly-Wiggly. She left her backpack on the seat and clambered out.

"Aren't you going to lock that up?"

She looked at him like he'd spoken Swahili. "What for?"

"That's a very expensive computer."

She laughed. "No one in this town would know what to do with it even if they did steal it. Besides, no one would bother Jemi's truck."

Alex followed her into the store. Wearing Ari's hand-me-down cutoffs, Hawaiian shirt, and thongs, he thought he looked almost like a local. He whistled a few bars.

Susannah shopped with efficiency. He looked for a printed list, but she said she'd simply memorized it since she didn't carry her printer to the Dew Drop Inn. Alex followed behind her, pushing the undersized grocery cart that fit into the narrow aisles of the store.

He was carrying the groceries to the truck when Susannah said, "I knew who you were from the first time I saw you, you know."

Alex turned around and regarded her with curiosity. "Yet you didn't say anything to anyone until today. Why not?"

"Ah, I figured you had a good reason for what you were doing. Someone as smart as you would have to."

She got back in the truck and he did the same.

"I only told Jemi today because Mr. Grandy said the time was right for Jemi to know, that it would make her happy." She sighed. "I do hope he was right."

"Me, too," Alex said and started the truck. "Do you know you're a most unusual child?"

"Do you think so?" She looked pleased, but then tried to act cool. "I'm just who I am. Granny says I can't help being different. She says my mother was always too smart for her britches, but that I've got more sense."

"And your mother is . . ." Alex didn't know whether the child was orphaned or abandoned.

"Gone." Susannah unwrapped a piece of Double Bubble, then offered him one.

He took it and said around the mouthful, "Gone?"

"She left me to Granny to raise."

"And how do you feel about that?"

She shrugged, but Alex saw the pain in her expression. "I do okay on my own, except for the days Granny gets real bad. But she buys me what I need."

Alex looked at the child's threadbare clothing and her crooked front teeth. He thought of her complaint the other day that her grandmother only cared about her monthly checks. Then he added that expensive computer into his equation. "Your mother sends her money?"

"Yeah, but granny puts most of it away. She said there's no need for me to be any more different than I am."

"Have you ever met your mother?" No matter how cold and indifferent his parents had been, at least they'd formed the framework of a family.

"Nah." She blew a bubble almost as big as her face, then sucked the gum back in with a whoosh. "And I never want to meet her. She had her chance to keep me and she didn't, so she'd better not come skulking around looking for me when I'm rich and famous."

"In computers?"

Susannah nodded. "That's how I knew who you were. I've been studying up on you. I can't be a pioneer the way you were in chip technology, but I've got some ideas of my own that as soon as I get a little more math behind me, I may be able to do something with."

"Would you like a job at Winston Enterprises?" Alex asked the question before he could even consider the consequences, something he never would have done before his trip to the Dew Drop Inn. But if he was going to persuade Jemi to return to California with him, he knew he'd need to provide for Susannah. Jemi had clearly taken the girl under her sheltering wings and wouldn't abandon her. And neither would he want her to.

"Would I?" Her eyes shone, but then she looked out the window and said, "But of course I couldn't do that."

He thought of her grandmother and the more than likely underequipped school in Dalton. "Why not? That is, if your grandmother agrees?"

"Well, you'd probably make me sign a noncompetition clause, then I couldn't start my own company." She blew another bubble and looked at him sideways, a grin on her face.

"Smarty-pants," he said, grinning. "Come back to California with me, and I'll find you a place to stay and I'll even get my lawyers to waive that clause."

"That's mighty big of you, A. G." she said, lifting a hand toward him, then dropping it quickly. "Thanks anyway, but I can't run off from my grandmother. She's my only family and I couldn't leave her to look after herself."

"Then we'll invite her too," Alex said, marveling that Jemi's inclinations to rescue people had rubbed off on him so thoroughly.

He took his right hand from the wheel, and they shook solemnly.

Susannah blew a big bubble to celebrate and hugged her backpack to her chest, her eyes dancing.

And somehow, Alex knew he'd made the second best deal of his life so far.

But the most important still waited to be settled.

After an annoyingly bumpy, noisy, and uncomfortable ride in a small plane from Arkansas to Dallas, Sharyn at last settled into her first-class seat for her flight back to Los Angeles.

As she waited for the attendant to return with her Dubonnet on the rocks, she rubbed the tiny crease that had only recently appeared between her eyes.

The first thing she'd do upon her return was schedule a facial.

Next, of course, she'd resign from Winston Enterprises. She was far too proud to stay where she wasn't welcome.

The attendant lowered the tray and set the drink in front of her. Sharyn didn't look up or acknowledge the service. When you paid for first class, you deserved what you got.

Her brow furrowed deeper as she thought of

the debacle that had occurred at the Dew Drop Inn. Her pride almost sank when she thought of A. G. discovering her in that dreadful pose with Quentin Grandy. The director meant nothing to her, he'd been nothing more than a diversion to help her not think about the memories the trip to Arkansas stirred. And even then, he'd almost brushed her off! She would have much rather A. G. found her in a scene that would be truly memorable.

She curled her lip and tasted the drink as a tinny voice in the background reminded them to fasten their seat belts and stow their drink trays. Sharyn nestled the drink in her hands and waited for the attendant to put the tray up.

There were benefits to being rich and powerful, benefits that helped ease the taunts she'd endured as the ugly duckling outcast of Dalton, Arkansas.

One thing was for sure, Sharyn told herself, smiling in satisfaction as the attendant almost managed to cover her annoyance when she scurried over to tuck the tray into the seat back, she would never go back again.

She might not become the first Mrs. A. G. Winston, but there were plenty of other men, much better prospects, now that she considered the situation, who would jump at a chance to slip a ring on her finger.

She could still accomplish her goal of marrying into monied society. As soon as she landed, she'd begin an in-depth study of corporate executives and company owners.

Taking another sip of her drink, she considered her failure at securing the secrets of the Dew Drop Inn from her wealthy counterparts. The hillbilly face of the young girl who'd brought her the towels swam into her mind. That child could have been Sharyn at age twelve.

She allowed her mind, only for a moment, to consider what had become of her own daughter. Her mother had told her if she walked out the door on the newborn, she'd better never look back, unless it was to send money. Unable to reconcile the squalling red-faced infant with her dreams of escaping Dalton, she'd left.

Sharyn took a sip of her drink and repressed a shudder. She rarely thought of her past. Since the earliest days she'd been able to spare the money, she'd sent it care of her mother and the local banker, to a trust fund she'd had her accountant establish. Sharyn refused to acknowledge guilt; but she couldn't stand the thought of another child enduring the drudgery of the poverty she'd escaped.

What if someone did link Sharyn to her past? She would give them her best wide-eyed look, and laugh. After all, she possessed the papers to prove she'd been born in California.

An idea came to her and she smiled. There was certainly more than one way to skin a cat.

Then she grimaced, remembering that had
been one of her mother's favorite expressions.
Thinking like that defeated old hag would get
her nowhere. If her mother hadn't fallen apart
after their father died, if she'd held herself
together instead of spiraling into drunken de-
feat, Sharyn's entire life might have been different.

But perhaps no better.

But truly, Sharyn thought, forcing herself to
stick to matters she could control, she wished
she'd thought of this idea earlier. It certainly
would have saved her a lot of time and trouble,
and she'd probably still be engaged to A. G.

A few well-placed criticisms, a conversation
with a travel editor here and there, and she
could easily squelch any enthusiasm for the
Dew Drop Inn. When she reported her dissatis-
faction with the rustic so-called retreat, and it
became known as not quite the place to go,
anyone she knew would drop it as a vacation
destination.

Honestly, Sharyn thought with disgust as the
plane pummeled down the runway and lifted
with a shudder into the air, she should have
thought of that plan much sooner.

That just went to show what happened when
you let your emotions cloud your judgement.

"Hey, sis," Ari said, walking into the kitchen
where Jemi pounded out her frustrations on a
huge batch of bread dough.

"Hey yourself," she said, summoning a smile for her big brother. "I thought you were going back to New York today."

"I needed to take care of some local business." He wandered to the refrigerator and returned with a bowl of grapes. "Why isn't your new helper making the bread?"

Jemi shrugged but kept her face pointed toward the bread board she used for kneading. Ari had always been too good at reading her mind. "I don't think he'll be here much longer."

"Want to tell me what happened?" Ari set down the bowl of grapes and she heard him walk toward her just as a tear splashed on the back of her hand.

"Drat it," she cried, and dried her hand on the back of her overalls. Then she turned to Ari and accepting the comfort of his shoulder, wailed out her sorrows.

"I took Alex in and I accepted him at face value and I-I—" she hiccupped, "well, I guess I fell for the guy and we made love and it was beautiful and then today this witch showed up and it turns out she's engaged to Alex even though Alex broke the engagement and he's some rich fancy man so it's no wonder he had no idea how to make a bed—" She hiccupped again.

Ari patted her on the back. "Your homeless man is A. G. Winston, *WorldView*'s most recent Person of the Year. I recognized him the minute

I saw him, and warned his ass not to play any games with you."

"Oh, Ari, I feel so stupid." Jemi sank onto a chair. "And I'm mad, too, because he acted like he cared about me, and all the time, he was engaged to marry a woman who has a stone in place of a heart. I ask you, what kind of man is that?"

Ari chewed on a grape. At last, he said, "Do you care for him?"

Jemi started to shake her head and disclaim any affection, but she was too honest of a soul to do that. "Yes, I do," she whispered.

"As long as he's no longer engaged, what difference does it make whether he's penniless or rich?" Ari selected another grape and popped it into his mouth. "I hate to point out the obvious, but isn't it better to be rich?"

"Oh, I don't know!" Jemi looked at him in exasperation. "What good does money do if you're not happy?"

"Ah, but money and happiness, that's a powerful combination."

She gazed at him. "You have money, don't you, Ari?"

He nodded. "I do okay."

"But you're not happy, are you?"

He studied the grapes in the bowl for a long time. His mouth twisted slightly, and he said, "No, I guess I'm not. But I manage, and that's that. And maybe that's one reason I want you to be happy."

"Oh, Ari, you're too good to be unhappy. All you need is someone to love you for yourself."

He smiled and shook his head. "You are a Pollyanna, aren't you, my littlest sister?"

She rose from her chair and squared her shoulders. "I don't think of myself that way. But I've been thinking and I'd like to come to New York, Ari, and work for you in your shop, the way we discussed last month."

He gazed at her, and she couldn't read the look behind his eyes. "Oh, you would, would you?"

"Yes, and I'll learn to dress and speak oh-just-so and carry on about the right fabrics and patterns to all your rich clients."

"And what if I tell you the job's not open any longer?"

"Oh, Ari, you wouldn't!"

He plucked another grape, and said, "If I thought it was better for you to stay here and face your demons, I'd say it in a second."

She pursed her lips. "Is that what you think?"

"I don't know, Jemi. But what's to become of the inn? Have you thought of what Susannah will do?"

"I won't shut down. I'll find someone to run the inn, and make them keep her on."

"It's more than just a job, Jemi; it's her home away from home."

"I know that better than anyone, and I . . ." Jemi dropped into a chair at the pine table. "I can't go," she said, lifting her head. "I can't run off and leave my responsibilities. I belong here."

Ari collected the bowl and put it away in the refrigerator. He stopped in front of Jemi and she looked up into his kind eyes.

"I'm at a crossroads, aren't I?"

Ari nodded. "Whatever you want to do, Jemi, there's a way to accomplish it. Just think it through. If it's coming to New York, then you'll figure out what to do about all your charges. If it's staying here, you'll find a way to be happy. And if it's listening to your heart, and letting yourself fall in love with A. G. Winston," he winked and said, "I think you can even do that!"

"Ari! Of all the outrageous—"

But Ari had gone, out the door, and back to his life.

Which left Jemi sitting in her chair, wondering why letting herself fall in love with Alex was the only option that appealed to her.

21 ~

"**D**on't you feel just the teeniest bit guilty?" Mia asked Quentin later that evening as they lay in the hammock watching the night sky overtake the last splashes of pink from a magnificent sunset.

Quentin lifted his lips from where he'd been nibbling on her earlobe. "What's to feel guilty about?" He squeezed her gently. "As long as you've forgiven me, all's right with my world. Besides, we did everything we could today."

"Are you sure?" Mia worried a fingernail across her lips.

Quentin kissed her fingertip. "We agreed after a good look at Jemi that she needed time to cool down. We found A. G. and Susannah hunched over her laptop yakking away about bytes and quarks. And since we're both invisible, we couldn't exactly drive into town to hunt for Queenie. Last year Mr. G provided a car with mysteriously dark windows but we don't seem to have the same luxury for this adventure."

He smoothed her brow with a kiss. "Let's wait until after the yoga class, then if A. G. doesn't have the sense to take advantage of this moonlight, I'll let you bop him over the head and we'll lay him out for Jemi to rescue again."

"I don't know—" Mia began.

Quentin trailed a finger across her breast, making it hard for her to concentrate. "Have faith, my little worrywart."

Then he grinned and said, "You did like skinny dipping again, didn't you, my sensuous sweetheart?" Quentin tickled her in the ribs and she caught his hand to stop him from distracting her again.

"True," Mia smiled. "Maybe I'm meant to be invisible. It sure frees me from inhibitions." She heated up, just thinking of the other night when she'd pleasured herself at Quentin's urging. Whether she could be that free in her normal state she didn't know, but somehow, she suspected Quentin intended to help her figure out the answer to that question. She shivered slightly in anticipation, then returned her mind to the very real concern of A. G. and Jemi.

"Seriously," she said, sitting upright so Quentin could see how serious she was, "Mr. G assigned A. G. to us and just because I've agreed to marry you despite your scandalous behavior doesn't mean we can abandon him."

"Absolutely not." Quentin sat up, too. "I don't know where my mind's been." Then he ruined his serious mien with a wink and a feathery light dance of his fingers up the inside of her thigh. When he did that, she had trouble thinking straight.

"When I stood you up," Quentin said, "were you ready to talk to me about it right away?"

"Absolutely not!"

"There you go," he said, transferring his attentions to her other thigh.

"So you think she needs all this time as a cooling off period?" Mia wrinkled her nose, but Quentin did have a good point. She'd seen the look of anguish and betrayal on Jemi's face when she learned of A. G.'s engagement. And not even a day had passed.

"Or a heating-up period," he murmured. "I know how I feel when I haven't been able to see you for a few hours."

She smiled but wouldn't allow herself to be distracted. Not yet, anyway. "Then there's Susannah. We agreed to help her and Queenie, too, and we haven't even made a plan. It's true she and A. G. have hit it off, which may be a good thing, but we still haven't solved the problem."

"I've been thinking about that, too," Quentin said, circling a finger on the back of her neck.

"You certainly have been doing a lot of thinking."

"That's because I couldn't do anything else,"

Quentin said with a grin. "Promise me you won't ever become invisible without me ever again."

"I hope it won't be necessary for either one of us," Mia said, but even as she said the words, she wondered whether she believed them. Being invisible did have its special moments. "There's another piece to this story that's been bothering me."

"What's that?"

"Why would a woman like Sharyn Stonebridge bother with the Dew Drop Inn? What's her connection to this corner of the world?"

"She planned to buy it only to shut it down." Quentin said slowly. "I'd forgotten all about her, frankly."

"Not your type, eh?" Mia couldn't help but tease him.

Quentin stuck out his tongue. "She'd close the inn possibly out of revenge or because she didn't want anyone she knew staying here."

"And the only reason for that is she's connected to this area and doesn't want people to know." Mia sat up and said excitedly, "And I think it's because she's Queenie's daughter."

"And Susannah's missing mother?" Quentin studied her, but he didn't give her that "are you nuts?" look.

"When I listened to her thoughts with the hanky, I could tell she had something to cover up here. But she never acknowledged in her thoughts any relationship to Susannah."

"I'm sure she wouldn't want the world to know she abandoned a baby twelve years ago. She probably lies about her age as it is. But just because the woman's beneath contempt doesn't make her the missing mother."

"No, but I think it's true." Mia knew she sounded stubborn, but she just knew when she was right about something. "All the pieces fit."

Quentin smoothed his hand over hers. "Even if it's true, maybe it's a truth that should remain a secret."

Mia thought about that, her first impulse to disagree. A child had a right to know her mother, especially when the father had disappeared from the scene, too. But then she considered Susannah and the hurt she'd feel. She thought, too, that sometimes the greater part of wisdom was leaving well enough alone.

She squeezed Quentin's hand to acknowledge that she agreed with him. "So that brings us back to Queenie and Susannah."

"Queenie, as I told you, used to run a sewing business." Quentin tapped his head. "I didn't get that hangover for nothing, you know. During our drinking spree, she told me about the dresses and suits she tailored. So—"

"Oh, Quentin, you're brilliant!" Mia threw her arms around the most clever man in America if not the world. "We'll offer her a job in Wardrobe! She'll have to apprentice but eventually I can get her into the union."

"Great minds do think alike," he said and kissed her.

Mia said against his mouth, "Do you think Susannah will be happy coming to California and leaving Jemi behind?"

Quentin broke the kiss and stared at her. Suddenly Mia realized she'd said the stupidest thing. She began to laugh. Quentin drove her on with a particularly devilish tickling attack.

She laughed so hard she cried. Quentin found the silk square, now fairly crumpled, and dabbed at her eyes with it. "Ready to go home, little one?" he asked. She nodded and they both held onto the hanky. Mia said, "On the count of three, say, 'Please let us go home.'"

It pleased her that Quentin accepted this request as seriously as she did. The Quentin of only a few days ago would have joshed at the thought of asking favors of a magic hanky.

Mia counted to three, then they both said, "Please let us go home."

Mia held her breath.

Nothing happened.

She gave Quentin a little smile, suddenly not feeling at all like laughing. "Maybe we have to be more specific."

"Maybe so. Maybe we have to ask to be visible again."

Mia shook her head. "I don't think it's such a step-by-step process. Now just isn't meant to be the time."

Quentin tucked the hanky behind them on

the hammock. "Let's not worry about it. Maybe we can't go home until our job is done."

"Then we'd better check on A. G. and Jemi right this minute. We'll feel pretty silly if we aren't visible in our wedding pictures!" Mia laughed nervously at her own joke.

"It's almost time for the evening yoga session," Quentin said, smoothing her forehead with a tender finger. "Let's walk down to the summer house and if A. G. doesn't show up, I'll pay him back for that right to the jaw he gave me this morning!"

Alex waited outside the summer house, listening through the open double doors to Jemi leading the guests in the nighttime yoga session. He knew little about the activity, but if the exercise would help to make him less clumsy, he'd embrace lessons eagerly.

Especially if Jemi agreed to be his teacher.

He peered through the door. The group kneeled in a circle around a purple cloth laid on the floor. Each person had his own mat. To his amazement, he saw all fifteen or so guests lean forward, sliding their hands down their thighs to their knees, eyes bulging, tongues extending past their chins.

They looked ridiculous!

But as Jemi relaxed her face from the pose, she smiled and breathed deeply and he could tell that what she'd done felt good.

Feeling extremely self-conscious, Alex got to

his knees on the hard boards of the porch and leaned slightly forward, resting his hands on the tops of his thighs as he'd just witnessed. Then he widened his eyes and extended his tongue. He held the position, counting to three in his head.

Then he sat back slowly and took a deep breath of the fresh night air.

He tipped his head back, then rolled it sideways and wiggled his jaw, and found to his pleasant surprise he felt lighter, as if some of the burdens of his day had been dispensed with by the silly-looking exercise.

Scooting around, he peered in the room. Now everyone lay on the mats, arms and legs at rest, eyes closed. Jemi lay in a similar pose, speaking in a low, calming voice, much the same voice she'd used the other night on the porch, when she'd cracked him on the back, then soothed his pain.

"As you walk through the night, remember you are at one with the universe," Jemi said, lulling them with her words. "As you lay your head on your pillow tonight, picture your body completely at rest, as it is at this moment. Breathe deeply and nourish your spirit with a long, deep breath, filling your lungs with the pure mountain air."

Alex sat down and leaned his back against the wall. Her voice flowed over him like maple syrup over pancakes, one of his favorite treats.

His shoulders unkinked and he believed, listening to her send her guests off into the night with that melodious voice, that all things were possible.

Quiet fell, and Alex enjoyed the sounds of the night time. A cricket chirped by his feet. He waited, but no one filed out of the summer house. After a few minutes, his relaxation turning into anxiety to talk to Jemi, he peeked around the door.

Everyone lay on the floor, chests rising and falling slowly. Then, as he watched, Jemi stretched her arms over her head and oh, so slowly, lifted her upper body and pulled into a cross-legged position still seated on the floor. She let her head drop forward and he experienced a jolt of desire as he saw her hair fall loose and free over her shoulders.

One by one the others sat up, then rose and headed out the door. He sat quietly in the shadows of the porch until only Jemi remained in the room.

The lights in the room were already dimmed. She switched them off, then stood on the opposite side from the doorway where Alex watched. Facing the broad windows overlooking the creek and swimming hole, she stood staring out, her arms wrapped around her upper body, her hands gently massaging her upper arms.

He studied her from the doorway. She belonged here, in the natural beauty of the woods. She moved as freely as the waters of the creek flowed by beneath the windows of the summer house.

Something broke inside Alex. What right did he have to ask her to leave this place where she belonged? Even though she'd spoken of selling and moving to New York, he hadn't been sure she would have done it.

He edged back out of the doorway.

He'd walk into town, find a way to the airport and return to life as he knew it.

Jemi would forget him quickly enough.

But a part of his brain knew he stood there making excuses to run because he feared rejection.

If Jemi had been willing to live in Manhattan, she might not mind Orange County. And they could visit Arkansas whenever she wanted.

Yet, he hesitated. When Jemi saw him in his own world, would she still like him?

Love him?

No woman had ever wanted Alexander Graham Winston.

He backed across the porch of the summer house, allowing himself one last longing look at Jemi's beautiful self.

Something hit him hard across the backs of his legs at the same instant he suffered a sharp crack to his head and toppled senseless to the porch.

* * *

Jemi cradled Alex's head in her lap, anxiously fanning his face with her hand. She'd tried to catch him as he fell but hadn't been able to move fast enough. He'd landed with a nasty thump to his head.

"If anything happens to you I won't be able to stand it," she said, smoothing her other hand over his fiercely craggy brows and tracing his crooked nose with a tender touch.

Not that she had any pretensions that he'd want her to continue to be a part of his life once he tired of pretending to be a pauper.

The vision of the glamorous black and white suit worn by the woman from California swam into her head. Jemi, with her overalls, undershirts, and bare feet, would never fit into the world of A. G. Winston.

She sighed, wishing for Alex, her homeless engineer, and for what might have been.

Not that she should forgive a man who'd made love to her while engaged to another woman, but she'd concluded, as the day had worn by, that either she didn't have enough sense, or perhaps too much.

But right now none of that mattered; an injured man needed to be revived.

"Wake up, Alex," she said, more loudly. If he didn't come around soon, she'd have to go for help. But that meant leaving him alone. She chewed at her lip then whispered fiercely, "If you love me, wake up this instant!"

His eyelids fluttered open. "Jemi?" Lifting a

hand toward her cheek, he said, "Am I dreaming?" Then a worried look crossed his face. "Or dead?"

She shook her head. "Neither. You're in the summer house. Maybe you should see a doctor about these passing-out spells."

Still rubbing his head, he said, "They never happened to me before this weekend." He blinked and seemed to realize he lay in her lap. "Of course, I've enjoyed quite a few new experiences since coming to Arkansas."

So that's what she meant to him, a new experience.

"Feeling better? Good." Before he could answer, she shifted his head from her lap and let it drop onto a yoga mat. "Lie there a few minutes before you stand up," she ordered, then rose to her feet.

She moved to the row of windows across the room, steaming.

What did she think? That A. G. Winston, America's wealthiest bachelor, would really fall for her?

He probably hadn't even been a virgin.

Jemi pictured him in the hot springs the night before. He'd sounded so sincere. Then she heated up, remembering how good he'd made her feel.

She reined in her hurt and anger and gazed out the window into the night, forcing herself to listen to her inner voice. Jemi closed her eyes and summoned a listening heart, calling on the ability to sense truth as her parents had taught her.

Alex watched her from across the room. His vision blurred, then steadied as he rose slowly to his feet.

"Jemi?" He spoke her name in a low voice as he passed the point in the floor where the yoga participants had formed their circle.

"Yes, Alex?" she said, without turning to face him. She placed her hands on what Alex recognized as a barre running along the wall. Ballet. That and yoga certainly explained her gracefulness. Alex shook his head and wondered whether he was out of his mind to think this woman might ever return his feelings.

Perhaps he'd been struck on the head harder than he'd realized, because his brain kept whispering to him that he had a chance.

A chance at happiness.

He crossed the floor and paused behind her. He lifted his hands to touch her, but something about the stillness of her back, the angle of her shoulders, warned him against such an encroachment.

Jemi, open-hearted, generous, loving Jemi, did not want him to touch her.

She turned around then and he would have known, had there been no light at all from the rising moon, that she glared up at him.

"Is there something you wanted to say to me before you leave?" she said in a controlled voice.

At least she spoke to him.

He thought of the speeches that had run through his mind all afternoon, he thought of the pretty words he would have liked to say, then his brilliant, well-trained mind went completely blank.

"I—uh—"

She tapped her fingers against her upper arm. "Cat got your tongue?"

He shook his head.

"What's the matter? You don't have any idea at all how to explain to me how you had the balls to make love to me when all the time you were engaged to another woman?"

He forced his lips to move, but only strangling sounds came from his throat. She meant too much to him to lose; he relived, in a searing miserable moment, all the horrible times in school the other kids had made fun of him because he couldn't think of the answer fast enough.

"Go ahead, let me hear it," Jemi said, beginning to tap her foot. "Let's hear your excuses. Oh, I would have told you. I meant to tell you. It slipped my mind in the passion of the experience." She stressed the last word and stared up at him.

"No," he said, "it wasn't that at all."

"Oh, no? You made love to me when you were engaged to that—that woman. So what was it?"

He could not argue the truth of that point.

"You just don't do that!"

"No," he said again, struggling to gain control of his tongue. What he had to say was the most important thing he'd ever said in his life and he wanted so desperately to say it right.

Jemi began to walk away.

"Wait!" he cried. "I love you!"

She turned halfway back to him. "What did you say?"

He swallowed. The words sounded so right to him. "I love you, Jemi Dailey," he said, reaching for one of her hands and clasping it in his. "I was engaged to Sharyn, but I had no concept of love. I won't give you a cartload of excuses; I'll simply say my eyes have been opened." He stroked her fingers in his and his heart took hope when she responded. "To so many things, many of them so very wonderful," he added, pulling her close.

He could feel her stiffen, even though she didn't pull away. "I haven't said the right thing, have I?"

Jemi wanted to tell him he'd said exactly the right thing, the words she wanted to hear and had doubted that she would.

She said nothing, gazing into his eyes, unable to detect anything other than shining sincerity.

"You really do believe you love me, don't you?"

"Yes."

Jemi bit her lip and wondered how to ask the question she really wanted to ask. Being held in his arms again felt so natural, as if she'd found the place on earth where she belonged. They might be anywhere, but as long as those strong arms embraced her, she would be safe.

But her own wisdom cautioned her. "Oh, Alex," she said, "I want to believe you but I'm afraid you only think you love me."

He blinked and smoothed a loose strand of hair from her cheek. "You mean because you're the first woman I made love with, don't you?"

"Yes, exactly!" To her great relief, he'd seen her point immediately. She forced herself to break away from his arms and hooked her hands to the retreat of the barre. "You should go home, meet other women. I have a feeling you won't be taken in by the Sharyns of the world anymore."

"I don't need other women," Alex said, with a stubbornness that made Jemi ease her stand and turn to face him. "Unless, that is, you're telling me to vamoose."

"Vamoose?" Jemi laughed. To her surprise, tears clouded her eyes. "You do talk funny, Alex."

"Jemi, what I am asking you is do you care for me? Could you possibly learn to love me?"

Jemi knew she should put him out of his agony quickly. "Kiss me, you fool," she whispered and moved into his open arms.

When Jemi opened her eyes again, she could have sworn the moon had risen several degrees during the length of that kiss. She toyed with his shirt front, slipping her hand between the buttons to play with the thick hair on his chest.

Alex smiled down at her, then suddenly said in a serious voice that quelled her heart, "You may be right about me needing to experiment," Alex said.

She stilled her hand. "Oh?"

"I may want to try all sorts of things I've only read about," he murmured.

"Then you should do that," she said in a stiff voice.

Alex caught her earlobe between his teeth and nipped ever-so-gently and before Jemi knew he'd even moved his hand, he'd slipped the top of her yoga leotard off her shoulders and down to her waist.

"Alex?"

"Yes, my love?" he said, halting what he was doing with his tongue to her nipple that was causing her to fast lose her breath.

"You mean you want to experiment with me?"

"And only you."

Jemi smiled. She could be a goose sometimes, worrying about things that left alone took care of themselves. She drew his head back to her breast and said, "What a lovely idea."

Alex lowered himself to his knees. He was so

tall he could kiss her breasts from there. Jemi started to join him on the floor, but he caught her hand gently. With a grin she would really have to describe as quite wicked, he said, "How 'bout we start experimenting now?"

"Now?" She wanted him to kiss her senseless and make mad passionate love to her, all pretty straightforward stuff. But that wicked glint in his eyes was doing strange things to her insides, melting them faster than any simple kiss. "Now?" she said again.

Alex slipped her tights past her hips and oh so slowly down her legs. He tossed them over his shoulder and smiled up at her. Then he placed her hands on the barre and tucked her fingers around the smooth wood.

"Hang on," he said with a wink.

She faced him, naked and vulnerable and trembling with anticipation. She licked her lips and nodded.

"First," he said, "a kiss to seal our bargain."

Jemi leaned forward, but he shook his head and nibbled on the inside of first one thigh and then another. Ever so tenderly he tucked her feet farther apart on the floor, then kissed his way back up her thigh. "A special kiss," he murmured, "to seal a very special bargain."

She almost cried out when his tongue flicked across her swollen, heated inner lips. "Oh, Alex, I like your experiment," she said, clutching the barre and giving herself over to the heat he sent spiraling with every stroke of his tongue.

He was, after all, a man of science, and who knew better how to conduct an experiment?

22 ~

"I don't think we need to worry about those two anymore," Quentin said to Mia about the time Alex began to ease Jemi's leotard down. He dropped the stick he'd used on Winston and said to Mia, "Pretty good teamwork on our part."

Mia clasped Quentin's hand in her own. "Partners always." She sighed, and as they walked down the steps of the summer house, she said, "Aren't those two precious?"

Quentin grinned at the idea of A. G. Winston being described as precious. But when the word came from Mia's lips, he had to agree. "Precious," he said, slipping an arm around her waist. "How about we do a little experimenting of our own?"

Mia smiled and said, "How about we see if we can tip over that hammock?"

"Last one to the porch is a rotten egg!" Quentin took off running, his stride hitting an easy lope immediately.

Laughing, her spiky hair waving like wheat

in a windstorm, Mia chased after him. He ran backwards, then circled round her, offering her a hand.

"Oh, no," she said, taking off again, "I don't want to be the rotten egg!"

He grinned. Mia did love to win.

And sure enough, she reached the Sunrise Cottage ahead of him. She dropped into the hammock as he took the steps two at a time.

"I'm all out of breath," she said, laughing.

"Not too winded to kiss me, are you?" He joined her in the hammock.

She answered him by sliding into his arms, pressing her lips to his and taking his breath away.

Quentin held her close. "Thank you, Mr. G," he said, then trailed his kiss lower, down the curve of her neck to the top of her breast.

Suddenly, he stopped.

"What is it?" Mia asked.

"Shh," he whispered and pointed to the edge of the porch. He thought he'd seen something or someone in the nearby bushes. He strained his eyes, but the moon had disappeared behind a stray cloud and he could detect nothing.

"Sweetheart," he said, speaking softly, "you know how you like to say things happen for a reason and the things that happen to us follow a certain logic?"

She was nibbling on his fingers, but she

paused to say, "Hmm-hmm," as she reached for the buttons on his shirt.

He covered his hand in hers. There, he'd seen it again, out of the corner of his eye, a movement beside the porch. "Do you think it's possible that we're visible again?"

Mia looked at him wide-eyed. "Because Alex and Jemi have gotten together! Oh, yes, we could be!"

Quentin kissed her again, then drew back. "Maybe we should retire to the privacy of the cottage before we proceed with our experiment."

"But if we're visible, we can go home!" Mia jumped up. "Quentin, we can go back to our wedding."

He smiled at her eagerness and climbed from the hammock. He wouldn't have minded one more interlude of their own before they left for the airport, but if she wanted to leave immediately, he'd not quibble. Mia had forgiven him and nothing else mattered. Pulling her close, he whispered, "I love you."

"I love you, too," she said and kissed him.

A light flashed.

"Gotcha!"

Quentin and Mia whirled around. The woman from the newspaper office, her gray bun bouncing, leapt up the stairs, flashing away with a camera almost as big as her bun.

"I knew you were on your honeymoon. You

can't pull the wool over a crack reporter!"
Flash! Flash!

Quentin started to laugh. "Mrs. Page, I presume?"

Mia stared at him as if he'd gone bonkers. "Let's go inside," she said, tugging on his hand.

He continued to laugh as the reporter snapped more pictures. Finally, he calmed down, and said, "So we're visible again."

Then Mia began to laugh, too. Looking down to her hand, she said, "Quentin, the crimson hanky is gone!"

He pulled her close, not caring whether Mrs. Page took more pictures or not. "From now on, we'll make our own magic," he said, then swept her inside the cottage.

Two hours later, Mia surveyed the rumpled covers of the valentine-shaped bed and smiled languidly at Quentin, who lay propped on an elbow, watching her with his heart in his eyes.

"I think," she said, "I'm ready to go home now." She patted the quilt. "It just seemed a shame to leave without making love at least once in this bed."

Quentin traced the side of her breast and flashed a wicked grin. "You mean at least once when we were both in the same state?"

Mia tossed a pillow at him and jumped from the bed. "Let's get dressed, tell Jemi and A. G.

we're leaving, and settle things with Susannah and Queenie."

Quentin flopped face down. "You mean I don't get to wake up nice and slow?"

Mia tugged on his arm, then let her hand drift to the firm line of his buttocks. "Tomorrow morning, Mr. Grandy, on the first morning of our honeymoon, I promise to wake you nice"—she sketched a feathery circle—"and slow and easy."

He caught her wrist. "Better stop now or we'll be here another two hours," he said and then rolled off the bed and climbed into his pants. "Your servant, ready for action."

When they were both dressed, Mia paused in the doorway and looked around the cabin. "I like to say good-bye to special rooms," she said to Quentin, who squeezed her hand and kissed the top of her head before they left the Sunrise Cottage.

No lights showed in the office cottage.

"They're probably in bed," Mia said.

"Or still at the summer house," Quentin suggested.

Mia heard the rustle in the bushes at the same instant Sugar streaked by, barking furiously. A camera flashed, then a woman cried, "Get away from me, stupid dog!"

Headlights from an arriving car highlighted the sight of Mrs. Page, bun bobbing, galloping toward them, making for the safety of the nearest cottage, which happened to be the office. Sugar dogged her heels, clearly as incensed over the woman's presence as Ari had been the other day.

Upstairs, lights flickered on.

"It's showtime, folks," Quentin murmured.

The cottage door opened. Mrs. Page ran in, and so did Sugar. From inside the room, Jemi told the dog to sit.

Car doors slammed and Ari, Susannah, and Queenie stormed onto the porch.

Mia and Quentin followed them up the stairs and into the cottage.

A. G., buttoning a garish Hawaiian shirt, cleared the bottom step of the inner staircase. He attempted to tame his long, quite disheveled hair, then looked around the assembled company.

Mrs. Page squealed and raised her camera.

"Oh, no, you don't." Ari reached her side in two swift moves. "You know Jemi's rules."

"But that's Alexander Graham Winston!" Mrs. Page looked like a kid who'd just had an ice cream cone taken away. "You can't deny me this coup!"

"Oh, I can't?" Ari took the woman by the elbow.

"One moment," A. G. said. Jemi crossed to his side and they held a whispered conversation.

"They're going to let her take the picture," Mia said to Quentin.

"Why now?"

Mia smiled. "Some things are meant to be."

"It's okay, Ari. A. G. doesn't mind and neither do I." Jemi leaned into A. G.'s arms and the smile she gave him glowed more brightly than Mrs. Page's flashbulbs.

Susannah stepped forward, hugging her backpack. "You may take my picture, too. I'm going to California and I'm going to be famous."

"Forget it, girl," Queenie said. "You're not riding on anyone else's coattails. You don't need any mug's charity."

Mrs. Page, not one to miss an opportunity, captured Susannah, her pigtails awry, her chin held high.

"I bet that photo is worth a lot of money some day," Quentin said so that only Mia could hear. "But how does she know we're going to offer her a chance to come to L. A.?"

A. G. knelt beside Susannah. "Does your grandmother not want you to come to California and work with me?"

"So it's your doing, is it?" Queenie made a face at the man. "Well, I don't know who you are, but I've made it good and clear to little miss two shoes Jemi that my family doesn't need any help. We take care of our own."

Susannah's chin, though still jutting at that defiant angle, had started to quiver. "But I can't learn enough here!"

A. G. rose and said to Queenie, "We agreed

she'd go only with your permission and if you would come, too."

"Making deals behind my back, eh?"

Ari, who'd stood back quietly while Mrs. Page took a whole roll of film, chose that moment to hustle her out the door. She started to protest, but when Sugar rose on her haunches, the reporter waved a hand and called, "Bye-bye! It's off to the darkroom for me!"

Quentin stepped forward from the back of the room where he and Mia had been watching. "Queenie! Hey, it's me, Dutch."

She blinked and stared at him.

A. G. gave him a questioning look and Jemi just shook her head. By this time, she probably had no idea who Quentin was really supposed to be.

"Dutch Moran." He winked. "From the jail, remember?"

"Dutch!" She threw her arms around him. "My buddy. What are you doing here?" To the others, she said, "Dutch is famous, ya know."

Mia smiled, proud of Quentin's quick thinking.

Ari walked back in the room. He watched Quentin talking to Queenie, then crossed to where Jemi stood by A. G. and Susannah, an assessing look on his face.

"So how ya been?" Queenie asked.

Quentin shook his head slowly, as if some problem weighed him down. "Not so good."

"What's a matter, Dutch? You're not in trouble again, are you?"

"Not right now. But I sure could use some help on this deal I've got brewing out in California."

Queenie's face lit up. She scratched her orange hair into a greater state of disarray. "What kind of help, Dutch?"

"Well, Queenie," he said, putting an arm around her shoulders, "when I'm not busy getting myself thrown in jail or running around the countryside kidnapping corporate executives"—he tossed a wink at A. G. and Jemi—"I have a job in the movie business."

She cackled. "Ya don't say."

Susannah had begun to grin and hop from foot to foot.

"Oh but I do say. And I've got this picture coming up that requires all kinds of special costumes."

Mia hugged her arms to her chest and thought there'd never been a more wonderful man born than Quentin Grandy.

"Costumes?" Queenie straightened, and the angle of her chin echoed Susannah's. "Dutch, that's no problem. You tell me what you need done and I'll see to it that it's finished in no time. I'm quite handy with a needle."

Quentin offered her his hand and they shook. "Thanks, Queenie, you're a trooper."

"So we can go?" Susannah glanced from her grandmother to Jemi to A. G. to Quentin.

Everyone nodded.

She burst into tears.

"There, there," Queenie said, stroking the top of her head.

Then she paused and looked over to Quentin, dismay clouding her face. "Dutch, a word with you in private?"

Quentin nodded and Mia wondered what the problem could be. But thankfully, Quentin herded Queenie into her hearing range.

"Ya see, Dutch, there's one sticking point to my leaving town and it's got to do with the girl's mother."

"Tell Dutch." Quentin tapped his chest. "I've never met a problem I couldn't lick."

"She sends these checks once a month to me and the banker. I've got the funds invested and the banker takes care of all that. What'll I do if I leave?"

Quentin stroked his chin. "Got that set up in some sort of trust?"

"That's it. That's exactly what they call it!"

So Queenie hadn't squandered the money. Mia thought of the empty envelopes tied in red ribbon. She would have loved to know how much the grandmother had saved for the child, but she figured that information really wasn't any of her business.

"You leave it to Dutch, Queenie; what with all the times I've been in the hoosegow, I know lots of lawyers and accountants. They'll be happy to fix it so you can handle the money from California."

"Dutch," Queenie said, chucking Quentin in the ribs, "you're a true friend."

"Mr. Grandy," Jemi said, "I'm really not sure who you are, but I can't thank you enough. And I hope everything works out for you and your sweetheart." When she said that, she slipped her arm through A. G.'s.

Quentin took Mia's hand. "Oh, but it already has. I'd like you to meet Mia Tortelli, the woman who's about to become my wife."

Jemi smiled. "Congratulations."

"Dutch, ya didn't tell me!" Queenie looked Mia up and down, then said, "Kind of skinny but I guess she'll do."

Ari cleared his throat. "Mr. Grandy, or Dutch, whichever you prefer, would you clear up two questions for me?"

Quentin nodded.

"Did you or did you not kidnap A. G. Winston?"

Quentin nodded again.

"And did you crack him over the head and leave him at Jemi's back door with a sign on his back?"

"I did that," Mia said.

Jemi stared. "But why?"

"Some things are meant to be," Mia said.

"I would have to agree with that hypothesis," A. G. said. "Jemi has agreed to return to California with me."

Ari smiled, then said in a voice that was all business, "Is there going to be a wedding?"

"Oh, Ari," Jemi said.

"Sorry, little sister, but someone's got to look after your best interests."

"Of course," A. G. said, "that is, if Jemi will marry me."

Jemi threw her arms around his waist. "Don't be silly!"

Quentin fished in his pocket and produced A. G.'s wallet and signet ring. He handed them to Winston.

With a smile, Winston slipped the ring onto Jemi's finger, then bent to kiss her.

Everyone applauded.

The front door edged open and a camera flashed.

And Mia could have sworn, in the light that filled the door, she saw the flutter of a crimson silk hanky.

Epilogue 〜

The strains of the wedding march lilted across the sunshine-kissed gardens of the country club. Mia reached for her father's arm.

He patted her hand, which she realized trembled.

After everything she'd been through, this should be the easy part, she scolded herself. But peering around the doorway at what looked like acres of guests, she experienced the urge to bite all ten of her beautiful nails to the quick.

She glanced at the clock on the wall.

Eleven-oh-one.

Mr. G, as always, had been true to his word.

So much had happened, she felt almost dizzy standing there waiting for her bridesmaids to lead the way.

They'd flown home in the MegaFilms jet, quite the merry crew. The pilot clearly had been disappointed to see A. G. Winston with a smiling redhead clinging to his arm, and surprised to see their party had grown by an old woman with orange hair, a buck-toothed little girl clutching a laptop computer, and a feisty German shepherd. Ari had stayed behind, canceling his return to New York to run the inn for Jemi until they decided on a permanent manager.

Mia glanced at the clock again. The guests stirred a bit. They'd all taken their seats and were clearly eager for the curtain to rise, so to speak.

Mia worried her chin with the tip of her fingernail. She didn't want to muss her lipstick.

Surely Quentin wouldn't be late.

Not this time.

Her father patted her hand again, then in his gruff voice, "Buck up, Mia girl, remember you're still a Tortelli."

She smiled at her father, and just then, the groom's party entered and took their places. Quentin, looking very much like a little boy about to burst from excitement and also very much like a man wise enough to know he'd lost his heart forever, had his eyes riveted toward the doorway, seeking her down the length of the white satin-draped aisle.

The orchestra increased in volume.

The first of the four bridesmaids stepped onto the runner.

"Oh, Daddy," Mia whispered, "I'm really getting married!"

"Don't be daft. What do you think we're here for?"

She heard a hacking cough, and grinned.

Mr. G sat in the back row, a crimson silk hanky looking quite dapper in the breast pocket of his old-fashioned suit. A. G., Jemi, Susannah, and Queenie sat alongside him, and Mia couldn't help but smile when she saw the child had kicked off her shoes.

"Some days, Daddy," she said, stepping forward as the orchestra swelled and the assembled guests rose, "you just never know what might happen."

Discover Contemporary Romances
at Their Sizzling Hot Best
from Avon Books

JONATHAN'S WIFE   *by Dee Holmes*
78368-1/$5.99 US/$7.99 Can

DANIEL'S GIFT   *by Barbara Freethy*
78189-1/$5.99 US/$7.99 Can

FAIRYTALE   *by Maggie Shayne*
78300-2/$5.99 US/$7.99 Can

WISHES COME TRUE   *by Patti Berg*
78338-X/$5.99 US/$7.99 Can

**ONCE MORE
WITH FEELING**   *by Emilie Richards*
78363-0/$5.99 US/$7.99 Can

HEAVEN COMES HOME   *by Nikki Holiday*
78456-4/$5.99 US/$7.99 Can

RYAN'S RETURN   *by Barbara Freethy*
78531-5/$5.99 US/$7.99 Can

Buy these books at your local bookstore or use this coupon for ordering:

Mail to: Avon Books, Dept BP, Box 767, Rte 2, Dresden, TN 38225   E
Please send me the book(s) I have checked above.
❑ My check or money order—no cash or CODs please—for $_____ is enclosed (please
add $1.50 per order to cover postage and handling—Canadian residents add 7% GST).
❑ Charge my VISA/MC Acct#_____ Exp Date_____
Minimum credit card order is two books or $7.50 (please add postage and handling
charge of $1.50 per order—Canadian residents add 7% GST). For faster service, call
1-800-762-0779. Residents of Tennessee, please call 1-800-633-1607. Prices and numbers are
subject to change without notice. Please allow six to eight weeks for delivery.

Name_____
Address_____
City_____State/Zip_____
Telephone No._____   CRO 0996

Avon Romantic Treasures

*Unforgettable, enthralling love stories,
sparkling with passion and adventure
from Romance's bestselling authors*

DREAM CATCHER *by Kathleen Harrington*
77835-1/$5.99 US/$7.99 Can

THE MACKINNON'S BRIDE *by Tanya Anne Crosby*
77682-0/$5.99 US/$7.99 Can

PHANTOM IN TIME *by Eugenia Riley*
77158-6/$5.99 US/$7.99 Can

RUNAWAY MAGIC *by Deborah Gordon*
78452-1/$5.99 US/$7.99 Can

YOU AND NO OTHER *by Cathy Maxwell*
78716-4/$5.99 US/$7.99 Can

WILD ROSES *by Miriam Minger*
78302-9/$5.99 US/$7.99 Can

LADY OF WINTER *by Emma Merritt*
77985-4/$5.99 US/$7.99 Can

SILVER MOON SONG *by Genell Dellin*
78602-8/$5.99 US/$7.99 Can

Buy these books at your local bookstore or use this coupon for ordering:

Mail to: Avon Books, Dept BP, Box 767, Rte 2, Dresden, TN 38225   E
Please send me the book(s) I have checked above.
❑ My check or money order—no cash or CODs please—for $_____is enclosed (please
add $1.50 per order to cover postage and handling—Canadian residents add 7% GST).
❑ Charge my VISA/MC Acct#_____Exp Date_____
Minimum credit card order is two books or $7.50 (please add postage and handling
charge of $1.50 per order—Canadian residents add 7% GST). For faster service, call
1-800-762-0779. Residents of Tennessee, please call 1-800-633-1607. Prices and numbers are
subject to change without notice. Please allow six to eight weeks for delivery.

Name_____
Address_____
City_____State/Zip_____
Telephone No._____   RT 1196